THE FLOWER DRUM SONG

is a brilliant and perceptive novel about the Chinese-Americans of San Francisco's Grant Avenue. Touched with humor and tenderness and pathos, it is filled with the drama of human conflict.

At its base is a beautiful and unusual love theme, the story of young Wang Ta, who was forced to break the age-old traditions of his people for the love of a woman.

But at its center, and dominating its pages, is the unforgettable figure of Old Master Wang, who refused to recognize the Western world around him—and resolutely shut his eyes to the crumbling walls of the House of Wang.

THE FLOWER DRUM SONG

A Novel by C. Y. LEE

A Dell Book

Published by
DELL PUBLISHING CO., INC.
750 Third Avenue
New York 17, N. Y.

Reprinted by arrangement with
Farrar, Straus and Cudahy, Inc.
New York, N. Y.

A portion of this book in a slightly different form
appeared originally in *The New Yorker* magazine.

The Chinese flower drum song verses quoted in this book
are from *The Flower Drum and Other Chinese Songs*,
copyright 1943 by Chin-Hsin Yao Chen and Shih-Hsiang
Chen, and are reprinted by permission of the publisher,
The John Day Co.

Designed and produced by
Western Printing & Lithographing Company

Dedication: *To the Staff*
of the Yale Drama School
and Drama 47

First Dell printing—October, 1958

PART ONE

1

To the casual tourists, Grant Avenue is Chinatown, just another colorful street in San Francisco; to the overseas Chinese, Grant Avenue is their showcase, their livelihood; to the refugees from the mainland, Grant Avenue is Canton. Although there are no pedicabs, no wooden slippers clip-clapping on the sidewalks, yet the strip of land is to the refugee the closest thing to a home town. The Chinese theatres, the porridge restaurants, the teahouses, the newspapers, the food, the herbs . . . all provide an atmosphere that makes a refugee wonder whether he is really in a foreign land. And yet, in this familiar atmosphere, he struggles and faces many problems that are sometimes totally unfamiliar.

Wang Chi-yang was one of those who could not live anywhere else in the United States but in San Francisco Chinatown. He was from central China, speaking only Hunan dialect, which neither a Northerner nor a Cantonese can understand. His working knowledge of the English language was limited to two words: "yes" and "no." And he seldom used "no," for when people talked to him in English or Cantonese, he didn't want to antagonize them unnecessarily since he had no idea what they were talking about. For that reason, he wasn't too popular in Chinatown; his "yes" had in fact antagonized many people. Once at a banquet, his Cantonese host claimed modestly that the food was poor and tasteless and begged his honorable guest's pardon, a customary polite remark to be refuted by the guests, and Wang Chi-yang, ignorant of the Cantonese dialect, nodded his head and said "yes" twice.

But Wang Chi-yang loved Chinatown. He lived comfortably in a two-story house three blocks away from Grant Avenue that he had bought four years ago, a house decorated with Chinese paintings and couplet scrolls, furnished with uncomfortable but expensive teakwood tables and chairs, and staffed with two servants and a cook whom he had brought from Hunan Province. The only "impure" elements in his household were his two sons, Wang Ta and Wang San, especially the latter, who had in four years learned to act like a cowboy and talk like the characters in a Spillane movie. At thirteen he had practically forgotten his Chinese.

Wang Ta, the elder son, was less of a rebel. Quiet and unhappy at twenty-eight, he was often embarrassed in his father's company. But he was reluctant to correct the old man's old habits and mistakes, for Wang Chi-yang was a stubborn man. In his house he was the "lord"; his words were the law. His servants still addressed him as Old Master Wang and worked for him seven days a week at ten dollars a month. They were loyal to him and respected him, although his stern looks, his drooping mustache, his large frame, his loose gown of blue satin, his constant cough, his unyielding demands and orders would have been very unpleasant to any servant hired in America. The only person who refused to be awed by him was Madam Tang, the widowed sister of his late wife. Madam Tang came often to give him advice. She regarded her sixty-three-year-old brother-in-law as extremely old-fashioned and backward. "Aiyoo, my sister's husband," she often said, "please put your money in the bank. And buy yourself a suit of Western dress. In this country you truly look like a stage actor in that satin gown."

But Madam Tang's advice went into Old Master Wang's one ear and promptly came out of the other. Not that Old Master Wang didn't trust the banks; he just couldn't compromise with the idea that one's money should be kept in strangers' hands. In China, his money had always been in the hands of his close friends, and it had always been safe even without a signature. And his friends had always brought him profit and interest twice a year and he had accepted them without a question. He believed that banks in this country would probably do the same, but in a bank everybody was a stranger. Money, in his opinion, was like one's wife; he just couldn't let a stranger keep it for him.

As for Western clothes, wearing them was out of the question. He had always worn long gowns, silk gowns in the summer, satin gowns in the spring or autumn, fur gowns or cotton-padded gowns in the winter. It would be unthinkable for him to change into the Western clothes with only two or three buttons and an open collar. Furthermore, a piece of rag tied around one's neck seemed to him an outrage, besides being ugly and an indication of ill omen. He would never dream of tying one around his neck. The Communists in Hunan Province had tried to discard the long gown and make everybody wear the Lenin uniform, which, in his opinion, was more formal than the Western dress since it had more buttons and a closed collar. To him, even that was too much of an undesirable change; and it was one of the reasons why he had escaped the mainland of China five years ago. No, he would never wear anything but the long gown. He was going to die in it and be buried in it. And he didn't think that his long gown would bother anyone but his sister-in-law. He had often walked on Grant

7

Avenue in it and nobody had paid much attention to him. Even the American tourists seemed to regard him as a natural phenomenon on Grant Avenue.

Old Master Wang loved to walk on Grant Avenue. Every other evening, after dinner, he walked down Jackson Street, turned south on Grant Avenue and strolled for six blocks until he reached Bush Street, then he crossed Grant and turned back. He regarded the section beyond Bush as no longer Chinatown but a foreign territory. At the border of Chinatown he stopped and looked at the brightly lighted Chinatown thoroughfare for a moment, at its skyline with the pagoda roofs, at the lantern-like street lights, the blinking neon signs of English and Chinese in red, blue, yellow and green. He looked at the cars which crawled endlessly into the heart of Chinatown, then he took a deep breath and started the journey back. The street was gay and noisy, and yet it had its tranquil quality, as no one seemed to be in a great hurry.

He strolled down the street and studied every poster and advertisement that was written in Chinese. During the New Year festivities he loved to read the orange couplet banners posted on the door of each shop. If he found the poetry on the banners well composed and the calligraphy having character and strength, he would read it aloud twice or thrice with his head shaking rhythmically in a scholarly manner, and then grade it. He graded all New Year poetic greetings on Grant Avenue, memorized the best ones and wrote them down when he came home.

He also enjoyed the articles displayed in the shop windows—the exquisitely carved furniture, the brass and earthenware bowls, the straw hats and bamboo baskets, the miniature trees, the lacquer, the silk, the tiny porcelain, the jade, the silk brocade of gold and lavender. . . . His great favorite was an intricately carved eight-foot tusk in a large gift store near California Street. He went in and inquired the price. The owner of the store, who spoke some Mandarin, managed to make him understand that it was a rare mastodon tusk that had been buried in Siberian ice centuries ago. The carvings, which told a story of a festival at an emperor's palace, took twenty-five years to complete. The price, therefore, was $15,000.

For three weeks Old Master Wang stopped in front of the window, admired the tusk and wondered whether he should buy it. Finally he made up his mind. He could enjoy the tusk on Grant Avenue as much as he could enjoy it privately at his home; why should he own it? Besides, it would be an act of selfishness to deprive others of the pleasure of looking at it by removing it from Grant Avenue. He was glad of the decision; for four years now he had enjoyed the tusk every other evening as much as if it were his own.

He didn't find much pleasure walking on upper Grant Avenue, for it smelled too much of fowl and fish. When passing Washington Street, he would take a quick trip to the Buddhist church that was being constructed a block down, make a five-dollar donation and then return to Grant. He seldom went farther to Kearny, for he regarded it as a Filipino town and he had no desire to go there. He always walked past Grant on Jackson and went home through Stockton Street or Powell Street, avoiding the chicken and fish marts on upper Grant.

Back home, he always sat comfortably in his rattan chair and waited for Liu Lung, the deaf manservant, to bring him tea, water pipe and the four Chinese newspapers. He subscribed to all the Chinatown newspapers for many reasons, the main reason being to see if there was any political fight among the editors. He always followed an editorial war with great interest; occasionally he would take sides and write an anonymous letter to the one with whom he sided, praising his reasoning and his fluency of composition. He always read all the papers from page to page, including the advertisements. He had no strong political convictions. He disliked communism for one reason only, that it destroyed Chinese traditions and turned the Chinese social order upside down.

9

After he had enjoyed his tea, the water pipe and the four newspapers, he was ready for his ginseng soup. Liu Ma, the fat, talkative woman servant, who was Liu Lung's wife and Old Master Wang's information bureau, brought in the soup, eased the Old Master's cough by beating his shoulders with the palms of her hands for five minutes, and in the meantime supplied all the household information of the day. "The cook had a visitor today," she said confidentially in Hunan dialect. "A crooked-looking man. I did not know what they talked about, but they talked for a long time in the cook's bedroom."

Old Master Wang grunted. "Has Young Master Wang San studied his lessons in his room this evening?" he asked.

"Yes. I saw to it that he studied."

"Are you sure he went to school instead of a motion picture?" he asked.

"He came home with many books this evening," Liu Ma said. "And went straight to his room and studied."

Old Master Wang grunted. "Has Young Master Wang Ta come home yet?"

"No, not yet," said Liu Ma, then she lowered her voice and confided, "Old Master Wang, when I cleaned Young Master Wang Ta's room this morning, I found a woman's picture in his desk drawer. A picture with five colors, the very expensive kind. On it were some foreign words I did not understand. I told Liu Lung this morning, 'No wonder Young Master Wang Ta has always come home late recently.'"

Old Master Wang grunted. "What does this woman look like?" he asked.

"She is a foreigner," Liu Ma said emphatically.

Old Master Wang stiffened. "What? Are you sure?"

"She has silk-colored hair, blue eyes and a large nose. She is a foreigner."

"Ask Young Master Wang Ta to see me when he comes home."

"Yes, Old Master Wang," she said beating his shoulders more energetically. "Do you want to talk to the cook too? I suspected that visitor of his is a bad character. Perhaps the cook is trying to find another job again and the crooked-looking visitor is trying to help him."

"No, I don't want to talk to him," Old Master Wang said. "He is permitted to receive visitors. It is enough beating. You may go now."

After Liu Ma had gone, Wang Chi-yang thought more of the foreign woman in Wang Ta's drawer than he worried about the cook. He knew that the cook wouldn't leave him again. A year ago his cook had been lured away by a Cantonese cook who made three hundred dollars a month in a restaurant. But two months afterward his cook returned, saying that he had been unhappy working in a restaurant as an assistant. He didn't understand their dialect and he had been pushed around; furthermore, he couldn't save any money although he had made two hundred dollars a month. The chief cook, who gambled, had often borrowed money from him. Now he realized that he had really been very happy in the kitchen in the House of Wang, where he was the chief. And he had always saved at least ten dollars of his fifteen-dollar monthly pay and during the past three years he had saved almost five hundred dollars. But he had lost all of his savings at the gambling tables during the two months when he was making two hundred a month. With tears in his eyes he had begged Old Master Wang to take him back. Wang Chi-yang remembered the cook's predicament and was sure that he wouldn't be so foolish as to work elsewhere and try to make two hundred dollars a month again.

But the foreign woman in Wang Ta's drawer bothered him. He waited for Wang Ta to come home but his son did not come. When the old clock on the marble mantel struck twelve he went to bed; he tossed under the huge square mosquito net, unable to fall asleep. He had brought the mosquito net from China and had slept peacefully for twenty years under it. He would feel naked without it. But tonight he felt disturbed as though hundreds of mosquitoes had been humming in his net. Was Wang Ta in bed with that foreign woman in some cheap hotel room now? He thought of it and he shivered.

The next morning he got up as soon as the clock struck eight, had his ginseng soup and inquired about Wang Ta. Liu Ma told him that the Young Master had come back very late and had gone out again early this morning. Old Master Wang was relieved, but he was still slightly disturbed by the fact that the younger generation was not obedient any more. His son should have at least waited and come to see him as ordered. Feeling a bit crabbed he dismissed Liu Ma and attended his miniature garden beside his bed. The garden was built on a huge Kiangsi plate, with a magnificent emerald mountain rising high above the water. There were caverns, roads, bridges, paths, pagodas and a monastery in the garden, with tiny goldfish swimming about in the lake. He fed the fish, watered the moss and the miniature trees in the mountain. He felt better. The beauty of nature always cured him of his bad mood.

Then he went to his large red lacquered desk beside the window and practiced calligraphy for an hour. He wrote famous poetry on his fine rice paper with great care and deliberation, his head moving slightly with the brush. Then he wrote the poetry all over again in grass style, his brush flying swiftly and smoothly on the paper. He was not satisfied with his grass style. For practice' sake, he wrote casually some folklore sayings on top of it: "Tight lips catch no flies," "Waste no time quarreling with women," "Loud bark, no good dogs; loud talk, no wise man" . . .

Then he suddenly remembered it was Monday, the day for his weekly trip to the Bank of America on Grant Avenue, not to deposit money, but to have a hundred-dollar bill changed into small bills and silver. He put his stationery away, put on a black satin jacket over his long gown, took a brand new hundred-dollar bill from his locked iron trunk in the closet and went out.

The teller in the bank knew what he wanted and, with a smile, she changed the money for him without a question. He wrapped up the small bills and the change in his handkerchief, and with an anticipation of the pleasure of counting the money, he hurried home. Counting money had become almost a hobby to him, and he enjoyed it as much as he did attending his miniature garden. After he had counted the total sum, he sorted the bills according to their denominations, then sorted them once more according to their degree of newness, putting the brand-new ones on one pile, the newer ones on another and the old ones on a third. He treated the silver coins with more deliberation, taking pains to examine them under a magnifying glass to see which was the newest. He would spend the old ones first and the new ones later; as for the brand-new ones, he would save them in an exquisitely carved sandalwood box locked in one of his desk drawers. When he had nothing else to do, he would sometimes bring the box out and enjoy counting the shiny half dollars, quarters and dimes until their luster began to fade, then he would spend them to make room for other brand-new ones. He counted the money until Liu Lung, the deaf servant, came to his bedroom to announce his lunch.

After lunch he took a nap. He was awakened by an itch in his throat and he coughed. He had been coughing for years and now he even began to enjoy that too. So he lay in his bed and coughed mildly and sporadically for an hour or so, then he heard his sister-in-law's voice calling for Liu Lung.

"Has the Old Master waked up yet?" she shouted.

"Enh?"

"I said, has the Old Master wakened from his afternoon nap?" she shouted louder.

"Oh," said Liu Lung after a moment, "I don't know. I shall look."

"Go wake him, I have something important to tell him!"

Wang Chi-yang lay in his bed waiting for Liu Lung to come in to wake him. The servant shuffled in quietly, opened the square mosquito net and called him cautiously, as though afraid of startling him. Old Master Wang opened his eyes slowly and grunted. "What is it?" he asked.

"Madam Tang has come," Liu Lung said.

"Ask her to wait." He seldom asked his sister-in-law to come in to talk in his bedroom where he received most of his guests. He always received her in the large living room furnished with the uncomfortable straight-backed teakwood chairs which often discouraged the visitor from staying long. Madam Tang had advised him to buy a few sofas and some soft chairs; he had said "yes" many times, but never bought them. He disliked sofas; sitting on a sofa often made him feel as if he were sitting in the arms of a fat woman.

He struggled out of the bed, took his water pipe and went to the living room where Madam Tang was sitting on one of the tall hard chairs waiting, her bright-colored umbrella and black leather handbag properly placed in her lap. She was fifty, but looked a few years younger in her blue silk gown with the short sleeves. She used no make-up except a little lipstick, and her hair was combed back and tied into a little bun, neat and well-oiled. "My sister's husband," she said as soon as Wang Chi-yang came in, "I have something very important to tell you." And she opened her handbag and fished out a little newspaper clipping in English.

Wang Chi-yang sat down next to her and smoked his water pipe, knowing that there was nothing very important. "Here is a piece of news I cut off from a foreign paper," Madam Tang went on, brandishing the newspaper clipping importantly. "I shall read it to you and translate it for you. It will serve as a good warning and make you realize that my advice concerning your money is sound." She cleared her throat and, with difficulty and her individual pronunciation, she read the news aloud. " 'Lum Fong, manager of Sam Sung Café on Stockton Street, told the police how a well-dressed man came into the café, ordered a meal, and when it came time to pay, slipped Lum Fong at the cash register this penciled message: "Give me all the money. I have a gun." The Chinese went blank. "So sollee," he said, "I no savvee." "You monee," whispered the bandit, trying to make the manager understand. "You monee! I have gun, I have gun!" But the manager was still puzzled. "So sollee," he said. "No savvee." The bandit, frustrated, started for the door. "So sollee," Lum Fong called out. "Checkee please!" The thug paid eighty-five cents and left!' "

When she finished reading she looked at Old Master Wang significantly with her lips tightly pursed.

"What does it say?" Old Master Wang asked.

"A bandit robbed a Chinese restaurant on Stockton Street," Madam Tang said. "The bandit had a gun; he almost shot Lum Fong, the owner of the restaurant. Fortunately Lum Fong had only eighty-five cents on him. The bandit robbed the eighty-five cents and escaped." She paused for a moment for emphasis, then went on, "My sister's husband, I have always told you to put your money in the bank. You will regret one day when a bandit comes in with a gun and robs you of everything. This piece of news will serve you as a good warning. I hope you will consider my advice and do as I have repeatedly told you."

Old Master Wang grunted and smoked his water pipe. He was only slightly worried. Nobody knew that his money was locked in an iron trunk in the closet. If a bandit came in, he would just yield to him the contents of his sandalwood box. No, he was not going to let any strangers in the bank keep his money. Nevertheless he grunted and said to his sister-in-law, "I shall consider your advice, my wife's sister."

2

Nobody knew how much cash Old Master Wang had hidden in his apartment, not even Wang Ta. All Wang Ta knew about his father's finances was that two years ago his late uncle Tang had remitted money to America from Hong Kong several times. Since his uncle's death, his father had not received any money from China. But his father never seemed to worry about money, and he seldom talked about his finances with anybody. When in a good mood, he was as quick with a hundred-dollar bill as a bandit with his pistol. During his four years' studying economics in the University of California, Wang Ta was often puzzled by his father's economic system. He had never received any checks from his father. Whenever he wanted money, it was always a brand-new hundred-dollar bill. He paid his tuition in hundred-dollar bills, paid his meals and lodging in hundred-dollar bills. Sometimes the bills embarrassed him.

But his father never tried to spoil him with money. The old man demanded a monthly account from him while he studied in the university. His pocket money was limited to a hundred-dollar bill every two months. He had to itemize all his spendings in his monthly account, not in great detail, but they must be honest. Once, out of curiosity, he spent five dollars on a street-walker recommended by a Filipino student. He hated the experience and it troubled him for days; besides, he didn't know how to itemize it in his monthly account. Finally he entered it as "A practical study of the sex life of the American college students from an economic point of view—$5.00." His father had never questioned it.

After four years of American education, Wang Ta adopted many American ideas, and being independent was one of them. He felt ashamed to receive money from his father after he graduated. This attitude puzzled his father considerably. In China it was either the father who supported the son or the son who supported the father, depending on who had the most money. They handed each other money as a matter of course, nobody should feel ashamed of that. "What do you intend to do?" his father asked him after he graduated.

"I shall find a job," he told his father. And armed with the brand-new college degree he paced California Street, Montgomery Street and Sansome Street for weeks trying to find a job that had something to do with his field. After more than thirty short interviews with potential employers, only an insurance company showed some slight interest in him. But when they discovered that he could not speak the Cantonese dialect, they decided not to use him. Knowing the odds against him, he made up his mind to broaden his scope and forget about his economics. So he landed a job as a dishwasher in an American restaurant at Fisherman's Wharf. When he went home to declare his independence his father was so shocked by the nature of the job that he almost fell down in a fainting fit. "I forbid you to take that job!" he shouted. "Nobody in my family shall wash somebody else's dishes . . ."

For more than two months Wang Ta hunted for a desk job, but his efforts were of no avail. Finally, through the mediation of Madam Tang, his aunt, he went back to school. He enrolled in the Medical School of the University of California. He wasn't too happy with the new field, but at least he wouldn't have to look for another job for five or six years. His father was contented. To him, being a doctor wasn't too bad a profession, although he didn't have a high opinion of the Western medicine.

At the University of California Medical School Wang Ta's major problem was love. He had fallen in love before and one love affair was more damaging than the other. He didn't know why, but he hadn't

17

thought of love too often when he had studied in Berkeley. Perhaps living in San Francisco provided more social life. Or perhaps he was taking life more seriously as he became older. Or was it that he was reaching the age when his desire for women was the strongest? He didn't know. He liked American girls; they had a strong appeal for him, especially physically. Some American girls had given him pictures taken in sweaters, and he loved them, but he knew that his father would not allow him to marry an American; and he also knew that many American parents would not allow their daughters to marry Chinese. He had dates with many American girls without serious intentions; he had enjoyed their company tremendously and thought they were gay and appreciative, different from most of the Chinese girls he had dated. The Chinese girls, especially those from China, were usually stiff and polite; some were downright conceited, knowing that the ratio of Chinese men to Chinese women was to the women's great advantage. Wang Ta knew that the "six men to one girl" situation was a social problem and he always held his horses whenever he met a girl from China. He had taken out a girl newly arrived from Formosa. But when the news got around, all of the old bachelors, including a flock from Monterey, flooded to San Francisco to date her. The girl, whose gown of blue cotton had cost her an equivalent of about two American dollars, now found herself wearing six-dollar flowers and going to concerts and operas. Wang Ta wondered if she would accept an invitation to a movie now, after being spoiled by so many anxious bachelors.

Then he met an American-Chinese girl, born in Stockton. She studied music at the City College. They went out many times. Wang Ta found her delightful, gay and appreciative like an American girl. After four months Wang Ta became serious. He was sure that his father wouldn't object to his marrying an American-Chinese. She was from a good family; her father owned a supermarket in Stockton and all her sisters and brothers had gone to college. She was the youngest and the prettiest in the family, with large sparkling eyes and long wavy black hair. One Saturday evening they had dinner in Chinatown. "Mary," Wang Ta said as they ordered a family dinner in a private booth in the Far East Restaurant on Grant Avenue, "let's not go to a movie tonight. Let me take you home and introduce you to my father."

"Oh, let's go to a movie," Mary said. "I'm anxious to see 'Rear Window.' If I miss it now I don't know when it will be shown again. It's already ancient, you know."

"But I want you to meet my father."

"Some other time, Lawrence," Mary said. "For four months I've been calling you Lawrence, and I'm still not used to it. It's a funny name. It sounds stiff. Why don't you use your Chinese name?"

"Wang Ta is all right in China," Wang Ta said; "but in this country everybody calls me Ta Wang. Ta Wang means 'bandit king' in Chinese. So I asked a schoolmate to give me an American name."

"Why did she give you Lawrence? Is she an old maid?"

"No, he is a man. He was studying Chinese. He gave me Lawrence to help him memorize Chinese."

"What do you mean?"

"Law-ren-ce means 'old man dies.' As long as he remembers me he remembers this Chinese sentence. Choosing between 'bandit king' and 'old man dies' I prefer the latter." He expected Mary to laugh, but she made a face instead. She was lovely even when she was making a face, especially the way she wrinkled her nose.

"Why don't you change it?" she said. "Why don't you use a more common name, like Tom, or George, or Larry? Yes, why not use Larry? It's pretty close to Lawrence . . ."

Wang Ta swallowed hard and said, his voice trembling a little, "Will you marry me, Mary?"

The waiter brought in the dishes. Mary sipped her

tea and waited until the waiter had left. "I'm already engaged, Lawrence," she said, lowering her beautiful eyes.

Wang Ta stared at her, then he swallowed again. "But you never told me," he suddenly said, his voice tinged with anger now.

"I never thought you were serious," Mary said.

"How could it be otherwise?" Wang Ta said heatedly. He was really hurt now. "I've been taking you out every week, isn't that serious enough?"

"A lot of other fellows have taken me out. It doesn't mean that I have to marry all of them."

"But you have let me kiss you!"

"Oh, let's not talk about it," Mary said. "Let's eat, the food is getting cold."

"You should have told me you were engaged," Wang Ta said.

"Oh, for heaven's sake, let's not talk about it. Must I walk around town beating a gong and tell everybody I'm engaged to be married? Dick is in Japan. He's just a soldier. I don't have to brag about him."

"You shouldn't have let me kiss you," Wang Ta said.

"Oh, you certainly are old-fashioned. Just like your name. I suppose all you fellows raised in China are like that."

"I suppose you kiss everybody!"

Mary threw her chopsticks down, grabbed her purse and overcoat and walked out of the restaurant without a word. For a moment Wang Ta was stunned. He quickly followed her. "Mary, Mary!" he called, catching up with her on Grant Avenue going south toward California Street. But she ignored him, crossed the street, got into a taxi in front of St. Mary's Church and was gone. That was their last date.

For two weeks Wang Ta studied hard in an effort to drive Mary out of his mind. Sometimes when he was reading a medical book, he wished someone had invented some medicine that would cure a man's love-sickness and his wounded pride. Mary had walked out on him; he was wounded, but he wasn't angry with her. Perhaps that's why it's so hard to forget a girl. Knowing that it was impossible to heal the wound with hard study, he went to a lot of movies and read many magazine articles on love and psychology. Sometimes he would enjoy reading a pocket book or a magazine short story in which the hero lost his girl, fought for her and won her back. He would identify himself with the hero and find some consolation through an illusion that girls were hard to grasp but they would eventually go back to their heroes with passion and love and humility.

But the formula fiction could only give him a temporary relief, just like a shot of whisky or brandy, and afterward the letdown was even harder to bear. Several times he attempted to call Mary but each time he dropped a coin in the phone he would change his mind. "What's the use," he would say to himself. "She is somebody else's girl. She is engaged to be married." He wasn't the kind of man to break people's engagements. And he wasn't sure that he could even if he wanted to.

Mary almost ruined his first year at the Medical School. His father didn't know anything about this romance and Wang Ta decided to keep it a secret. He became terribly lonely and unhappy, and his grades went downhill. He wrote to Chang Ling-yu in Los Angeles. They had been close friends at the University of California where Chang had worked for his Ph.D degree in political science. They had spent many week ends together in Berkeley, sipping coffee and discussing politics. Chang, a heavy-set man with a broad jovial face, was always a great talker whenever he touched the subject of women. Wang Ta had the impression that Chang must have once been a great Romeo in China, knowing so much about women. After having received his Ph.D degree in political science, Chang had left for Los Angeles. Now Wang Ta suddenly missed him and wrote him a letter inviting him to San Francisco for a week end.

Chang didn't answer his letter, but three weeks later

he called Wang Ta on the phone. "I'm in town," he said. "I've moved. I didn't get your letter until I went to my former landlady to redeem my trunk." He told Wang Ta that he had owed his former landlady thirty dollars' rent and she had kept his trunk as a "hostage." "Don't worry about me now," he went on jovially. "I'm wealthy now. I'll treat you to a tea lunch at Hsiang Yah. Meet me there in twenty minutes."

Wang Ta chuckled as he hung up the phone. Chang hadn't changed—still talkative, spirited and straightforward. He remembered the breakfast and lunch combinations they had had years ago at Hsiang Yah teahouse in the nameless, obscure alley across the street from the Chinese Y.M.C.A. It was in a basement with an insignificant entrance, opening for business only from 10 A.M. to 3 P.M. The American tourists would never find it unless they were guided, and few Americans were guided there. Perhaps the citizens of Chinatown wanted to keep it an exclusive Chinese teahouse, or perhaps they were afraid that the Americans wouldn't like the food there. Wang Ta had never thought of taking an American girl there.

Hsiang Yah Teahouse seemed to him a Chinatown within Chinatown; its atmosphere was typical Chinese, with customers sipping tea and talking noisily in typical Chinese manner. A Caucasian American struggling clumsily there with a pair of chopsticks would seem out of place, spoiling the atmosphere. Years ago he and Chang used to go there on Sundays, eating and chatting and sipping aster tea until closing time. They used to devour eight dishes of *deem sum* and special delicacies, their favorite being *har gow,* the bonnet-shaped transparent pouches with shrimp filling; *fun gor,* the half-moon-shaped pouches filled with pork, chicken and bamboo shoots; braised duck feet and chicken giblets and pig stomach; grilled Chinese turnip cakes; sweet rice cakes and many kinds of buns and steamed dainty dumplings. The food was expensive but good and typical Cantonese, with no compromising effort made to meet the taste

22

of "the foreigners." He and Chang used to eat to their hearts' content and come out of the teahouse staggering.

Chang was waiting for him at a table in a corner in the teahouse which was decorated with couplet scrolls and red lacquered overhanging carvings. They greeted each other warmly like long-lost friends. Wang Ta never felt quite at home in front of his father or in the company of a sophisticated girl, but with Chang he always relaxed, as though all the little knots of inhibition and restraint in his mind suddenly dissolved. Talking to Chang, he didn't have to choose his words or be cautious of his opinions, and above all, he could enjoy casualness of manners since Chang was very casual with his.

"What are you doing now?" Wang Ta asked after they had ordered.

"I'm a grocery clerk," Chang said cheerfully. "Perhaps the first grocery clerk with a Ph.D degree in political science. Hope I can claim it as a kind of world record."

"I hear there is a Ph.D washing dishes at Fisherman's Wharf," Wang Ta said. "I would have become his subordinate if my father didn't smash the rice bowl for me."

"What are *you* doing?" Chang asked.

"I've gone back to school. The U.C. Medical School. If the professors there have no regard for human lives, they will let me become a medical doctor in seven or eight years." He paused, then added half-mockingly and half-bitterly, "I'm pretty sure I can render a better service for my fellow man by washing their dishes."

"Don't you like medicine?"

"I chose the course because it takes the longest to finish. At least I don't have to look for another job as long as I'm in school. Do you like your job?"

"I'm happy with it," Chang said. "It pays better than a professor. And the butcher gives me the best cut at wholesale prices. By eating well and regularly, and having a lot of physical exercise carrying potatoes, I

23

intend to cut drastically the business of future doctors. Besides, my new profession is either my own salvation or our compatriots' good fortune, depending on how I look at it."

"What do you mean?"

"I've gone through a lot since I got this awe-inspiring Ph.D degree. I discovered it was the heaviest burden I've ever shouldered, something like a wife and her eight children by a former husband. It was a great hurdle of life. Once I almost became a hotel clerk—the nearest thing to a white-collar job, but when my prospective employer found that I was a Ph.D he fired me as promptly as he hired me. His son told me frankly that my degree gave his old man an inferiority complex. Ever since that day I've been convinced that my degree was my only jinx. It has at least smashed ten good prospective rice bowls for me; it has brought me nothing but frustration. Well, that day I tossed my Ph.D into the gutter. I became an ordinary layman, reading who-done-its, loving a good lowbrow joke and haunting the bowling alleys. My luck began to turn. I joined a bowling team, and a week later one of the team members, whose father is the manager of a market chain, got me this job—"

"Is that what you mean by self-salvation?" Wang Ta interrupted.

"No," Chang said, pouring tea for Wang Ta. "Let me tell you, the trouble with most of us Chinese refugees is that we take life too seriously. We cling to our old standards, ignorant of the fact that we are only a bunch of White Chinese, like the White Russians; we refuse to adjust ourselves to a new environment. We dream a lot. I would have been very unhappy if I hadn't adopted a new philosophical attitude toward life and discarded many of our ancient habits, including the habit of loving one's face. The new attitude helped me see my course clearly. If I still lamented my great unfathomable learning as being a waste, I probably would have gone back to the mainland." He

24

gulped down a mouthful of tea, swallowed a *har gow,* wiped his mouth with a napkin and went on:

"So, not going back to the mainland is my self-salvation; refusing to go back to Formosa is our compatriots' good fortune, for with my uncle's influence, I might actually work my way into the government and become a rotten official. I don't know. But I don't want to see that happen. So I am happiest to become a grocery clerk. Let's change the subject before I turn this happy little gathering into a tedious lecture session. How is your love life?"

"Not so good," Wang Ta said grimly.

"Tell me something about it."

"I would rather not talk about it."

"Hm, I can tell you this," Chang said, biting into a duck foot. "You are committing the same mistake by taking love too seriously. You have to remember that you are a White Chinese. You are facing many odds against you in the love business as you are in many other things. I always say that to us the girl situation is just like a grocery store in a year of bad inflation. The few items in the store are so highly priced that they are beyond our reach. I don't blame the local-born Chinese girls for their reluctance to associate with us. What have we to offer them? Nothing. Take me, for instance. I am over forty. I am not better-looking than any of the local-born boys, the sons of a grocer or a restaurant-owner. What I have got that they haven't got is probably my Ph.D degree, which cannot be eaten, like a loaf of bread. But there are a lot of things that they have got and yet I haven't got—cars, television, family properties, youth—things too numerous to name!"

"Guess you are right," Wang Ta said, staring gloomily at the asters in his tea.

"Knowing the situation," Chang went on, "you again have to analyze the girls and then set your policy accordingly. If the girl is the playgirl type, it will be suicidal to get serious with her. If the girl is the serious type, you have to ask yourself honestly whether you like her enough to continue the association. Some girls will play hard-to-get, and they can afford to, too, since there isn't any competition. Others will shop around, just like the old Chinese saying goes, 'Riding on a horse to look for a better horse.' If you find a girl who is looking for something better by riding on your back, you'd better throw her off as quickly as possible. However, this type of girl is easy to detect."

He gulped down another mouthful of tea. "In fact, such a girl is too simple-minded and too practical to be subtle. If you call her on the phone to ask for a date, she will accept it if she thinks she has nothing better to do. If she thinks John or George might call and take her out, she will *humph-ah-humph* for a while on the phone and tell you to call her again tomorrow. If she is entertaining somebody in her apartment when you call, very likely she will say, 'I can't talk to you now, Chang, I'm frying a lamb chop, it will get burned.' And you can be sure that the lamb chop is either John or George, her favorite boy. There is another type which is downright mercenary. However, you don't have to worry about this type, for they will come to you if they think you are a gold mine. You can enjoy the free entertainment without yielding any gold, if you're clever. Of course, there are a lot of nice girls, but we are not talking about nice girls. No matter what type you meet, just remember this rule: Don't plunge yourself headlong into the whirlpool of love so quickly and anxiously."

"I know," Wang Ta said. He picked out an aster from the tea and crushed it between his fingers. "But sometimes you just can't control love. You just can't switch it off and on like an electric light."

"Then you need to have your brains washed," Chang said. "Your attitude toward love must be changed. As I said, you mustn't take love too seriously in the first place. I don't mean everybody should take this attitude. I only mean us, the White Chinese bachelors who are approaching middle age. You have to be callous and prepare yourself to deal with the worst situation. Ah, I've talked too much and ignored my eating. Let me hear some of your stories so that I can eat." He threw his chopsticks down, picked up a large white bean-paste-filled lotus bun with his hand and bit into it hungrily.

"I decided to forget about my past romance," said Wang Ta. "It is a painful failure and it is my own fault."

Chang suddenly stopped chewing the bun and his eyes narrowed, looking intently at a girl in a booth nearby. "I know her," he whispered. "She speaks Mandarin, Shanghai dialect, Cantonese, some English and three or four words of French learned from a French sailor at Hanoi. We came by the same boat seven years ago."

Wang Ta looked. In the booth were two women sitting opposite each other and talking animatedly with hand gestures. One was middle-aged, plump, with heavy make-up on her round face; the other was young and beautiful, dressed in a tight, light-blue gown of shiny material that revealed an excellent slim figure. "Which one?" Wang Ta asked, swallowing.

"The one who looks like a movie star," said Chang. "Do you want to meet her?"

Wang Ta swallowed again. "What type is she?"

"I don't know. I never found out. I met her on the *President Cleveland* seven years ago. In those days I didn't know anything about types." He rose to his feet. "Come on, I'll introduce you to her. You'll never have a dull moment with her. She never stops talking. Perhaps she can cure your unpleasant memory of your past romance for a moment."

They went to the booth. Chang said cheerfully in Mandarin, "What wind has blown you here, Miss Tung?"

Both women turned. Miss Tung stared at him and suddenly her face brightened. "Oh," she said, flinging a slim forefinger at him, a finger with a long silver fingernail pointing slightly downward, "you are Mr. Wu from the Chinese Consulate!"

"Guess again," said Chang, smiling. "My surname is the same as that famed general who had sixty-three wives."

Miss Tung withdrew her finger, placed it on her full crimson lips and thought for a moment, her large dark eyes fluttering. "Oh," she said, her forefinger shooting out again, "you are Mr. Wang of the Five Continent Import and Export Company!"

"No," said Chang, chuckling and shaking his head slowly. "People of a noble breed are oblivious, as the good old saying goes . . ."

"Don't tell me," said Miss Tung hastily. "Give me another hint."

"My surname is one of the most popular and celebrated in China," said Chang. "More corrupt generals and warlords were born with this name than with any other. See if you can remember the young marshal who advocated ballroom dancing and kidnapped Chiang Kai-shek . . ."

"Oh, oh," cried Miss Tung, "you are Mr. Chang! We played poker on the *President Cleveland!*" She laughed. Then she turned to Wang Ta and her long eyelashes batted. "Who is this gentleman?"

Chang introduced them. Miss Tung looked at Wang Ta for so long that Wang Ta almost blushed. "Let me introduce Madam Wu," she said, her eyes fluttering again, and she introduced them to her plump companion.

Chang and Wang bowed to Madam Wu, who nodded her head with a smile. "Sit down and join us," invited Miss Tung. Madam Wu is going to adopt me. We were discussing the adoption ceremony. I would like to have your opinion. Sit down, please."

She turned her eyes to Wang Ta and fixed them boldly on his face while he sat down. When Wang Ta returned her gaze she fluttered her eyelashes and smiled. Wang Ta's heart started beating violently now. He found her very sexy, especially when she smiled. Her white even teeth and her deep dimples were the best asset of her smile. "Madam Wu is from Szechuan

Province," she went on. "Her husband was a great general who fought both the Japanese and the Communists in China. Please eat something with us, Oh, waiter, please bring two more teacups. And chopsticks. Now he is one of the most wanted men on Mao Tsetung's blacklist—I mean General Wu, Madam Wu's husband. Now Madam Wu wants to adopt me. Mr. Chang, what ceremony do you think is suitable? I insist on giving her three kowtows, but Madam Wu says three bows would be enough, with three more bows to heaven and earth. What do you think?"

"Kowtow is more serious," said Chang, "more binding. Don't forget to invite us to the ceremony."

"Madam Wu is going to give a banquet," Miss Tung said. "We'll invite you to the banquet. Give us your addresses and telephone numbers." She quickly opened her handbag, fished out a golden address book and handed it to Wang Ta. "Do you live in San Francisco, Mr. Wang?"

"Yes."

"You should come and visit Madam Wu's new house," Miss Tung said. "It's in the Marina, the most beautiful residential section in San Francisco. I'm going to move in with her as soon as we become mother and daughter." She filled up Madam Wu's teacup, then selected a piece of chicken liver with her chopsticks and placed it on Madam Wu's plate. "You like chicken liver. Here's a good piece. Mr. Chang thinks I should kowtow to you, Madam Wu. I refuse to become your daughter unless you accept my kowtows. Oh, waiter, more chicken liver. What do you like to eat, Mr. Wang?"

"I have had plenty at our own table," said Wang Ta. "Thank you. I'll just have a little tea."

"Oh, eat a little more," she said. She picked up a large white bun and placed it on Wang Ta's plate, which the waiter had just brought to him. "Please try this *char sil bow*—it is the best in San Francisco. And I am told that the barbecued pork filling is made from a secret recipe. Please try it. If you like chicken fried

29

noodles, you have to go to Kuo Wah Restaurant on Grant Avenue. It serves the best chicken fried noodles in San Francisco. Madam Wu, what else would you like to eat, please?"

Madam Wu smiled. "No more. I have had enough to last me two days."

Miss Tung placed another piece of chicken liver on Madam Wu's plate. "This piece is also good, please try. The argument is settled, Madam Wu. I'm not going to accept anything from you unless you accept my kowtows."

"Oh, this is America," Madam Wu said. "Kowtow is too old-fashioned. The foreigners might laugh at us."

"Oh, don't mind the foreigners," Miss Tung said. "We shall only invite a few of them. My voice teacher and your piano teacher—Mr. Clark and Mr. Rogers." Then she turned to Wang Ta and added, "Mr. Rogers is Madam Wu's piano teacher. He is very good. He is teaching her how to play the piano without reading the music notes. You should come and listen to Madam Wu play. She can play 'Yankee Doodle' and 'Dixieland' just like Mr. Rogers. Do you sing, Mr. Wang?"

"A little Chinese opera," Wang Ta said. "That was years ago . . ."

"Peking opera?" Miss Tung said excitedly. "Good! Madam Wu sings Peking opera too. And I know somebody who can play *fu chin*. He played for Mei Langfang in Peking. I'll invite him to play at our house. You and Madam Wu can sing to the accompaniment of his famous *fu chin*. I shall call you when he comes. Have you written down your telephone number in my address book?"

"Yes," Wang Ta said, handing the golden address book back to her. She put it back into her handbag and suggested, "Let's go to the park. The sun is beautiful today. Let's drive to the beach. My brother bought me a new car. I'm teaching Madam Wu how to drive. Do you have time this afternoon, Mr. Chang, Mr. Wang?"

Wang Ta waited for Chang to accept the invitation,

but Chang made an excuse saying that they had to visit some friends across the bay. Miss Tung expressed her sincere regret. "Please come to see us," she repeated, then paid the check and left the teahouse arm in arm with Madam Wu.

"Why didn't you accept the invitation?" Wang Ta asked as they walked out of the teahouse. "I think she's interesting."

"You mean she's sexy," Chang said, chuckling.

"We might have a good time if we went with them," Wang Ta said.

"She talks too much," Chang said. "With her I couldn't even get a word in. I love to talk, you know, and also love to listen; but she says nothing that is worth listening to. She is only good to make love to, I presume. But to me it's the case of 'a frog which dreams of eating the flesh of a swan,' as the old saying goes. Don't worry, you'll see her soon. She is going to call you. Did you notice, during the one-sided conversation, that she kept looking at you and asking you to go to her house, or her would-be mother's house? Probably you look very sexy to her, too. Just watch your step, and remember the rule."

As they walked down Sacramento Street and reached Grant Avenue, they saw Miss Tung and Madam Wu get into a brand-new red Buick parked half a block away. "Let's go up to Clay Street," Chang said, turning left. "If she sees us, she might stop the car and talk for another half an hour and maybe block Chinatown traffic."

"Do you think she is a gold digger?" Wang Ta asked.

"She puzzles me," Chang said. "If she was, she would have tried to find out where you work, or who your father is. But she didn't show any interest in your work or your father. Likely she is just a playgirl."

An automobile horn blasted twice and Wang Ta turned. The flashy red Buick was passing them by. Miss Tung waved at him; her white bejeweled hand on the ivory-colored steering wheel, her bright smile with the dimples, her dark wavy hair and her sporty red

31

scarf framed in the car window presented a picture as pretty as an advertisement in a national magazine. Wang Ta waved back and swallowed. He wished he were in a car, driving to Golden Gate Park, to Ocean Beach, then passing the Cliff House, turning into Lincoln Park. . . .

"What a car," Chang said. "Probably the flashiest in Chinatown. Her brother must be as wealthy as Ali Khan."

"I don't think she's a gold digger." Wang Ta suddenly found himself defending her. "She's just a happy, naïve girl who likes to talk and be friendly."

"Hope you are right," Chang said after a moment. "Yes, I think she is a playgirl. She doesn't have any of the characteristics of a gold digger. Do you want to know the characteristics of a gold digger?" He stopped to light a cigarette. "Well, a gold digger first looks at a man's shoes. She has an infallible eye for a man's shoes. She knows the price of a man's shoe better than a shoe salesman. A man who wears a pair of shoes under twenty-five dollars, or whose shoes need a twenty-five cent shoe-shine or a change of heels, is in her eyes a poor 'security risk.' If your shoes pass the test, then she will study your shirt. If you are well-dressed but your shirt collar has a little dark rim or is slightly worn out at the back, she will pass you up as another—well, let me use an American expression—as another phony. If your shoes and shirt are all up to her standard, then she will find out—in a very subtle way, of course— whether you have a car. If you have one, good; she will then ask you to take her home, or give her a ride, the doctor says she needs plenty of fresh air. If your car happens to be a rattletrap, she will have a sudden headache and tell you that the doctor is just around the corner . . ."

Wang Ta hardly listened to his friend. He was thinking of Miss Tung, and wishing they had accepted the ride. In his mind's eye he could see himself sitting beside her . . . the car was coming out of Lincoln Park, driving along the scenic coast and into the Presidio, then turning into the highway lined with yellow lights, crossing Golden Gate Bridge and going straight into the beautiful green valleys in Marin County. . . .

3

For two years Madam Tang had been attending the American citizenship class at the Marina Adult School. She had no idea when the Immigration Service would write to her asking her to go for the preliminary hearing; Madam Tien, one of her close friends, had waited for six years before such a letter reached her. However, Madam Tang kept hoping and studying, memorizing every word of the American Constitution. Her teacher, Miss Shaw, had commented in her class that Madam Tang was the only student who hadn't missed a single class during the past two years and could recite everything she had learned, although her English was a bit hard to follow. But hastily she added, "Her English has improved a great deal. Two years ago when she talked to me in English, I didn't know whether she was talking Greek or Chinese. Now I understand practically every word she says."

Madam Tang was very pleased with this comment. And she couldn't help looking to her right and left and smiling proudly. She still had a lot of difficulty in reading and speaking the English language, but now she could at least answer her teacher's questions without hesitation. During the past week she had made only one mistake. Miss Shaw had asked her what were the advantages of being an American citizen. She stated all the privileges fluently until she hit the last one: "I can find a joke in the government." It puzzled Miss Shaw for a moment, but soon it dawned on her that Madam Tang, in a moment of great fluency and enthusiasm, had used the word "joke" instead of "job." She had just hit the wrong key, like a pianist.

It was a sunny afternoon and Madam Tang came out of the school feeling good. She decided to visit her sister's husband to see whether he had put all his money in the bank. She had been worried about his money ever since reading that robbery news in the paper. Luckily, her late husband had managed the old man's finances and had wisely invested most of his money in sound business, otherwise Wang Chi-yang would probably have tucked all his half million dollars away under his bed. She wondered why the old man was so stubborn, and how her late sister could have tolerated him. She also wondered whether all the people from Hunan were like that, being the greatest red-hot-pepper eaters in China. The province had certainly produced a lot of strange characters, including the Communist, Mao Tse-tung.

While entering Chinatown by the Sacramento Street bus, Madam Tang decided to say a prayer first, at the Temple of Tin How. She believed in Jesus Christ and also, taking no chances, in Tin How, the Chinese Goddess of Heaven. She got off the bus at Grant Avenue and walked to Waverly Place, the street crowded with many colorful, tile-faced buildings with long balconies and black-and-gold ideographs, buildings belonging to wealthy family associations.

The temple was on the top floor of the Shew Hing Benevolent Association. Madam Tang climbed the narrow stairs at least once a month to visit the Queen of Heaven, who guards the fortunes of all those who travel and live in a foreign country. Today she made this special trip to pray for the safety of her brother-in-law's cash stacked somewhere in his house. The old man's money was also her late sister's money; she somehow felt responsible for its safety. She knelt on the straw cushion in front of the gilded, elaborately carved altar of teakwood on which the Goddess sat with both hands holding her scepter in blessing. A thread of blue smoke from the incense bowl rose to her benevolent face. Madam Tang kowtowed three times to the Goddess, said her prayer and then took the can of fortune sticks from the long offering table, shook it until one stick fell out of the can. She read the fortune on it and smiled. The Goddess of Heaven was kind; she promised to look after her brother-in-law's welfare.

Then she rose to her feet, put a dollar of incense money under the incense bowl and left the temple in an excellent frame of mind. She felt hungry, and decided to eat a Peking duck at Tao Yuen on Clay Street. The restaurant was in a basement, with a right-angled downward stairway designed to prevent evil spirits from entering, as evil spirits couldn't turn corners. Madam Tang had been to Peking and thought the duck served here was pretty close to real Peking duck. And the chef at Tao Yuen was honest enough to give the customer not too much of the unwanted part—duck meat. According to real Peking standard, a Peking duck should contain nothing but the skin of the duck, crisp, fragrant and roasted brown, and a bowl of fine soup made from its bones. While waiting for the duck, Madam Tang ordered a glass of hot san shui wine. This was to put her in a state of tranquillity necessary to appreciate fully the fragrant dish.

After dinner, she decided not to visit her brother-in-law. She had prayed to Tin How, the Goddess of Heaven; whether his money was still in his bedroom or had been deposited in the bank, it would be safe.

But when she arrived home, Liu Lung, her brother-in-law's deaf servant was sitting on the steps of her house, dozing. She kicked him lightly on the leg and asked, "What has brought you here, Liu Lung?"

Liu Lung jerked his head up. Seeing Madam Tang, he quickly rose to his feet. "How are you, Madam Tang?" he greeted her politely.

"Not good, not bad," Madam Tang said. "What are you doing in front of my house?"

"Enh?"

"Oh, I forgot you are deaf," she said, and she shouted the question into his ear.

"Old Master Wang invites you to his house," Liu Lung said.

"I am not going. I have had my dinner."

"Enh?"

"All right, I shall go," Madam Tang said despairingly. "It is much simpler to go there than to ask you to carry a message to him."

She started for her brother-in-law's house, which was only three blocks away to the north. Liu Lung followed her at a respectful distance. When she arrived, she waited for Liu Lung to open the door. She went into the living room and sat down in one of the straight-back chairs in which she had always sat. She glanced at the dining room. The round table had not been laid yet. She was glad she had already eaten. She seldom enjoyed the food in the house of Wang anyway; there was red-hot pepper in every dish and she always hiccuped whenever she ate it.

"Madam Tang," said Liu Lung, coming out of Wang Chi-yang's bedroom, "Old Master Wang invites you to his room to talk."

Madam Tang felt strange. Her brother-in-law seldom invited her to his room. When she stepped into the room crowded with the huge mosquito net, the miniature garden, the bookshelves, the desks and many rattan chairs, she knew there was something wrong. Wang Chi-yang, sitting in his chair behind his desk, looked ghastly pale. "My wife's sister," he said with formality, his voice trembling slightly, "I was robbed today."

The news hit Madam Tang like a blow in the face. She was so shocked that she was tongue-tied for a moment. She grabbed the back of a rattan chair and sat in it as though she were sick. "When did it happen?" she asked.

"This morning," Wang Chi-yang said. "When I was returning from the bank."

"Were you robbed of everything?"

"Everything. Every copper of my hundred dollars which I had changed at the bank."

Madam Tang inhaled deeply and sighed. "Ah, only a hundred dollars. I thought a bandit had broken into

36

the house and robbed you of all your cash. How did it happen?"

"A strange foreigner followed me from the bank," Wang Chi-yang said. "When I reached a corner on Powell Street, he put something hard against my back and said something that I did not understand. I knew he was a robber. I quickly raised my hands. He snatched the money from my hand and fled around the corner. My wife's sister, I suspect that the robber had been following me for a few weeks; he might know where I live now. Can you report it to the American government? I want two guards to guard the house day and night."

"My sister's husband," Madam Tang said heatedly, "the American government is a democratic government; it is for the people and by the people, with three principles of the Constitution which are liberty, equality and justice. You just cannot order the government to send you two soldiers to guard your house day and night as though you were a feudal lord. This is not China. You had better get that idea out of your mind. Besides, the American government has three departments: the legislative, the executive, and the judicial. All you can do is to ask the police department of the Executive Department to catch the thief. As for your money, it should be kept in a bank, as I have repeatedly told you." She looked at him narrowly and asked, "Have you deposited your money in the bank?"

"No, not yet," Wang Chi-yang said. "That is why I invited you here to . . ."

"I am glad a robber has robbed you of a hundred dollars!" interrupted Madam Tang angrily. "It will be a good lesson for you! Luckily I prayed for the safety of your money at Tin How Temple a moment ago, otherwise the bandit would have broken into the house and robbed you of all your cash in the house! *Aiyoo,* my sister's husband, why are you so stubborn? Why don't you listen to my advice?"

"I have decided to deposit it today," Wang Chi-yang said. "I do not know the foreign talk, that is why I invited you here . . ."

"Not today," Madam Tang interrupted again. "The bank is closed."

"Closed? Why?"

"The bank closes at three o'clock. Do not you know it?"

"No," Wang Chi-yang said. "I always go there at lunch time. My wife's sister, can you call the manager and ask him to open it?"

"*Aiyoo,* my sister's husband," said Madam Tang despairingly, "the bank manager is not a black-market money-changer, how can you call him and order him around like that? Besides, I do not know his home telephone number. Please get the idea out of your mind that you are still in your backward Hunan Province. We shall go to the bank at nine o'clock tomorrow morning. That is when it opens. Tell Liu Lung not to let anybody in tonight. And tell Wang Ta and Wang San to stay at home. You do not have a pistol, do you?"

"No."

"Well, I do not think the bandit will come to the house tonight, since he has already robbed you of a hundred dollars. It ought to last him a few days. And I am going to call the police to catch him. What does he look like?"

"I do not know what he looked like," Wang Chi-yang said. "He is a foreigner. All foreigners look alike."

"Since you do not know what he looks like," Madam Tang said firmly, "I shall not call the police. The police are not going to arrest everybody in San Francisco to find out who the robber is. Do the servants know that you were robbed?"

"No. I did not tell anybody. That is why I invited you to my room to discuss it."

"Good," Madam Tang said, rising from her chair. "Keep quiet. I shall come tomorrow."

The next morning, Madam Tang came promptly at nine o'clock. Old Master Wang had got up an hour earlier than usual to wait for her. He had put an extra lock on the trunk in which the money was kept. He hadn't slept well last night because of the robbery. Every little noise in the house had startled him. He had not told Wang San to recite his lessons as he often did during the evenings when he stayed at home. He had heard Wang Ta come in late in the night; he had also heard Liu Ma scold her husband in their room upstairs. And the old clock on the mantel had seemed noisier than usual. No, he had not slept well at all. "You do not look well," Madam Tang said. "Are you sick?"

"No," Wang Chi-yang said. "This is all the cash I have in the house."

Madam Tang looked at the huge iron trunk and frowned. "What? A whole trunk of it?"

"No, it is not full." He unlocked the three locks on the trunk and opened it. Packed in a corner were stacks of brand-new hundred-dollar bills. "Only eighty-seven thousand and seven hundred dollars here. I shall tell Liu Lung to carry the trunk to the bank."

"Carry a trunk to the bank?" Madam Tang said. "Nobody has ever carried a big iron trunk to the bank. We shall bring the money to the bank in an old shopping bag. It is much safer this way. I am going to borrow a shopping bag from the cook." She went to the kitchen and asked the moon-faced cook to show her all his shopping bags. The cook had five of them. Madam Tang selected the shabbiest-looking one and brought it to her brother-in-law's room. She stuffed the bank-notes into the bag and covered them with a Chinese newspaper. "I shall carry the bag," she said. "Let us go now."

They came out of the house and went down the hill to Grant Avenue. The Bank of America China-town branch was crowded in the morning. Madam Tang didn't wait on lines. She told a girl across the counter that she wanted to see the manager. The manager, a plump, amiable Chinese lady wearing glasses, looked up from her desk, and when she saw Madam

Tang she quickly rose from her chair and greeted her. "I have brought a little business to you, Mrs. Hu," Madam Tang said in Cantonese. "Can we come in and talk to you in private?"

"Certainly, Mrs. Tang," the manager said, opening the counter door for them to come in. Madam Tang introduced her brother-in-law to the manager, then they went to the manager's corner, where Mrs. Hu invited them to sit down. "My sister's husband intends to have some money deposited in this bank," Madam Tang said, handing Mrs. Hu the shopping bag. Mrs. Hu peered into the bag, then fished out a stack of hundred-dollar bills from under the old newspaper and her eyes popped. She switched her eyes between Wang Chi-yang and the money a few times without saying anything. "This is not fake money, Mrs. Hu," Madam Tang said. "I can vouch for it. There are eighty-seven thousand and seven hundred in the bag. My sister's husband wants to open a savings account for eighty thousand, and a checking account for the rest of the money."

The manager smiled. "It can be arranged," she said. She turned to a small, pretty Chinese girl at a desk, called her over and asked her to count the money in the bag. Then she started gathering information about the depositor. When the girl returned with a slip of paper stating the amount of money in the bag, Wang Chi-yang glanced at it and nodded his head in approval. "The girl is honest," he said to Madam Tang. "Good."

Madam Tang coughed in embarrassment and said hastily to the manager, "My sister's husband cannot sign his name in English. If he signs a check, is a Chinese signature all right?"

"I'm afraid not," Mrs. Hu said. "Some of the tellers do not read Chinese. But some of our depositors use a seal. Does Mr. Wang have a seal?"

Wang Chi-yang had many seals, and he always carried one of them with him in a little pouch chained to a button on his long gown. When the business was completed, Madam Tang, smiling broadly, thanked the manager and left the bank with her brother-in-law. The great load on her mind was finally off. But something else still bothered her. When they reached a street corner a block away, she turned into a haberdashery and said to Wang Chi-yang, "I shall show you how to use a check. Come in."

In the store the manager greeted them cordially. "How much is your best suit?" Madam Tang asked in Cantonese.

"A hundred and twenty dollars," the manager said, "imported from England."

Madam Tang took out the checkbook and wrote a hundred and twenty dollars on a check, then told her brother-in-law to put the seal on it. "See? How simple!" Then she handed the check to the manager and added in Cantonese, "Endorse it before he changes his mind. And please show him the best suit you have."

When the manager brought out a dark-gray worsted suit, smiling and blowing dust off its shoulders, Old Master Wang's face reddened. "What is this for?" he said angrily. "I do not want any foreign dress."

"*Aiyoo,* my sister's husband, why are you so stubborn? You have a prominent stomach. You will look nice in a suit of foreign dress. Please go and try it on."

"No, I do not want it!"

"Whether you want it or not, it is already paid for," said Madam Tang firmly. "It has cost a hundred and twenty dollars, and you have already put your seal on the check."

"That is right," said the smiling manager in Mandarin with a heavy Cantonese accent, "and I shall pay the sales tax for you as a friendly gesture to a new customer. Come this way, please. Any alteration is free of charge."

4

On Saturday morning everybody in the House of Wang was doing something different, or in a different mood. Wang Ta was out; Wang San was hungry and had his ball game on his mind; the cook was shopping; Old Master Wang was still in bed; Liu Ma was worried.

Since Old Master Wang had bought the Western suit, Liu Ma had been talking about it, creating a rumor that the Old Master was going to Westernize the household. She expressed her fear to Liu Lung early in the morning when her deaf husband was still sleepy and deafest. So nobody heard her complaint but Wang San, who hated bed and was already in the kitchen raiding the icebox.

"Did you hear what I said?" Liu Ma shouted to her husband as they came into the kitchen from the back yard where they had done some cleaning.

"Enh?" Liu Lung asked.

"Oh, I wasted my breath the whole morning trying to tell you what is going on in the house," Liu Ma said. "If the Old Master discharges you and hires a foreign servant, don't tell me I have not warned you!"

"You warn me? What?"

"Oh, why am I wasting my time talking to a deaf and dumb old turtle like you?" Liu Ma moaned. When she saw Wang San she frowned. "Eating raw ham again?" she said. "You had better not let the cook know that you are eating his ham. He might tell your father and you know what the Old Master will do to you. He will whip your palm with that bamboo stick again." Wang San swallowed the ham without much chewing and gulped down a bowl of cold water so fast that it made Liu Lung wince. "I wonder why the cook still has not come back from the morning shopping," Liu Ma went on. "If he still kills his time in a teahouse every morning, one day he will find his bedroll at the front door and a foreign cook in the kitchen."

"Will my father hire an American cook, Liu Ma?" Wang San asked, his face brightening.

"He has bought an American suit," Liu Ma said emphatically. "That is only the beginning. He is going to Westernize the household and have all of us discharged. I have wasted the whole morning trying to tell Liu Lung about it and this deaf-dumb old turtle did not hear even a word of what I said!"

"Oh, boy!" Wang San said in English. "No more chop suey, goody goody!"

Wang San had no school today. But he hated Saturdays and Sundays because he had to eat all his meals at home. Whenever he saw the typical Hunan dishes he lost his appetite. Sometimes he would sneak out and eat a hot dog or a hamburger before meals. If he had no money he would raid the icebox when the cook wasn't in the kitchen. When he was very hungry he would raid it anyway, cook or no cook. Usually he was the hungriest when the family dinner was the richest, for there were so many delicacies on the table that Wang San hated. The only food he enjoyed at home was the raw Chinese ham in the icebox.

Now that he had learned his father was going to Westernize the household, he was excited. There were a lot of things he would like to do at home but had never dared, such as reading comic books on the living-room floor, chewing bubble gum, shooting birds in the back yard with an air gun, and so on. Now perhaps he could do all these things without arousing his father's anger.

At lunch time he boldly brought home a loaf of bread. Instead of eating rice he made sandwiches with the Chinese dishes. While he was enjoying his sandwiches his father looked at him with a deep scowl. "What kind of food is that?" Old Master Wang asked.

"Sandwich, father," Wang San said.

"What a barbarous way of eating it," his father said. "Use your chopsticks!"

"You are not supposed to eat sandwich with chopsticks, father. This is American food."

"What is wrong with the Chinese food on this table?"

"I like American food better."

Old Master Wang's scowl became deeper. "I am told that you often eat raw ham, is that true?"

Wang San said through a mouthful of food, "Yes, but I was hungry."

"You used to have good table manners," Old Master Wang said, "eating sparingly and quietly. Now you eat like a mountain bandit; furthermore, only cannibals eat raw meat; if the cook tells me you eat raw ham again, you might as well move to the hills and live like one. Did you study this morning?"

"Yes, father."

"Come to my room and recite your lessons to me after lunch," Wang Chi-yang said, rising. Wang San's sandwich and table manners had ruined his appetite. He couldn't eat any more.

After his father had left the table Wang San enjoyed his sandwich even more. He didn't know that the Chinese dishes, which he had disliked, could taste so good with bread. He was glad that his father hadn't said anything about forbidding him to eat sandwiches.

Having had a good lunch, Wang San felt it was the best Saturday he had ever had. And he couldn't wait to get into the ball game. He wished he was grown up like Wang Ta, who could come and go without having to ask his father's permission, and always had enough money to eat outside. He wondered where his brother was now. He seldom saw him, especially on week ends. He envied his brother's life and was sure he always had a good time; besides, Wang Ta didn't have to recite his lessons to their father. Although the recitation routine was nothing difficult, for his father didn't understand a word of what he was reciting anyway, yet it was annoying and often made him nervous.

He was glad he was to recite his lessons in the privacy of his father's room, for nobody could hear what he was reciting except his father. But sometimes his father would have him recite his lessons in the living room. It was always a dreadful experience, for his aunt Madam Tang might drop in and listen to him. His aunt understood English and could easily find out he was cheating a little.

He took his school books and went to his father's room. Old Master Wang was sitting in his rattan chair enjoying a mild cough. Wang San waited until his father finished coughing and went to his desk stiffly. "What lessons have you studied this morning?" Old Master Wang asked, groaning and clearing his throat.

"Geography and arithmetic," Wang San said.

"Put your books down," his father said.

Wang San laid his books on the desk and waited. "Which lesson of geography have you studied?" his father asked.

"Lesson nine."

"Recite lesson nine."

Wang San recited lesson nine about North America, and when he began to stammer, he quickly switched to the American Declaration of Independence, which he had memorized and could recite fluently. When Wang San finished, Old Master Wang nodded his head with approval and grunted, "Hm, not bad, not bad. Which lesson of arithmetic have you studied?"

"Lesson ten," Wang San said.

"Recite lesson ten."

Wang San didn't argue that arithmetic lessons were not to be recited. He knew his father, who believed that anything a student learned at school must be memorized. It was the system practiced in China for thousands of years, and Old Master Wang firmly believed it was the only system that could help the student learn anything. "Lesson ten, go on," he said.

Wang San cleared his voice and repeated the American Declaration of Independence, twice this time. When he finished he shifted his legs restlessly and waited anxiously for his father to dismiss him. He didn't want to be late for the ball game. He was getting more uncomfortable now. Old Master Wang roughed and asked, "Is that all?"

"Yes."

"Next time study more."

"Yes, father. May I go now?"

Wang Chi-yang looked at his son sternly and asked, "Why are you so anxious to go?"

"M-my aunt wants me to visit her," Wang San said.

Old Master Wang couldn't object to his sons' going to their aunt's for fear he might displease his sister-in-law, who had insisted that relatives should visit each other as often as possible. But he didn't let Wang San go until after he had given him a lecture on manners, honesty and filial piety.

After Wang San had left Old Master Wang coughed for a time and felt contented. In a good frame of mind he practiced his calligraphy, tended his miniature garden, and then decided to take a walk in Chinatown.

He walked down Stockton Street and turned onto Sacramento. The afternoon was sunny and the air was warm and fresh, many Cantonese women were sitting at their doorsteps watching the street, as Chinese women used to do in China. Old Master Wang missed the hawkers and the rickshas. As he was going down the hill and passing the Chinese playground, feeling nostalgic, he suddenly saw Wang San throwing a leather ball over a net with a group of youngsters. He blinked a few times to make sure it was his son. Yes, it was he. Was that how he visited his aunt?

Old Master Wang felt anger rising in him. He hated his son's dishonesty, especially after he had just lectured him on the subject of honesty. He controlled a strong desire to go over to his son and box his ear for lying. He coughed to attract his son's attention, but Wang San was so engrossed in the game that he never noticed his father. Wang Chi-yang's anger was rising fast as he watched his son, but soon he was

46

amazed at Wang San's skill in hitting the leather ball. He ran, fell and leaped like a monkey, saving the ball from falling to the ground with great agility. Old Master Wang watched for a while, fascinated, and gradually found himself secretly rooting for his son's team.

Feeling somewhat ashamed of himself for enjoying a children's game he quickly left the playground, glad that Wang San had not seen him. He wondered if he could find a place where he could watch the game without being seen. It would certainly create a scandal if people talked about Old Master Wang watching a ball game every Saturday afternoon. He would like to solve the problem. It was the first time in his life he had discovered that hitting a leather ball over a net could be so interesting.

On his way home, he made another discovery: Wang San's hands must have been toughened by this game. No wonder the boy had become less afraid of his bamboo stick. Next time he punished him he must hit harder.

5

As Chang had predicted, Miss Tung called Wang Ta three days after they had met at Hsiang Yah Teahouse. She invited him to her small but luxurious apartment and cooked him a five-course dinner, with four of the courses ordered from The Express Kitchen on Broadway. The course she cooked herself was an egg flower soup, which was pretty good except a bit too salty. Wang Ta enjoyed the meal and helped clean the table. He insisted on washing the dishes, but Miss Tung pushed him out of the kitchen, guided him to the cozy living room and turned on the television. For two hours Wang Ta watched four dramas and didn't have the slightest idea what they were all about. All he noticed was that two of the main characters in the four television plays were murdered. He couldn't concentrate. He was in love. His heart was beating violently as he watched the screen and his mind floated; whereas Miss Tung, seated beside him, enjoyed the plays tremendously. During the tense scenes she would grip his arm and catch her breath; sometimes she would sigh or groan or laugh or urge the hero to go on, especially during a love scene in which the bashful hero hesitated too much.

Wang Ta sat there fighting a strong urge to put his arms around the soft warm body beside him; the fragrance of her hair was so good and strong that he inhaled deeply in secret, adding toughness to the fight.

After that evening, they went out together many times, going to the movies, dancing at night clubs and eating at the drive-ins. Each time they went out, Wang Ta had to fight the desire to kiss her. Once he almost did but at the last moment he backed out. He was afraid. Once he had wanted to kiss a girl but the girl had said. "Oh, let's not spoil the fun." What if Miss Tung says the same thing? No, he couldn't act too hastily. He mustn't spoil the good friendship and the fun by acting like a wolf.

Miss Tung seemed very busy, but she always accepted his invitations, although some evenings she said she couldn't stay out too late, for her brother was home. Wang Ta had never met her brother. When he asked where her brother worked, she said he was an officer on a big steamship, and then promptly changed the subject. Wang Ta had met a few of her friends, and they played mah-jongg in her apartment; it seemed that none of them had met her brother, either. He wrote to Chang and reported to him about his dates with Miss Tung, and asked him whether he knew her brother. Chang replied that he knew nothing of him. All he had guessed was that he was pretty wealthy. He had bought her a brand-new Buick, hadn't he?

At the mah-jongg table, Wang Ta met a certain Miss

Chao, a pockmarked woman, who seemed to be very intimate with Miss Tung. She and Miss Tung had known each other in Shanghai and had gone through a lot together during the war. Wang Ta befriended Miss Chao in hope that he might be able to find out something about Miss Tung's mysterious brother from her. He was sinking deeper in love every day and losing his appetite on account of it. To him Miss Tung was a perfect girl, gay and extremely attractive. The only thing that bothered him a great deal now was this shadowy brother of hers. He invited Miss Chao to dinner several times and inquired about Miss Tung's brother, but Miss Chao was noncommittal. She liked to talk about art and philosophy. She told Wang Ta that he was the only person with whom she could really enjoy talking. Reciprocating his friendship, she invited Wang Ta to her apartment to enjoy her home-cooked Shanghai dishes. Wang Ta liked her cooking and enjoyed her company, so he went to see her often, knowing that he would never fall in love with her. He was also sure that Miss Tung wouldn't be jealous, for Miss Chao was badly pockmarked, and was probably ten years his senior. He liked her as a sister, and didn't doubt for a moment that she was treating him like a brother, too. She told him of her family, her friends and all her happy days in China. She talked about everything but Miss Tung and her brother.

One evening, Wang Ta and Miss Tung had a date. When they came out of the movie, Wang Ta suggested that they go to a drive-in and have a milk shake, but Miss Tung was tired of drive-ins; besides, milk shakes made her fat. Why not do something else for a change? So they drove to Coit Tower on Telegraph Hill to enjoy a panoramic view of the San Francisco Bay and the East Bay area. The new Buick climbed smoothly, with music blaring. On the scenic dome of Telegraph Hill they found a parking space between two cars; it commanded an excellent view of Alcatraz Federal Prison and the long Bay Bridge that gleamed with thousands of yellow lights. In the distance, across the bay, were the cities of Berkeley and Oakland, glittering against the starlit evening sky like the contents of a pirate's jewelry chest. A steamer tooted somewhere in the bay; an airplane with red and yellow lights blinking circled the city leisurely, humming like a thundering bass in a strange symphony composed of hundreds of other city noises.

Miss Tung turned the music off, pushed the seat back and half-turned to Wang Ta. "Let's talk," she said. Wang Ta turned to her, putting his left arm on the back of the seat behind her, touching her long soft hair. His heart thumped. Through the window on Miss Tung's side he saw the occupants in the next car wrapped up in each other's arms, kissing. He looked at Miss Tung; she was looking at him. In a sudden surge of courage he took her in his arms, and before he knew it, Miss Tung's soft lips were on his, her hands clutching him tightly. He didn't know how long the kiss lasted, but it was the longest kiss he had ever experienced with any woman in all his life, and the most enjoyable one. When he opened his eyes the car next to theirs had gone, the airplane had returned. He looked into the bay and felt as if he had just made a round trip to Utopia where one's sense of time was completely lost. He kissed Miss Tung's neck boldly and asked, "Will you marry me, Miss Tung?"

Miss Tung tossed her head up, laid it on the seat back and laughed. "Why are you laughing?" Wang Ta asked, bewildered.

"You are the first man who ever proposed marriage to me and called me Miss Tung at the same time," she said, laughing. "It sounds very funny."

"I have always called you Miss Tung. I think proposing marriage should be serious and formal. Calling you miss is appropriate."

"Yes, but you have never called me anything else but miss. And you never kissed me until a minute ago. You act very strange, but I like it. You are so different from the others. Now, since we have kissed, you may call me Linda and be less formal. My voice teacher gave this name to me. Linda Tung will be my professional name if I become a professional singer. Linda Tung—does it sound like a famous singer?"

"You haven't answered my question yet," Wang Ta said. "Will you marry me, Linda?"

Miss Tung patted his cheek. "Of course I will marry you, but I'll have to ask my brother's permission. He is a tyrant . . ."

"I have never met your brother," Wang Ta interrupted. "Where is he anyway? Can I meet him?"

"Of course you can meet him. He is in Europe now."

"What does he do in Europe?"

"I told you, he is an officer on an ocean liner. Oh, your poor memory." With a laugh she hastily changed the subject. "Do you know why a woman bears a baby boy, and why she bears a baby girl?"

Wang Ta was puzzled by this irrelevant question. "Why? Because she is married, I guess."

"Yes, but when a woman bears a baby boy, why is it a baby boy, not a baby girl?"

"Why? Because the male sperm contains . . . oh, let's not talk about it. It's biology. It will become either too dull or too vulgar if we keep talking about it."

"You know what my voice teacher said?" She laughed again. "Oh, he has the funniest ideas about baby boys and baby girls. He says, in the process of making a baby, if the man enjoys more, it will be a baby boy; if the woman enjoys more, it will be a baby girl."

"Let's not talk about it, Linda," Wang Ta said, somewhat embarrassed. "Let's talk about your brother. How old is he? Do you have his picture in your apartment?"

"Of course," Linda said. "I'll show it to you next time. Somebody told me you and Helen are seeing each other very often, is that true?"

"Who is Helen?"

51

Miss Tung poked her face with a forefinger. "You know . . . you know who she is."

Wang Ta was more puzzled now. "I don't know who you mean."

"*Aiyoo*, don't you know?" Miss Tung said impatiently, still poking her face with the finger. "The woman whose face has got a lot of little holes . . ."

Wang Ta laughed. "Oh, you mean Miss Chao! Why didn't you say Miss Chao in the first place?"

"Do you like her?"

"Why, yes. We are just like sister and brother!"

"Perhaps she doesn't think of you as a brother. Somebody said she is very sexy. Do you know the old Chinese saying about pockmarked women? 'Nine pockmarked women out of ten are sensual' it says."

"It is just an old saying. It has no scientific proof."

"Helen is sensual," Miss Tung said. "I know all about her. I've known her for fifteen years. Somebody said . . ."

"Oh, please, let's not talk about her. She is just a sister to me. I like her, but I don't think I could ever fall in love with her. Let's not talk anything bad about her."

"Being sensual is not exactly bad," Miss Tung said. "Men like women being sensual. Don't you? You know what my voice teacher said the other night? He said . . ."

"Let's talk about our marriage," Wang Ta interrupted. "Do you think your brother will approve of it?"

"Naturally," Miss Tung said, giving Wang Ta's face an affectionate pat. "He's always wanted me to get married. Let's listen to some music." She quickly turned on the radio. "I like South American music, especially the rumba, don't you? I never get tired of listening to it. I can dance the rumba all night. A lot of women don't know how to twist their hips when they dance the rumba . . . oh, here is a jitterbug." She clamped her front teeth, snapped her fingers and jerked her shoulders to the beat of the music, humming, her eyes rolling. Wang Ta watched her, his heart thumping, pumping blood and love all over his body. He swallowed, fighting another strong urge to take her into his arms and kiss her and swear that he would never let her go. But he controlled himself. Oh, what a lucky man he would be if he could possess her for the rest of his life. His hands began to sweat as he watched her humming and jerking her shoulders, her breasts bouncing slightly under the red wool dress with the low-cut neckline. When the music ended, Wang Ta grabbed her. She quickly planted a kiss on his cheek and pushed him away. "Let's go. I have to get up early tomorrow," she said, starting the car.

"Shall I see you tomorrow?" Wang Ta asked.

"Oh, no," she said. "I have a singing lesson early in the morning. I'll see you Saturday. Let's drive to Carmel and spend a week end there. Oh, I love Carmel. Have you been there?"

"Yes, a few times."

"Oh, I love to spend week ends there. So peaceful. So beautiful."

Wang Ta swallowed. "All right, we'll go to Carmel this week end."

"We shall stay at the Highland Inn," Miss Tung said. "It's my favorite hotel. We can register there as husband and wife. Oh, here's a rumba!" She turned the music louder, clicked her tongue to keep the rumba beat as the car followed the winding road down the hill. . . .

Wang Ta didn't sleep well that night. He tossed in bed dreaming and thinking of Miss Tung, alternately loving and worrying. He hoped her brother would return soon; and yet he was afraid of meeting him. He was afraid he might turn him down. There were a lot of men in the market, independent men, young and good-looking. Her brother might know dozens of them. Why must she have her brother's permission? he wondered. She was over twenty-two. Probably her family was just as old-fashioned as his. He also had to have his father's permission to get married. But he

53

was ready to revolt if his father refused to give his permission. He would pack and leave the house. He had always wanted to be independent anyway.

The next morning he got up early. As he didn't have a class until eleven, he went to see Miss Tung. Perhaps he could accompany her to her voice teacher's house and watch her taking lessons for a while. He would like to meet her voice teacher, whom she had talked so much about. He had the impression that the teacher was a strange character. Well, most artists are strange characters anyway, he thought.

He got dressed, made his toilet quickly and drove to her apartment on Vallejo Street. He rang her bell for a solid minute before she answered it. When he got into her apartment she was in a pink silk robe, looking half-awake. She touched her hair with the palm of her hand and yawned. "Oh, it's you," she said. "You woke me up."

"I thought you had singing lessons early in the morning," Wang Ta said.

"What time is it?"

Wang Ta consulted his watch. "Eight thirty."

"Only eight thirty?" she cried. "It's not dawn yet."

"Can I watch you take singing lessons this morning?"

"No, you can't," she said. "My voice teacher says it's bad to have visitors. I can't concentrate when I'm being watched. But you can have breakfast here if you want to. Oh, it's early. Only eight thirty, heavens!"

"I'm sorry," Wang Ta said apologetically. "Let me cook the breakfast for you."

"You can stay here for only an hour," she said. "Come and help me make my bed first."

He followed her to her bedroom. It was luxuriously furnished, but by no means tidy. On the light-green dresser that matched the color of the whole room were brushes and combs and cosmetics of all types, lying in a state of litter as though a cat had chased a mouse among them. On the wall and on her other dresser and desk were a number of her glamour pictures taken on

54

beaches and beside her car, each showing a great deal of her shapely legs. "Now, be a good boy and change the sheets," she said, smiling. "I'll be with you in a few moments." She tossed two clean sheets on the bed and went out of the room, yawning.

While he was changing the sheets in her wide, fragrant bed, Wang Ta noticed that on the lamp stand beside her bed was a plate of melon-seed shells and a Chinese book. He chuckled. The girl really knows how to enjoy life, reading in bed and cracking melon seeds. Curiously he picked up the book, and his eyes widened slightly as he read its title, *Madam Fang's Secret Romance*. There were illustrations in the book, too. He almost blushed as he looked at some of them. He sat down on the bed and read a few paragraphs of the book, his heart pounding. ". . . after the long, ecstatic kiss, she felt her blood boiling in her veins and her bones melting with the burning desire of love. He pushed her down on the couch breathlessly and his masculine hands started to explore the curves of her soft, warm body . . ."

He devoured the paragraphs until he heard the water run in the bathroom and then a door click. He quickly put the book away and with his heart pounding more violently now, he started making her bed. When he finished he put his head out of the room and listened. The water in the bathroom had stopped running. He took the book, sat on her bed and read a few more pages. Suddenly the bathroom door clicked again; quickly he put the book away. "I've had my bath," Miss Tung said, coming into her room. She pulled her robe sleeve up and put her arm to Wang Ta's nose. "Does my skin smell good? I washed myself with a special kind of soap. My brother sent it to me from Paris."

Wang Ta took her soft bare arm and smelled it. The fragrance was pleasant and mellow. He pressed his lips on the arm but she quickly pulled it away. "Now get out," she said, smiling and fluttering her eyelids. "I'm going to get dressed. You can go to the living room and watch television. Or read the movie magazines. I have all the movie magazines in the world. The ones from Hong Kong are bad. The movie stars printed in them are too skinny. Their chests are as flat as a washboard. No figure." She loosened the belt of her robe and Wang Ta caught a glimpse of her fully developed breasts and her pink, scanty underwear. "Now get out and let me get dressed." Laughing and batting her eyelids, she pushed him out of the room with one hand, holding her robe loosely together in the other.

"I'll cook breakfast now," Wang Ta said.

"All right," Miss Tung shouted from behind the door. "I want two soft-boiled eggs. My voice teacher said they are good for my voice." As Wang Ta went to the kitchen he heard her scream, "Boil only three minutes!"

Wang Ta took some food out of her huge new refrigerator. He fried some bacon and made toast, then boiled her eggs, looking at his watch constantly to make sure it was three minutes. He was happy. She had a perfect figure. Too bad she hadn't let him take a longer look at it. Well, it would be his sooner or later. He was sure that, after they were married, he would never be tired of looking at her or loving her. It was such a soothing feeling, such gratification to anticipate the day when she would be his, all his alone.

He set the little oblong table in the kitchen, boiled some water for tea and waited. When Miss Tung came in, she was dressed in a light-blue sweater and a white skirt, a pink silk scarf tied around her neck. "How do I look?" she asked. Wang Ta looked at her and swallowed. She lifted her skirt a little and whirled around. "You like it?"

"Beautiful," Wang Ta said. He couldn't take his eyes away from her.

"Let's eat," she said, sitting down at the table. "You must go in twenty minutes." She ate her eggs quickly and gulped down her tea.

"You seem to be in a great hurry," Wang Ta said,

eating very little and devouring her with his eyes.

"Let's go to the living room," she said, rising from the table. "No time to wash the dishes now. You can stay ten more minutes." She came to the living room, threw herself on the davenport, put her legs up and her hands behind her head. "You can kiss me before I put on my lipstick," she said, her body wriggling slightly.

Encouraged, and his heart pounding, Wang Ta sat on the edge of the davenport, put his arms around her willowy waist and kissed her. The softness of her body and lips seemed to electrify him, giving him a tickling sensation that he had never experienced before. Miss Tung held his head tightly with both her hands and moved her head slightly up and down. They kissed as though they never wanted to stop. Miss Tung pushed his head away to take a breath, but soon their lips were together again.

Wang Ta didn't know how long they had kissed; he was willing to continue it for the rest of the day, but the doorbell suddenly rang. It buzzed until Miss Tung removed her lips from his. "Oh, bother," she said. "I'll have to answer the door."

"Let it ring," Wang Ta whispered.

"No," she said, "my car is outside. They know I'm at home. They will get ideas. Everybody is as suspicious as a fox these days. Oh, bother!" She pulled Wang Ta's head down and kissed him hungrily.

The doorbell rang persistently. "Let's drive out," she said into his lips, "let's go to Marin County."

"How about your singing lessons?" Wang Ta asked.

"Oh, my voice teacher won't mind. I'll make it up some other time." The doorbell was still ringing. "Guess I'll have to answer the door now. Let's drive out to the country." She got up from the davenport, went to the hallway, pushed a button, and opened the door. Then she quickly returned to a chair and smoothed her hair. Presently a short, middle-aged man with a red face came into the apartment with a bunch of roses. "Oh, Mr. Poon," Miss Tung said in Cantonese, rising from her chair, "you are early. I was in the bathtub. I didn't even have time to put lipstick on. Oh, meet my brother." She jerked a hand at Wang Ta. "He just returned from Europe. This is Mr. Poon."

Mr. Poon eyed Wang Ta suspiciously. Wang Ta rose to greet him but Mr. Poon handed the roses to Miss Tung and said, "I came at ten. Let's go."

"I'm sorry, Mr. Poon," Miss Tung said, "I can't go with you today. My mother is sick, I have to see her. Oh, what beautiful roses! Oh, thank you, Jack."

"Why, don't you want to buy that overcoat this morning?" Mr. Poon asked, scowling.

"Yes, but my mother is sick!"

"Since when did you have a mother?"

"Oh, you suspicious old turtle," she said, pinching Mr. Poon's short chin, "she is that Szechuan general's wife, don't you remember? She adopted me. She is sick."

"Oh, yes," Mr. Poon grunted. "Where is she?"

"In a hospital in Oakland. I must take my brother to see her. We'll have to go now. Call me tomorrow, will you, Jack?" She turned to Wang Ta and said, "Let's go!"

On the street, Mr. Poon got into his shiny yellow Cadillac and slammed the door. Miss Tung pinched his chin through the window and said, "Please call me, will you, Jack? Call me tomorrow. I'll cook you a mushroom chicken dinner and tell you how my mother feels. All right?"

Mr. Poon grunted, "All right." The Cadillac roared and darted away.

"Come to my car," Miss Tung said cheerfully to Wang Ta as she went to her Buick parked on the other side of the street. "Your car might break down."

"Why did you say I was your brother?" Wang Ta asked as he got into her car.

"So he won't get ideas. He is already suspicious, can't you see?" She started the car and drove down to Kearny Street. "Oh, it's a beautiful day. Let's drive to Carmel today, all right? I'll buy a few things and then we'll go, all right?"

Wang Ta was a little disgusted. The middle-aged man and Miss Tung's lies bothered him. Nevertheless he said, "All right. But I'll have to go home and get some money."

"Oh, don't bother, I can cash a check somewhere. I need some gas. The tank's practically empty." She swung her car and drove into a Shell station. "Have you got some money for gas? I don't have a dollar cash with me."

Wang Ta dug out his wallet and checked. "I have two dollars."

"Oh, no," Miss Tung said. "It takes seven dollars to fill my car up. I'll cash a check here." She turned to the attendant and asked in English, "Do you take a check?"

"A personal check?" the attendant asked.

"Yes."

"Sorry, miss, we don't take personal checks."

"Oh bother," Miss Tung said in Mandarin. "I'll make a phone call."

She got out of the car and went to the station to make the call. Wang Ta got out to go to the restroom. But when he passed the office he heard Miss Tung say into the phone in Shanghai dialect, "I'll take you for a ride. Come over right away. Yes, the Shell station on Kearny. . . . All right . . . wait for me at the door. I'll come right away."

Wang Ta scowled. He wondered what this was all about. When he returned to the car Miss Tung had already started it. "Let's go pick up a man. He lives around the corner," She drove around the corner and turned to Montgomery Street. Sure enough, a neatly dressed little man was waiting in front of a building, waving. She stopped the car and the man got in. "This is my brother," she said in Shanghai dialect, then she turned to Wang Ta and added in Mandarin. "He is Mr. Liu. He can't speak Mandarin." She turned the corner and drove back to the Shell station. "Fill it up," she said to the attendant.

While the attendant was filling up her car and wiping the windows, Miss Tung gabbed away in Shanghai dialect, which Wang Ta understood a little. Mr. Liu laughed and was highly amused, when the attendant came to the window to announce "Six dollars" he quickly dug out his wallet and paid. "I'll make a call," Miss Tung said and got out of the car. Wang Ta and Mr. Liu sat in the car without saying much. All Wang Ta found out about Mr. Liu was that he was a merchant seaman waiting for his ship to sail. Presently Miss Tung returned. "I'm terribly sorry, Tom," she said to Mr. Liu. "I just called my mother. She is terribly sick. She wants me to go there right away . . ."

"I'll go with you," Mr. Liu said.

"Oh, no. I don't know whether we'll be back tonight. She is terribly sick. Maybe we'll have to send her to a hospital. Call me tomorrow, will you, Tom?" She started the car and drove around the corner to Montgomery Street. "Please call me. I'll cook you a shark's-fin dinner." She stopped the car in front of the same building. "Will you call me tomorrow, Tom?"

Tom got out of the car and slammed the door. But he was polite. "I'll call you," he said, smiling. "Give my best regards to your mother."

"Now we've gotten rid of everybody," Miss Tung said as she drove the car away. "Let's do some shopping. I have a charge account at the White House. Then we'll start for Carmel. We'll spend the whole week end there."

"That's how you make people pay for your gas?" Wang Ta asked grimly.

"Why not?" Miss Tung said cheerfully. "I never buy gas myself."

"And you told both of them to call you tomorrow."

"What's wrong with that?" Miss Tung said laughing. "Let them call. It's not a crime if I'm not in."

"Let me out at the next block," Wang Ta said.

"Why? Do you want to buy cigarettes?"

"No, I want to get out. Just let me off."

"What's the matter? Are you sick?"

"No, I'm not sick. Please stop the car and let me off."

"Don't you want to go to Carmel with me?"

"No. I have a class at eleven. Please stop the car."

Miss Tung slammed on the brakes angrily. Wang Ta got out of the car and hurried away without another word. He was disgusted now and terribly disappointed. The beautiful balloon was pricked, and his heart exploded with it. He remembered Chang's remarks and wondered why he couldn't take love less seriously, as Chang had advised. He must talk to someone. He dropped into a drugstore, went to the phone and dialed Miss Chao's number.

6

After Wang Chi-yang had deposited his cash in the bank, he began to sleep better. One day, in an attempt to show his appreciation for his sister-in-law's advice, he put on the Western suit which Madam Tang had tricked him into buying. But he acted very stiff that day. He felt uncomfortable in the foreign suit. The trousers seemed too tight; the open collar of the coat made him feel naked and cold, as though the front part of the clothes had been torn away in an accident. And when he lifted his arms, the sleeves seemed to pull them down; furthermore, the heavy shoulder pads bothered him, making him feel as if someone were putting his arm around his shoulders. After that day, he packed the foreign suit at the bottom of his trunk and never wanted to wear it again.

Because he felt safe now, he sometimes sauntered out of Grant Avenue and ventured to some side streets and back alleys. He discovered, to his surprise, many sights and noises that were both strange and familiar to him. The clatter of mah-jongg behind the closed doors, the operatic music of drums and gongs from basements with signs saying "Music Clubs," the noodle factories, the tailor shops with children playing around their working mothers, the pawnshop with the high counter, the barbershops with all the traditional services, including cleaning the ears and beating the shoulders, the retired old men reading the Chinese newspapers in little stores which sell nothing . . . all these were familiar to him, reminding him of China. But the bars with the neon signs and the foreign music blaring inside them; the smokeshops with the blinking machines; the loud-mouthed young people who talked the foreign tongue, laughed, and drank brownish liquid from bottles all seemed to him somewhat strange. One evening when he was walking out of a back alley, a female voice coughed. He turned and looked. A fat woman with silk-colored hair was standing beside a doorway smiling at him. She tossed her cigarette away and said something he didn't understand. Then she pointed at him and pointed at herself, jerked the middle of her body and whispered, "Mama make happy. Good time, savee?" Quickly Wang Chi-yang turned away and hurried to brightly lighted Grant Avenue. The woman reminded him of the picture in Wang Ta's room that Liu Ma had talked about. Both women had silk-colored hair. Had Wang Ta been going out with prostitutes? he wondered. He had to find that out.

By venturing to the side streets and upper Grant Avenue which he had decided to familiarize himself with despite the fowl and fish smell, he found many items of food that he had missed very much since he had left China. He made a mental note to tell the cook to buy them when he got home, especially the taro roots, the lotus roots, and the dried snake meat and the salted fish, which had always been his favorite dishes.

When he was passing by another store, he discovered many other foods imported from China that he had also wanted to buy. In the window of the store were displayed at least a dozen items, with their names written on red paper pasted on the plates and jars which contained the food. He went in and selected ten items—sea dragon and sea horse, the great nourishing herb to be cooked with lamb or pork; dog tail and tiger tail, the sex organ of male seals and male tigers which are believed to have great rejuvenating power; heavenly heroic lizard from Kwangsi Province; horse hoof from Kwei Ling; water chestnuts imported from the capital of Kwangsi; tiger-bone medicine wine; clean hair vegetable, the hairlike seaweed with great nourishing power; old-fruit skin, the dried, fragrant tangerine peels; first-grade bird's-nest from the South Seas; the stomach of eels imported from Canton. Writing them down, he ordered these items, the prices of which added up to ninety-eight dollars. He paid for them with a hundred-dollar check which Madam Tang had written for him for emergency use. He asked the manager of the store to deliver the food to his house, and to tip whoever was to deliver the goods two dollars, the balance of the check.

Having made such exciting discoveries, Wang Chiyang explored upper Grant Avenue some more. His cough wasn't getting better and he decided to find some herbs that would ease it a little during the night. He didn't want to have it cured completely. Coughing, in his opinion, was sometimes a pleasure and it seemed to increase a person's authority in his household.

He stopped in front of a herb store and examined the advertisement pasted on the window. It was a public letter cut from a Chinese newspaper, written in classic language by a grateful patient. It said, "Younger brother (the letter-writer himself) toured Mexico during his younger years. On account of the hard work and his indulgence in sex and lewdness, he found himself in later years lacking of spirit and energy, and feeling drowsy most of the seasons; his heart and kidneys being thus damaged, they gradually lost their ability to function . . ." The letter went on and told how the herb doctor in the herb store had built him up again and saved his life with a miracle prescription and the first-class herbs purchased at this store.

The herb doctor might be good, Wang Chi-yang thought. He looked into the window and saw some of the rare tonics imported from China. Displayed in large Kiangsi plates were these items: Genuine deer's-horn from the North; genuine fungus from the East; selected ginseng from the Old Mountain; deer's-tail from Hwei Chung; effective spiritual cinnamon bark; great nourishing lizard tea from Wu Hsi. He had been dissatisfied with the ginseng soup he had been drinking; perhaps he should look into the price of the ginseng here. And the deer's-horn, which looked genuine enough. He had tried most of these tonics in China and they had been effective.

He went into the store and was greeted by the manager behind the shiny counter. "Are you interested in buying some genuine tonics from China, sir?" the manager asked. Wang Chi-yang studied him and thought he was honest. He had a straight nose and clear eyes, although he was wearing glasses; he looked about sixty but spirited and straight, with good, healthy color in his face. Wang Chi-yang wouldn't trust a tonic merchant who had a sickly look himself. He asked for brush and paper and ordered some ginseng and a pair of deer's-horns, in writing. The manager packed the selected tonics in paper boxes and tied them with red cord, then brought his old black abacus to the counter and his fingers worked dexterously on its little balls for a moment. Knowing that the customer didn't understand Cantonese, he wrote the total price on the rice paper with the brush: Thirty-six dollars.

After Wang Chi-yang had paid he glanced at the hundred little drawers of the red-lacquered cabinets that covered the whole wall and reached the ceiling; he read the couplet scrolls that flanked the door leading to an inner room; he sniffed the air, blended with the fragrance of the herbs. It must be a reputable place, he thought. He picked up the brush and wrote, "Is the herb doctor in?"

The manager read the words, nodded and smiled. He pointed at the doorway beside the counter and nodded again. Wang Chi-yang went into the inner room through the doorless entrance and was greeted by a middle-aged man with a thin drooping mustache sitting behind a large red-lacquered desk. He was thin but his eyes were shiny and the color of his face was healthy. "Sit down, please," he invited, indicating a chair beside the desk. "What is your honorable ailment, sir?"

Once again Wang Chi-yang asked for brush and paper. In classic Chinese, with a secret intention to show off his calligraphy, he stated his trouble. The herb doctor pushed his horn-rimmed glasses to his forehead, took the paper under the bare light and read the writing aloud; then, with a smile, he picked up the brush and wrote in grass style the following comment, "A cough of ten years' standing is a serious matter, but without resorting to cutting into the abdomen to cure it as a Western doctor will undoubtedly prescribe, Shen Nung, the ancient father of plants who a thousand years ago tasted a hundred herbs to discover their medicinal value, has handed down a cure for coughs of even twenty years' standing." He handed the paper back to Wang Chi-yang, watched his face intently for his reaction. Wang Chi-yang studied the herb doctor's grass style and thought it was good, although lacking strength. His composition was faultless, although tinged with the characteristics of a broker. But an herb doctor was not a poet, he thought. With such writing ability this one at least wasn't a quack. He was satisfied and asked him to diagnose. The herb doctor put a little embroidered cushion in front of him and motioned him to lay his wrist on it. Having examined the pulse in both his wrists, he asked to look at his throat and tongue.

When all this was done, the doctor opened the middle drawer in his desk, took out a piece of fine rice paper with his Chinese letterhead printed on the side. He carefully laid it on the table in front of him, closed his eyes, folded his hands, leaned back in his chair, and thought for a moment. Suddenly he opened his eyes, picked up his brush and wrote the introduction of the prescription, "Back of everything there is a cause. Every plant that grows on earth is a blessing to mankind if it is correctly utilized with skill and wisdom. The patient has a cough of ten years' standing, caused by a stubborn wind and a wild fire in the lung, as indicated by his pulse and the color of his tongue. In order to uproot the cause of the trouble, the herbs that will neutralize the wind and the fire in his lungs are therefore prescribed." Then he proceeded to write the names of the herbs, with their weights marked under them.

Wang Chi-yang paid three dollars for the prescription. Before he left, he exchanged a few more pleasant remarks with the doctor in writing, and at parting they bowed to each other politely. He fully agreed with the doctor's diagnosis and had gained considerable confidence in him.

Coming out of the doctor's office, he went to the manager of the herb store. The manager took the prescription and filled it, weighing each item carefully with a tiny hand scale. He wrapped the herbs in many little packages, then wrapped the many little packages in a large package and tied it with a red cord.

Wang Chi-yang took the medicine home and handed it to Liu Ma, who had brewed herb medicine for the family of Wang for more than twenty years. She had become an expert in herbs, and knew exactly what to do with them. Sometimes, by examining the medicine, she could tell from what ailment the patient was suffering. As she opened the packages ready to brew the medicine in an old earthen pot, she knew that the Old Master had had his cough treated, for among the items she found some mint leaves and a few dried cicadas; the former was to fight fire and the latter was to control the wind in the human body.

When the medicine was brewed, Liu Ma brought it to Wang Chi-yang's room and poured the black juice into a large rice bowl in front of him. Old Master Wang drank the bitter juice with a slight scowl and then ate a piece of sugared winter melon to take the bitterness off his tongue.

"I have bought some ginseng from the Old Mountain and a pair of genuine deer's-horns," he said to Liu Ma as the maidservant finished telling him some household news of no significance. "I want you to keep them in a safe place and brew the ginseng for me on the following dates: the 11th, the 15th, the 28th of the 9th moon, and the 2nd of the 10th moon. I want to eat the deer's-horn on the 21st of the 10th moon. I have consulted the lunar calendar and it said that these dates are the best to take medicine and tonic."

Liu Ma remembered the dates and took the expensive tonic away, pleased with the fact that Old Master Wang still trusted her more than anybody in the house. She had for a long time dreaded that the cook had been gaining favors fast in the family. Ever since the cook had left his restaurant job and returned to the House of Wang, he had doubled his efforts to please the Old Master with his cooking. And judging from the Old Master's slightly improved appetite, the cook had apparently been doing a good job. That had worried Liu Ma considerably. Sometimes she had wished the cook would make a bad mistake and displease Old Master Wang, recently she had even thought of sneaking a tablespoonful of salt into the Old Master's favorite dish now and then and putting the blame on the cook. Now that she had been reassured of the Old Master's trust she felt better and decided to postpone this little scheme.

Wang Chi-yang visited the herb doctor a few more times, although his cough seemed to be better. He found it a pleasure to visit the doctor and converse with him in writing. Both enjoyed calligraphy and admired the same ancient poets. One afternoon, Wang Chi-yang visited the herb doctor but the doctor had been called away to treat a woman patient in her house. Wang Chi-yang didn't want to wait. He came out of the herb store and walked north on Grant Avenue. He was in a good mood and decided to venture farther north to the foreign territory called North Beach. It was one of the rare times he had walked beyond the boundary of Chinatown. He sauntered along the sidewalk with apprehension, glancing into the dark bars without turning his head. It seemed to him there were more bars than anything else on the street. Sometimes a whiff of an alcoholic smell would invade his nose, making him scowl and quicken his steps.

When he was waiting for the traffic light to change at the intersection of Columbus Avenue and Pacific Street, a heavily made-up woman winked at him and said something he didn't understand. He ignored her, and the woman snorted, then walked across the street without further waiting, swinging her hips. Suddenly Wang Chi-yang felt bad about it. She might be a nice woman asking directions. He had acted rudely and put a black mark on the friendship maintained between Chinatown and the foreign territory. He followed the woman, hoping he could catch up with her and offer her an apology. The woman entered the International Settlement and disappeared. Wang Chi-yang walked into the Settlement and was amazed by the strangeness of the street. It was full of bars and clubs, with pictures of nude foreign women hanging outside the doors like the poetic banners posted outside the Chinese stores during the New Year.

As he looked at some of the pictures, feeling somewhat embarrassed, a man with a false red nose and a black hat hustled him into a club in which a gaudily dressed woman with golden hair was wriggling on a little platform. A three-man band was supplying strange music that sounded like the thumping of a steamship engine. Promptly a slim girl met him and escorted him to the table nearest to the platform. The wriggling girl with the golden hair smiled at him as she started taking off her gaudy gown. "What'll it be?" the slim girl asked him, smiling.

In an effort to contribute something to the friendship between Chinatown and North Beach, Wang Chi-yang smiled back, dug a five-dollar bill out and handed it to the girl, who took the money and asked again, "What'll it be, sir?"

Wang Chi-yang shook his head to indicate that he didn't understand her foreign talk. The girl smiled and went away. Presently she brought him a tall glass of yellowish drink with a cherry on top and a black plate on which were three old dollar bills and some change. He waved at the money; the girl was puzzled. He pointed at the money and at the girl, and waved again. The girl's face brightened; she took the money and thanked him warmly, smiling happily. Wang Chi-yang was satisfied. He had been friendly to the girl and at the same time had got rid of the dollar bills which were too old to keep.

By this time the girl with the golden hair had taken off her gown and was prancing on the little platform, jerking the middle of her body to the beat of the loud music, her hands flying, touching her breasts and thighs, or tossing up her long wavy golden hair that resembled the flame of a fierce fire. She smiled and rounded her lips alternately as if she were blowing something. Wang Chi-yang had never seen such an act in all his life; in fact, he had never in his life seen any woman so scantily dressed as this one. He looked at the jerking white body and suddenly felt terribly embarrassed. He wanted to go but was afraid of being rude. He took the glass and sipped at the yellowish drink. It was so cold that he almost spat it out. Never in his life had he drunk liquor mixed with ice water. He swallowed it and shivered. It tasted even worse than the bitterest herb juice. He wondered whether it was impolite not to drink the foreign concoction.

Now the girl on the platform was going further by

taking off the little cover on her breasts, exposing her enormous breasts fully, except the nipples, which were covered with a piece of golden paper the size of a half dollar. That didn't bother Wang Chi-yang too much for he had seen many women's breasts in China, bared to feed their babies. But when the girl started to take off the small piece of cloth with golden tassels that hid her middle Wang Chi-yang almost jumped. He watched her with wide eyes as she threw the piece of cloth behind the black curtain, pranced to the front stage, and *tong, tong, tong, tong,* she jerked her almost completely nude body right above Wang Chi-yang's head to the beat of the drum which was rising to a crescendo.

Wang Chi-yang shot up to his feet, upsetting the small table, and hurried out of the club, wildly wiping his forehead with his silk handkerchief. His face red with anger, he strode rapidly out of the International Settlement and kept wiping his head. It was bad luck to have a woman jerk the lower part of her body above his head like that. He must hurry home and bathe himself and fumigate his head with incense. He quickly crossed the street and took the same route back. While passing a bar beside a little alley, he saw, through the glass window, his son Wang Ta and a woman sitting at a table talking intimately to each other. He halted and turned slightly to take a look at the woman. She was well-dressed in a gray foreign suit, her black hair swept up and knotted at the top of her head in the fashion of a Taoist priest. She not only looked like a Taoist priest, she was also badly pockmarked. A female Taoist priest with a pockmarked face and dressed in a foreign suit . . . what was she if not a demon? Greatly shocked, Wang Chi-yang turned and walked away hurriedly. He wondered what was happening to his two sons these days. One stayed out late, associated with foreign women and haunted public bars with a she-demon like this; the other talked a foreign tongue, ate with his hands, read strange picture books and tossed an ugly ball around every day.

He must do something about his sons before they became too wild and foreign. He must talk to his wife's sister concerning Wang Ta and have her help in disciplining him; as for Wang San, perhaps he could deal with him alone. He would first order him to study Confucius and thus impart to him the fundamental Chinese morals. . . .

He walked hurriedly, thinking and worrying, without any idea where he was going. At the intersection of Broadway and Columbus he was completely lost. There were six streets meeting at the same point; unable to read the names of the streets, he looked around with panic. The lights blinked and the traffic roared by. It was not until he spotted a pagoda roof of a tall family association building that he finally found Grant Avenue. With a deep sigh, he plunged into the milling crowd. Once back in Chinatown, he swore that he would never venture to the foreign territory again without first consulting his lunar calendar. It had been a bad day; he had been followed by the devil, as everything had indicated ill omen. He must hurry home and fumigate himself with incense.

Back in his house he mobilized his servants. He ordered Liu Ma to prepare his bath and burn some incense in his room; he sent Liu Lung to invite Madam Tang over for urgent conference; he told his cook to cook a vegetable dinner tonight, for he must prepare himself to ask for the Buddha's blessing.

Madam Tang arrived after Old Master Wang had bathed and fumigated himself thoroughly. He received her in the living room and told her of his adventure outside Chinatown, omitting the nude dancing girl. Madam Tang listened to him with her lips tightly pursed and shook her head with disapproval. "You should not have gone to North Beach," she said after Wang Chi-yang had finished. "That place is for people who look for song, women and wine. It is a shame for a man of your age to set your feet there. I am glad that nobody robbed you again and no bad woman trapped you. And there are obscene shows in that In-

71

ternational Settlement, I am told. You were lucky that you did not wander in that direction . . ."

Wang Chi-yang coughed and quickly changed the subject. "My wife's sister, do you see Wang Ta very often?"

"No, the only time I see him is when he comes to my house to borrow money. My sister's husband, you are a generous man, but it seems to me that you are very stingy toward your sons . . ."

"Did he say that?" Wang Chi-yang interrupted angrily.

"No, of course not," Madam Tang said. "Wang Ta has always respected you. But you have not treated him correctly. How much do you give him for pocket money every month?"

"Fifty dollars every month. He never asked for more."

"Still fifty dollars a month? Did you not know that the price of everything has risen twofold? No wonder he is always short of money. For the last several months he has been borrowing money from me. Since he is going to inherit all my money, I did not tell you anything about it and I did not keep an account . . ."

"You are spoiling the boy, my wife's sister," Wang Chi-yang interrupted. "Do you know what he has been doing? He has been inviting women to foreign bars!"

Madam Tang looked slightly shocked for a moment, but soon she nodded her head and defended her nephew. "A young man should have some pastime, my sister's husband. They are living in a modern world. I do not see any harm in inviting a girl friend out and treating her to a drink or two."

"This afternoon he took a pockmarked woman to a foreign bar," Wang Chi-yang said. "And they drank and talked practically on the street, with every passer-by looking at them like animals in a cage. Do you know that woman, my wife's sister? She wears foreign dress and has her hair dressed like that of a Taoist priest. She looks just like a she-devil."

"I know her," Madam Tang said. "She is a seamstress at a clothing factory, studying to be a fashion designer. Wang Ta has told me about her. There is nothing between them. They enjoy each other's company like sister and brother."

"Why can't he invite somebody else out? Invite somebody better-looking?"

"It is lucky that he can invite anybody out at all," Madam Tang said. "There is a shortage of Chinese women in America. Even I, at my age, often receive invitations to go to a motion picture. My sister's husband, Wang Ta is a good boy. I hope you will not interfere with his social life, and you can trust his words that there is nothing between him and Miss Chao."

"I shall see to it that there will be nothing between them," Wang Chi-yang said. "I do not want a pockmarked woman for a daughter-in-law. Her broken physiognomy will bring ill luck to the household. My wife's sister, the reason why I invite you here is to ask you to keep an eye on the boy. I seldom see him since he goes out early in the morning and eats most of his meals outside. And he seems to be afraid of me. This is good; but he is afraid of me to the point of avoiding me, that is bad. However, I must do everything to keep him from going astray. Since he seems to be closer to you than to me, I shall leave his private life to your supervision. And I must remind you, my wife's sister, giving him too much money to spend is not good supervision."

"I am not concerned about that," Madam Tang said. "He is an independent boy. He has promised to repay every dollar he has borrowed from me. That shows he will not squander his money, a virtue inherited from my sister." She looked at Wang Chi-yang narrowly. "By the way, what happened to your foreign suit. You have not worn it for a long time."

Wang Chi-yang coughed. "Oh, oh, I accidentally burned a hole in it while smoking my water pipe," he said, trying not to stammer. "About Wang Ta, I hope . . ."

"We shall not talk about Wang Ta now," Madam Tang interrupted. "There is nothing wrong with the boy. Please bring out your foreign suit and let me see the hole. Miss Chao is a good seamstress; I shall ask her to mend it for you."

"It is beyond mending. I shall buy another suit when I find a lucky day in my lunar calendar."

"You cannot throw an expensive suit away like that. It cost you a hundred and twenty dollars. Please bring it out. I am a woman, I am the one to tell whether it is beyond mending or not."

To avoid argument, Wang Chi-yang went into his room, but he was determined never to wear that foreign suit again. He opened his iron trunk, dug out the suit from the bottom and proceeded to burn a hole in the coat with a lighted paper spill. He first burned a hole the size of a half dollar near the right pocket, then burned a bigger one on the other side to make sure it was beyond repair. He pressed the holes with the palm of his hand to make them look old; after this was done, he sprinkled a little water from his water pipe on the coat to kill the new burning smell. Feeling somewhat dishonest and guilty, he brought the coat to the living room, his face grim and his heart beating fast. Madam Tang examined the damaged coat with a deep scowl. "Hm, what happened?" she asked, looking at him suspiciously. "Did you fall asleep while smoking your pipe?"

"The material is made of wool," Wang Chi-yang said. "It burns easily."

"It must have burned long enough to cook a meal. I am glad the house did not catch fire. Well, I shall take it to Miss Chao and see what she can do about the damage. She is a very good seamstress, extremely deft with thread and needle."

After Madam Tang was gone, Wang Chi-yang went back to his room, feeling sulky. He had had a bad day; on top of that he had burned a brand-new suit that had cost him a hundred and twenty dollars. If that pockmarked woman was clever enough to mend the holes, perhaps he would have to wear the suit again and the burning would be a waste. He wondered why he had let his wife's sister meddle with his life. Perhaps he had depended on her too much. In China he would have told her to go to the devil a long time ago.

The next day his cough seemed to be worse. He decided to break his daily routine and pay the herb doctor a visit in the morning. He felt that in the whole of Chinatown only the herb doctor had something in common with him. He wanted to visit him as a friend rather than as a patient.

The doctor welcomed him warmly and poured a cup of medicine tea for him. They inquired about each other's welfare in their own dialects without understanding each other; but knowing it was some polite remark of no significance they let it go, and proceeded to converse seriously on other matters in writing. "How is your honorable cough?" the doctor wrote in grass style, purposely making the characters hard to read to show his scholastic achievement. Without hesitation Wang Chi-yang took over the brush and replied, "The humble cough was gradually retreating after your noble medicine descended upon it, but unfortunately, owing to my own negligence and an incident of ill nature that occurred in my humble home yesterday, the evil illness seemed to regain power this morning."

The doctor read the writing over his glasses, nodded his head, and produced his embroidered cushion from a drawer. He examined Wang Chi-yang's pulse carefully with his eyes closed, pressing his fingers hard on his patient's wrist. With the small finger extended like a petal of a blooming orchid, he tightened and relaxed his fingers intermittently as if trying to detect the slightest irregularity of Wang Chi-yang's pulse. After he had examined the pulse in both wrists; he grunted and produced his special prescription paper with the letterhead; he laid the paper in front of him, leaned back in his chair and thought for a moment, his face expressionless. A moment later he opened his eyes, pushed the glasses to his forehead and picked up the brush.

"The negative and the positive of nature must be in harmony," he wrote; "any irregularity of the body function is caused by the disharmony of these two sides of nature. The patient's pulse, weak at times, shows this discord and therefore it is wise to first balance the nature in his system . . ."

It was a long introduction to an elaborate prescription. Wang Chi-yang read it and thought the composition was even better than the last; the handwriting was also smoother with quite a few strokes containing real strength, an indispensable quality of good calligraphy. Having gained more confidence in the doctor he doubled the fee, which the herbalist accepted after an appropriate amount of argument and refusing.

"I do not hope that the cough will be cured completely," Wang Chi-yang wrote. "It is a pleasure to retain a mild cough as long as it does not harm the health and shorten my life."

"It is hard to cure completely a cough of more than ten years' standing," the doctor wrote. "But your honorable cough will not affect your longevity, which is indicated in your physiognomy. You have a prominent chin, which dominates your late years, and you have no fear for evil influence invading your late years because of your good mustache, which wards off the evil; therefore, longevity is safely predicted."

"Do you know horoscope too?"

"Yes, it is part of my profession. But you do not need a horoscope analysis, since your physiognomy is as clear as a heavenly book."

"I have a dog son who has reached the marrying age," Wang Chi-yang wrote. "I would like to have his horoscope analyzed and see what type of wife he will have. He was born on the hour of *hai,* on the second day of the eleventh moon, in the year of the Sheep."

76

The herb doctor studied the birth date of Wang Ta, counted the years on his fingers with his lips moving slightly. "He is under the influence of fire and water. He is leading a stormy life with many women involved. But these women are not predestined to marry him. It seems to me his predestined lot is in the East. Unless he finds a woman from the East, his married life will not be too happy; as he was born in the year of the Sheep, he must not marry anyone who was born in the year of the Tiger."

"Will he marry a woman with a broken physiognomy, such as a pockmarked woman?"

"Very unlikely," the doctor wrote. "But your son has a soft nature, being born in the year of the Sheep; it is possible that an ill-destined marriage might develop if he is not properly married soon. Since his lucky star is in the East, why not send for a picture bride from Hong Kong? That will eliminate all the evil elements that might enter his life."

Wang Chi-yang considered the suggestion for a moment, nodding and grunting, then he wrote, "Ever since my humble relative Mr. Tang, the husband of my wife's sister, passed away two years ago, I do not have anyone in Hong Kong whom I can trust with such a matter."

"Perhaps I can help," the herbalist wrote. "I know a go-between who is noted for his wide connection and honesty. Perhaps he can find a suitable woman for your son; and to insure a safe marriage, I shall send him your son's birth date and his horoscope as I have analyzed it."

Wang Chi-yang's face brightened. Quickly he picked up the brush and wrote, "Your kind help will be greatly appreciated. Please proceed with the arrangement and assure the go-between that he will be amply rewarded if the correct woman is selected. My dog son, although not born with unusual talent, is intelligent and passably good-looking. He is honest and knows filial piety . . ." He stopped. He wanted to write more of his son's virtues, but he suddenly became unsure of them. Mutual honesty, he thought, is of prime importance in such a matter.

The herb doctor nodded and smiled. "I have no doubt of your son's virtues," he wrote. "In order to shoot two vultures with one arrow, perhaps you will also like to consider a woman for yourself? If your honorable lady is still living, please regard this suggestion as nonsense, for in this foreign land a concubine is not permissible."

"My cheap wife passed away years ago," Wang Chi-yang wrote. "But I am too old to take another woman."

"No one is too old to marry again," the herbalist wrote. "This herb store sells genuine seal's-whip, which I strongly recommend. It is the undamaged sex organ taken from a male seal at the prime of its years, guaranteed to make a man in his sixties feel as if he were forty; and it is possible that a man in his late years who takes the tonic regularly will be blessed with three or four more children."

"It is a blessing to have more children," Wang Chi-yang wrote. "But children born in a foreign land always lack filial piety, it is better not to have them."

"Perhaps you are right," the herbalist wrote. "But there is no harm in taking a young wife who will serve the sole purpose of warming a cold bed."

"The foreign house in which I live," Wang Chi-yang wrote, "equipped with foreign contrivances and boilers supplying a steam heat day and night, is already too hot."

Both laughed and nodded in agreement. Wang Chi-yang offered five dollars for the horoscope; the herb doctor refused it three times before he finally accepted it. They parted happily, and as Wang Chi-yang went home he felt a warm friendship was growing between them. He had achieved a great deal this morning.

When Old Master Wang entered his house, he heard a noise that could only be heard in the house of quarrelsome coolies. He hurried into the living room and found, to his surprise, that Liu Ma and the cook were having a heated argument, whereas Liu Lung was busy rubbing Tiger Balm oil on a lump on the head of Wang San, who sat on a chair with some cotton stuffed in his nose. "What is all this?" Wang Chi-yang asked.

Both Liu Ma and the cook stopped shouting for a moment, and Wang San squirmed slightly, then Liu Ma, quicker with her tongue than anyone else in the house, said in one breath that Wang San had been beaten by a wild boy in the Chinese playground on Sacramento Street and she wanted the cook to go out there to give the wild rascal a beating, as this was certainly a great insult to the House of Wang, but this ungrateful and cowardly turtle's egg refused to do her bidding because he said his job was only cooking. . . .

"Wang San," Old Master Wang interrupted this soliloquy angrily, "come to my room." With this he went to the kang, took from behind it a bamboo stick about four feet long, and entered his bedroom, his face red and stern. In his room he took out from his trunk in the closet the Four Books of Confucius, then he went to his chair and sat down, put the books beside the bamboo stick on his desk and waited. What he hated most was his son's having a street fight. That would be like telling the whole of Chinatown that the family was of a low breed and the father had no control of his wild children, a great face-losing condition. He must discipline the boy and start feeding him with the fundamental morals and virtues of Confucius. "Wang San," he thundered, as he had waited for a few moments without seeing the boy come in.

Wang San was standing outside the door trying to work up enough courage to step in. He tumbled in as he heard his name called. "Come closer," Old Master Wang ordered, his hand on the stick. "How dare you debase yourself by fighting with street urchins?"

Wang San shifted his legs and said in Chinese with an English accent and English grammar, "Our teacher says if somebody hits me I must hit back. I don't want nobody to call me sissy."

When Wang Chi-yang finally digested the statement he was somewhat shocked by this odd teaching. It was then he decided to send the boy to one of the Chinese middle schools in Chinatown after his American school, plus an hour of private lessons of Confucius every other evening at home. That perhaps would make the boy act and talk more like a Chinese. As he stared at Wang San's bleeding nose and the growing lump on his forehead he suddenly became sympathetic. The boy has had enough beating today, perhaps he should omit the physical punishment this time. "Wang San," he said, his voice softer now, "our sage has well said, a genuine hero always avoids a fight when confronted with a strong enemy. In order to have you protected in this wild society, I decide to send you to the Chinese school and give you a private lesson of the Four Books of Confucius."

When Wang San saw his father's hand move from the bamboo stick to the Chinese books his face whitened. Just as he was about to protest, his father had already opened one of the books and started the first lesson. "The Doctrine of the Mean," Old Master Wang read aloud with piety after clearing his throat. "Chapter One. Confucius says there is nothing more visible than what is secret, and nothing more manifest than what is minute. Therefore the superior man is watchful over himself, when he is alone . . ."

7

Wang Ta found a great deal of warmth in Miss Helen Chao's tiny apartment. Although furnished with a second-hand davenport, a repainted desk and a few chairs, the living room was cheerful with its fresh flowers, goldfish, and Chinese etchings painted by Miss Chao herself. Her bedroom was so small that it resembled a closet, with three sides of her double bed surrounded by walls. Spread on her bed was a beautiful silk cover with an old pine, a peacock, and a few chrysanthemums embroidered on it. It was her own masterpiece, but for some reason or other she had never done another stitch of embroidery since her arrival in America eight years ago. Wang Ta had suggested that she take up embroidery again, but she always avoided the subject as though it pained her to talk about it. When pressed for an explanation she would always say there were a few sad stories in her life she didn't want to be reminded of.

She had the most completely equipped kitchen, very neat and clean, with utensils to prepare a Southern banquet, a boatman's dinner of Central China, or steamed buns and onion cakes of the North. She often invited Wang Ta to dinner in her apartment and each time the menu was different. Wang Ta loved her tsa-chiang-mein, chiao-tze and lao-ping, the famed Northern food which had been introduced to Italy by Marco Polo as spaghetti, ravioli and pizza. She could make the best red-cook pork of the South; the fragrance of such a dish would fill the apartment for hours, and Wang Ta, when breathing it, would feel hungry even if he wasn't.

Wang Ta ate many times at her apartment. He didn't know why he spent so much time with Miss Chao; perhaps his school life was very boring and his frustrations so great that he found Miss Chao's cozy little apartment a temporary shelter, a resting place after a day's drudgery. The only unpleasant time was once when Helen Chao encouraged him to take becoming a doctor more seriously, but since she sensed his feelings about medical school she never mentioned it again. Once he wrote to Chang about his school work. Chang replied:

". . . My dear man, it seems to me that you have an excellent dinner served to you and yet you still have no appetite for it. I've thought of your plight and found there isn't anything others can do to develop

81

your appetite for your medical school. Perhaps marriage can help. But again it depends on whom you marry. Sometimes love can be a great driving force, but where to find love? That's what we've been wondering for years.

"Sometimes I also thought of your studying medicine as like a very unhappy marriage. You, the wife, are suffering an acute case of frigidity. The only thing for you to do is to learn from the frigid wives. You either get a divorce or stay with your husband and fulfill your duties. Fulfilling your duties is the only way to save the marriage. It is disgusting work but you must think that you get paid for it and are assured of a comfortable old age. That's what many frigid wives are thinking, I guess. And in order to squeeze a bit of pleasure out of life, they organize hen clubs, bridge clubs, they collect minks, study modern painting, visit handsome psychiatrists etc., etc. Why don't you do the same? Acquire for yourself some hobby—hunting, fishing, dancing, swimming, bowling, perhaps even whoring, if it can oil your squeaking scholastic machine and make it less uncomfortable . . ."

Wang Ta tore up the letter and decided not to talk to Chang about his school again.

One evening he had an elaborate meal in Miss Chao's apartment. The small table in her kitchen was heaped with dishes from the North, the South, and Central China. She also served him with genuine tigerbone wine; after two glasses of it he felt as if he were flying in the air. He protested when Miss Chao poured him a third glass, but Miss Chao was persistent. "What is the occasion, Helen?" he asked.

"No occasion," Miss Chao said. "I just like to feed you tonight. Please drink up."

"Let me pour another glass for you," Wang Ta said, picking up the lead wine pot and filling her glass with the white, warm wine.

"Don't try to make me drunk," Miss Chao said, smiling. "I have an unusually large capacity, inherited from my great-grandfather, who was a wine merchant and went bankrupt by drinking." Then she urged him to drink up. *"Kan pei, kan pei,* please."

Wang Ta drank another glass and the world began to whirl around under his feet. Miss Chao turned out the light and lit two candles. The kitchen was warm and full of the fragrance of food and wine. "Drink a little more soup," Miss Chao said, filling his bowl with her delicious bird's-nest soup. "The soup will dilute the wine so that you can have another glass. Life is short, we might as well enjoy ourselves."

After a fifth glass Wang Ta forgot where he was. The kitchen became a technicolor picture out of focus; everything swayed in a delightful blur, and Miss Chao became a double image, which seemed to dance, swim, fly in front of him like Siamese twins. She was beautiful, graceful, angelic. She came to him, said something into his ears that sounded like a soft song, and touched his burning face with the palm of her hand. She kept talking but he didn't understand what she was saying. Presently, she brought him a cup of hot tea, fed him with the spoon, and gradually the heavy drowsiness began to disappear. He felt deliriously happy and lazy and carefree. "You need a little sleep," Miss Chao said; "hold me, so you won't fall. Hold me."

He held Miss Chao's shoulders and let her help him up to his feet. "Will you call a taxi for me?" he said. "I'm too lazy to drive."

"All right, I shall call a taxi for you." She helped him to her bedroom. "Lie down on my bed for a while. Take a little nap. I'll call a taxi for you as soon as you wake up."

Wang Ta fell upon the soft, wide bed; every muscle, every bone in his body felt relaxed. He had never enjoyed such complete relaxation in all his life before. He closed his eyes and felt he was the happiest man in the world; he was so lazy that he never wanted to open his eyes again, or to move even a small finger for the rest of his life. Miss Chao took his shoes off; moved his feet to the middle of the bed, then covered him with a perfumed blanket. He didn't know how long he stayed in the bed in such a delightful semiconscious state and he didn't care. He wouldn't care even if the house had caught fire and the sky had crashed down. He heard little rustling noises as though Miss Chao were busy doing something. He didn't care; he wasn't at all curious about what she was doing. All he wanted was just to lie there and enjoy the present semiconscious state of well-being.

Presently he felt one side of the bed sink a little. Someone had crept into the bed beside him. A whiff of strong perfume invaded his nose; he didn't stir. Then the soft warm body beside him moved closer, nestled against him tightly. And it was a completely nude body; he wasn't surprised, he didn't care. . . .

He spent the whole night in the bed. It was not until next morning, when he found himself lying in it without any clothes on, that he remembered how much had happened. As he recalled the happenings he was shocked. Feeling guilty, ashamed and angry he quickly jumped out of the bed, threw his clothes on, and without bothering to wash, or comb his hair, he stormed past the living room toward the front door. "Why in such a hurry?" Miss Chao called. She had followed him to the living room from the kitchen. "I am preparing a breakfast for you."

He couldn't bear to look at her. "No, I'm going." He quickly stepped out of the apartment, slamming the door.

For ten days he didn't call Miss Chao, but the guilty feeling gradually disappeared. He felt that he had acted crudely. Miss Chao had treated him extremely well, cooking for him and consoling him whenever he was unhappy and disillusioned. Besides, that night had not been a bad experience for him, there was no reason why he should be angry and act rude and cruel. He paced the floor in his room, unable to decide what to do. Should he call her or write her a letter of apology?

He went to the hallway and picked up the phone. But just as he had dialed half her number, he threw the phone back into its cradle again. He couldn't talk to her; he was afraid that he might sound silly. He went back to his room and started to write a letter to her, but how to begin? "Dear Miss Chao . . ." Not right. He tore the paper and took out another sheet. "Dear Helen . . ." No. Too intimate. Perhaps he should write her a Chinese letter. In a Chinese letter he could be polite without being stiff; he could be close without being intimate; and above all, he could be impersonal.

He wrote the Chinese letter, read it to himself and found it satisfactory. He sealed it in a plain white envelope and slipped it into his coat pocket, ready to mail after dinner. While he waited for dinner, he tossed on his bed and his thoughts returned to that night at Miss Chao's apartment. Her passion, her acts, her endearing words, which had shocked him before, came back vividly to him. He could feel the warmth of her body, the smoothness of her skin. In the semi-darkness she wasn't bad-looking, and she had an excellent round body, with medium-sized firm breasts that hardly showed in her clothes. In fact, he had never noticed before that she had such a good figure. When he thought of all these things, his heart began to beat violently and his face burned. He got up from the bed, took a drink of cold water, paced the floor, tried to read, took another drink of water, tightened his shoelaces, paced some more floor . . . oh, damn it, he wasn't hungry at all; he wondered why he was waiting for something he didn't want. He went to the hallway again, picked up the phone and dialed her number. Her voice was warm. ". . . I have been wondering what had happened to you. Do you like salted fish steamed with ground pork? I have just steamed one. Why don't you come over and help me eat it?"

"All right," he said after a moment's hesitation. "I'll come in about a half an hour." Back in his room he tore up the letter and tossed it into the wastebasket. His heart beat violently, and he wondered why he was so excited. When he got into his car and started it, he found his hand trembling.

After that evening, Wang Ta visited Miss Chao regularly twice a week. He would go there before dinner and stay with her until after midnight. But he never took her out again. Miss Chao suggested many times that they go to a movie or go dancing, but Wang Ta always told her that it was more cozy staying in the apartment. He told her that he seldom enjoyed dancing and he loathed movies. He hated these lies, but since his relationship with Miss Chao had changed he somehow felt a strong reluctance to be seen with her in public again. "What's the matter?" Miss Chao asked irritably one evening. "You never want to go out with me anymore. It won't cost much to go to a movie. If you need money, I have it."

Wang Ta stiffened. He was hit by the remark as if he were stabbed with a knife. "Which movie do you want to see?" he said, rising to his feet quickly, fighting an aversion and a strong desire to walk out on her.

"Any movie," Miss Chao said, smiling. "I just want to go out with you, it doesn't matter which movie we go to. Let's drive to Market Street and see what pictures are being shown there tonight."

They drove down Market Street quietly. The brightly lighted thoroughfare was a wonderful sight on a Saturday night. The traffic was heavy, with people milling around on the clean, wide sidewalks, colored lights blinking, taxis roaring through narrow gaps between cars trying to make the green light, impatient drivers honking their horns. A woman driver turned into a one-way street the wrong way, and brakes were heard screeching; a motor cop came out of nowhere and gave chase to an unknown car for unknown reasons; a siren screamed somewhere and soon disappeared in the distance. Wang Ta loved Market Street, but he hated driving through it. "What picture?" he asked. "Have you made up your mind?"

"Any picture," Miss Chao said. "It doesn't matter."

Wang Ta turned his '48 Plymouth sharply into Ellis Street and drove into a parking lot. After the car was parked they walked back to Market Street. "Why do you walk so fast?" Miss Chao asked. "The movies are continuous. You won't miss anything." Wang Ta didn't say anything. He walked to the nearest movie, and without consulting the colorful posters that flanked the theater in a gaudy display, he bought two tickets. They went into the movies without a word.

It was a technicolor picture with costumes of splendid colors and a foreign background. There were a lot of tortures and brutal killings, mingled with love-making, sexy dancing, oratory and incredible feats and bravery. There were slave girls and women soldiers, who fought on horseback with swords and lances and in the meantime didn't forget to bare their legs. The picture depressed Wang Ta. He fidgeted in his chair. He had never been so restless and uncomfortable before. When the picture was over he got up quickly and said, "Let's get out of here."

"We haven't seen the news yet," Miss Chao said.

"You have already read it in the newspaper," he said. "Let's go."

Outside the theater Miss Chao consulted her watch. "It's still early. Let's go to Chinatown and have a bowl of won ton."

Wang Ta was anxious to go home. He realized that it had become a torture to go out with her. He said, "Sorry, Helen, I must go home early."

"Why?"

"I've got to get up early."

"You were never so conscious of time before."

"I need more sleep."

"It's only nine. And this is Saturday night. Let's go to Chinatown and take a short walk on Grant Avenue. I haven't walked on Grant Avenue on a Saturday night for a long time."

Wang Ta started for Ellis Street. "Come on, let me drive you home."

Miss Chao stood beside the theater glaring at him. "Come on," Wang Ta said impatiently. "Let's go!"

"Go where?" Miss Chao asked, her voice angry.

"Go home!"

"All you want is that, eh?" she said.

"What do you mean?" Wang Ta asked. He felt a strong revulsion when he thought of his illicit relation with her. "What do you mean? Listen, I'll drop you home and go right back to my own!"

"You are ashamed of me!" she said. "You are ashamed of going out with me and being seen with me in Chinatown. I began to suspect it since last week, and now I know it!"

Wang Ta became more angry because she was right. "Listen, Helen, be reasonable . . ." But she ignored him. She turned abruptly, walked away and disappeared into the crowd. He attempted to follow her but a great reluctance held him back. He stood there staring at the milling crowd. Yes, he was ashamed of her. He could never treat her like an elder sister again, and he could never again appear in public with her without feeling uncomfortable and painfully self-conscious.

For two weeks he didn't see her, but Helen Chao kept calling him and apologizing, asking for his forgiveness and inviting him to dinner. Wang Ta remained cold; in two more weeks she stopped calling. As time went on, Wang Ta's conscience began to bother him. Somehow he felt that he had done a great injustice to Helen. His brutal attitude toward her made him feel like what the Americans called a "stinker." He wrote her an English letter asking for her forgiveness. But the letter was never answered. Then he bought a dozen roses at a Chinatown florist and had them delivered to her apartment but, again, they were not acknowledged. Several times he attempted to call her on the phone, but each time he picked up the phone he changed his mind. He thought that if she had refused to answer his letter, she certainly would refuse to talk to him on the phone. Well, he told himself with a shrug of his shoulders, that was that. He had apologized to her in a long letter and there was no reason why he should feel bad about it any more. He found how surprisingly easy it was to forget a woman when there was no love involved.

Two months passed. Wang Ta studied hard and

stayed at home most evenings. Sometimes he helped Wang San with his arithmetic in Wang San's room. Sometimes Wang San was so irked by his study of Confucius that he complained of it to Wang Ta. "You haven't got anything to complain about," Wang Ta told him. "What d'you think I'm studying? Medicine. That's a hundred times more complicated than Confucius. And I have to live on it too, one of these days."

"Yeah, but you don't have to memorize every word of what you've studied," Wang San said. "I have to recite all Confucius' books, and I don't understand a word of all that junk."

"But you don't have to kill others with what you've studied. I might," Wang Ta replied. "When you recite Confucius the only man you might kill is yourself and Confucius himself, and he is already dead for thousands of years. Now, concentrate on your homework."

Old Master Wang noticed the change in Wang Ta and was pleased. One night he called him to his room and praised his good behavior, then followed with a long lecture on the virtues of Confucius. Wang Ta listened intently and controlled a strong desire to argue on a few points which he regarded as somewhat out of date. He thought that Confucius' moral codes were actually some clichés universally accepted and still preached by different religions. The Ten Commandments in the Christian Bible, in his opinion, could have been written by Confucius. His main objection to Confucianism was that the sage had put too much emphasis on severity, which created unnecessary inhibition in the human mind and hindered the freedom of thinking. He found out that a man would be happier in this world if he could be more callous and less serious toward life, as Chang had often said. Somehow he felt that his own unhappiness was born out of a formidable inhibition, which created many mental blocks and caused his behavior sometimes to look shy and ridiculous. He always felt obliged, indebted, ashamed, remorseful, and sometimes angry with himself, for the voices in his conscience, dictated by Confucius' moral codes, kept crying that he was wrong, that he had done a great injustice. . . .

"Are you listening?" his father asked, coughing.

"Yes, I'm listening," he said. Suddenly he was worried by his father's coughing. "You should see a doctor about your cough, father. Your cough is getting worse."

"My cough is being treated by a successful herb doctor. He is a good friend . . ."

"I don't think a herb doctor can find out what is really wrong with you, father . . ."

"You do not know anything about coughing," Wang Chi-yang said, "right now I am talking about your ambition, please lend your ears to me." He coughed, cleared his throat and went on: "A man should have ambition, and there are four essential steps for a man of ambition to take, as advocated by Confucius. First, he should purify and mold his mind; second, he should complete a home. Unless he has successfully taken the first two steps, he will not be able to take the third and the fourth, which are: To serve one's country unselfishly and to bring peace to the world. I am glad that you have been doing well in taking your first step. Concerning the second step, I and a friend, who is the successful herb doctor I just mentioned, will help you when the time ripens."

Wang Ta had no idea what his father and the herb doctor had been doing in helping his career, but he wasn't too optimistic about his own future. When he returned to his room he found a letter on his desk with both his Chinese and English name written on it in a delicate handwriting. He tore it open and found a short note in it:

"Mr. Wang:
    Thank you very much for your kind letter and the roses, which have lain beside my apartment door for two months, as I have been away for that long.

                                        Helen Chao"

For a moment Wang Ta wondered why she had left San Francisco for two months. Had she been sick? Or had he hurt her so much that she must go away and have a change of scenery? He called her on the phone; at first her voice was cold, but after Wang Ta had apologized once more for his unbecoming behavior she warmed up a ltitle.

"Where have you been?" he asked.

"I have been away," she said.

"Were you sick?"

"No."

"You sound very mysterious."

"Thank you for calling. I'll see you some day." She said good-bye and hung up.

Wang Ta felt relieved. She was all right, he thought; he felt that he had finally paid a debt that had weighed heavily on his mind for a long time. He wrote Chang a letter, telling him of his new attitude toward life. "Never owe anybody anything," he said, "either emotionally or materially. I definitely·believe now that I shall be happier if everybody owes me a small debt or a slight apology. When I owe somebody something, the debt seems to move into my mind like a cowbird forces its way into another bird's nest and occupies it, keeping peace, its legal occupant, out of it permanently. I don't know what you think of it, and I'm afraid that this attitude would be strongly opposed by American loan companies and department stores with installment plans . . ."

Three days later Chang replied, ". . . Toughen yourself, my boy. I still can see that you have a heart that is too soft and comfortable a nest for the cowbird to occupy it permanently. Toughen yourself, I say. I'll write the following message in English so that in case your old man reads your letter he will not set the F.B.I. on you. Do you know who that Miss Tung is? A dancing girl from Shanghai's A Hundred Happiness Dance Hall. Came to this country as a G.I. bride; divorced her husband three years ago and has been 'free lancing' ever since. Don't fall for her 'brother' hoax. It's purely fictitious. A fellow here has learned all these facts through some bloody experiences. Said she wanted to get even with men. Her attitude is exactly the opposite of yours. Some say she has an iron ball for a heart. Just watch out! By the way, how far have you gone with her? . . ."

Wang Ta answered this question immediately. ". . . I have gone as far as becoming her 'brother.' We were about to go to Carmel as husband and wife, but the car broke down. It's the will of heaven. I took a hint from providence and stopped at the 'brother' stage . . ."

Wang Ta never told anyone of his affair with Miss Chao, although he almost confided it to Chang in a letter. Now he thought the whole thing was over and he was glad of it.

One morning when he was sorting the morning mail, he found a small pink letter addressed to him in a delicate handwriting. He frowned slightly as he opened it. As he had guessed, it was from Miss Chao: It was an intimate letter, written in Chinese, inviting him to a *ho-kuo* dinner in her apartment. "I have finally succeeded in buying a *ho-kuo* from Hong Kong," the letter said. "It is not as good as a Shanghai *ho-kuo* but it is made of good bronze with a good-sized charcoal compartment in the center. The boiler itself is large enough for six bowls of water. The food cooked in it will be more than enough for you and me. Do you like meat dumplings cooked with white cabbage and rice noodles? It is my favorite *ho-kuo* dish. Will you come to share it with me, dear?"

The letter made Wang Ta uncomfortable. It sounded too intimate; probably because it was written in Chinese, a conservative language. A slight show of sentiment would sound natural in English, but in Chinese it sticks out uncomfortably. The word "dear" bothered Wang Ta a great deal. He decided to refuse the invitation. He wrote her a polite letter saying that the coming examination would keep him very busy. Just as he was ready to go out and post the letter, the phone rang. He went to the hallway and answered it. It was Miss Chao, and her voice was unusually cheerful. "Have you received my letter?"

"Yes," Wang Ta said. "I've just written you a letter . . ."

"Can you come tomorrow?" she asked enthusiastically.

"I'm afraid I can't. The winter examination . . ."

"Oh, please come," she interrupted. "It is my birthday. Please don't bring anything. I always refuse presents on my birthday."

Wang Ta was trapped. Nobody could refuse a birthday invitation without a good reason; besides, she mentioned a present; if he didn't go she might think he was trying to avoid buying her a present. He accepted the invitation, feeling slightly irritated at her statement about refusing any present. It was just like saying, "Oh, you can come. I won't ask you for anything."

The next day he bought a pair of jade earrings for her, but returned them and bought a silver cigarette box instead. Earrings were too intimate, he thought. He didn't want to give her any birthday present that would be misleading. He decided to stay there for only a few minutes. Lucky it was a party, he thought, not a date. He could leave a party anytime without offending anybody.

He arrived at her apartment at seven P.M. When she answered the door he was a little shocked. She was beautifully dressed in a gold brocade Chinese gown, with pearl earrings and a necklace, but her face was so red that he almost didn't recognize her at first. If she hadn't greeted him, he certainly would have thought that he had come to the wrong door. What the devil has happened to her face? he wondered. "Come in," she said cheerfully. "The *ho-kuo* is almost ready."

He came into the living room and gave her the present. "Oh, I told you not to bring anything," she said, looking at him affectionately. When he quickly looked away, there was a moment of awkward silence. The room was dark; only two candles flickered at the top of the radio-phonograph combination in a corner. There were no other guests in the room. "Am I too early?" he asked.

"No, no," she said after a moment. "You are just on time. I asked you to come at seven, didn't I?"

"Where are the other guests?"

"I haven't invited other guests. The *ho-kuo* is only big enough for two. Please sit down. I shall bring you a glass of wine."

"No, no," he said hastily. "I can't drink tonight. I have to study. I can only stay for a little while."

There was a moment of silence. "Of course," she said. "I'll have dinner ready in no time." She put the present on the radio combination, almost upsetting one of the candles. With a nervous laugh she hurried to the kitchen.

Wang Ta was bothered by the change in her face. It was so red that it looked funny to him. He almost wanted to turn on the lights and take a good look at it to see what was wrong. Had she burned her face? Has she just recovered from scarlet fever? He sat on the davenport and wondered. Waiting for dinner uncomfortably, he picked up some magazines from under the tea stand beside him. As he leafed through the magazines, he discovered a little pamphlet entitled "The Sandpaper Treatment," lodged between the pages of a woman's magazine. He looked at the illustrations in the pamphlet and suddenly realized what it was. He brought it close to the candles and read a few paragraphs in it. No wonder her face is as red as a monkey's bottom, he thought. She just had a sandpaper treatment, the newest treatment for a pockmarked face. He seemed to have read about it in a digest magazine some time ago. With a chuckle he quickly replaced the pamphlet, put the magazines under the tea stand and turned on the radio. Presently Miss Chao came into the living room and announced dinner. Her voice was a little too cheerful to be convincing. That made Wang Ta more uncomfortable.

The kitchen was even darker, for there was only one

candle, not on the table but on the icebox fifteen feet away. Miss Chao nervously poured a glass of wine for him as he sat down at the table. "Just one glass," she said. "It's longevity wine. You must drink it. We are going to have some longevity noodles besides the *ho-kuo*."

She lifted the lead lid of the bowl-shaped *ho-kuo*, which was set on a wooden square in the center of the table. The charcoal was burning in the charcoal compartment in the center, with the food boiling mildly around it. She then picked up a large spoon and served Wang Ta a bowl of soup from the steaming *ho-kuo*. "Please help yourself to the meat dumplings and the cabbage," she said. "The rice noodles in it are long, you have to stand up when you pick them out." She laughed nervously and hurried away to attend to the longevity noodles which were boiling on the stove. The kitchen was hot and filled with the smell of spicy food. Wang Ta wasn't hungry, but he found the food in the *ho-kuo* delicious. "Please sit down and eat the *ho-kuo*," he said. "It is wonderful."

"Do you really like it?" She sounded pleased. "If I had some genuine *chin-chin* and *mo-erh*—you know, the imported dried flowers of the lilylike species and the black fungus—I could make a much better *ho-kuo* dish. But I didn't have time to shop for these delicacies in Chinatown. Next time I shall prepare a real *ho-kuo* for you."

Wang Ta wanted to inquire about her treatment, but on second thought he changed his mind. It was a touchy subject. She might be very sensitive about it since she had turned all the lights out. The whole thing seemed pitiful and wretched. Her nervous laugh, her efforts to hide and to please all seemed to contribute to his discomfort. He was anxious to finish the dinner and leave.

The longevity noodles were cooked with shrimps and dried mushrooms. They were served in delicate bowls. "The noodles are also long," she said, bringing him a dish of soybean sauce. "You can roll them around your

95

chopsticks and eat them. Please don't bite them in two. I'm superstitious tonight."

"Please sit down and eat something yourself," Wang Ta said. He picked up his wine glass and proposed a customary toast: "Wish you a longevity comparable to that of the South Mountain, and a fortune as wide as the East Sea."

She sat down and tossed down her drink. "Thank you, Ta," she whispered. The grateful quality in her voice made Wang Ta scowl nervously. Why should she feel grateful and make such an effort to please him? She just made him more uncomfortable. He stole a glance at his watch, but it was too dark to see what time it was. He had intended to stay only for a few minutes; now he must have stayed over half an hour. How he would have enjoyed the food and the evening if their relationship had remained purely platonic! he thought. They had had a great deal to talk about before. They had discussed everything under the sky and above the earth; now, every moment seemed to be awkward and it was such a strain to find anything to say. He put down his bowl and chopsticks and said apologetically, "I really have to go now. I have to study for my examination. Thank you very much for the *ho-kuo*."

Miss Chao put down her chopsticks and picked them up again, her hands were shaking. Wang Ta was glad that it was so dark in the kitchen. He didn't want to see the hurt expression on her face. "Of course," she said cheerfully after a moment, but there was a great effort in her voice. "You can go after a cup of tea. I'm going to boil the water. You must taste my Black Dragon tea with the aster flowers. A friend sent it to me from Formosa. It will be ready in three minutes. She got up from her chair and hurried to the stove. "You can wait for it in the living room if you wish."

Wang Ta went to the living room. He decided to stay ten more minutes, not more. Soon she came in with two glasses and a bottle of whisky. "You haven't finished my longevity drink yet," she said. "It is bad luck not to finish it." She put the glass on the tea stand beside him. He noticed that she had added some liquor in his glass. *"Kan pei, kan pei,"* she said, lifting her own drink up in a great effort to appear cheerful.

"Sorry, I can't finish the drink," he said. "I must go home and study—"

"Just this glass," she urged. "The tea will be ready in a moment. *Kan pei,* please."

Wang Ta took a sip from his drink, while Miss Chao tossed hers down and poured herself another, her hands were shaking so badly that the glass and the bottle rattled. Wang Ta watched her and found the change was really shocking. She seemed to be a nervous wreck now. She sat down in a chair opposite him, gulped down another mouthful of drink, put the drink on the floor and picked it up again as if fighting a mental battle. "Will you marry me, Ta?" she suddenly said, looking at Wang Ta anxiously.

For a moment Wang Ta was dumfounded. "Please marry me, Ta," she said again, flinging herself at his feet. She knelt down on the floor and grabbed both his hands, looking at him pleadingly. "Please marry me. I'll do anything for you, Ta." Strong revulsion made Wang Ta want to withdraw his hands from her grasp but she refused to let them go. "Look at my face," she went on anxiously. "I'm cured now. I took the bandage off this morning. The doctor gave his guarantee that I shall regain my normal color in a month or two. I have his written guarantee. I can show it to you if you want me to . . ."

Wang Ta ransacked his brains for something appropriate to say—something that would not hurt her. "I'm not independent," he said, trying to avoid her eyes. "I can't get married until I finish medical school."

"You don't have to support me," she said hastily. "I can make a good living."

"No, I can't do that, Helen."

"Why? Tell me why?"

"I—I—don't want to get married, that's all."

"Love will grow, Ta," she said, tightening her grip. "Love will grow after marriage."

Wang Ta stiffened. He didn't know why, but the word "love" repelled him. "No, I'm sorry," he said bluntly. "I can't marry you. Let's not talk about it any more." He made an attempt to get up but Miss Chao wouldn't let his hands go.

"All right, don't marry me," she said, her voice a bit hoarse now. "But come to see me every week. You don't have to take me out. We'll stay just in my apartment. I'll cook for you, do anything for you—"

"I think we should not see each other any more. Please let me go . . ."

"Promise to come once a week, Ta," she said, her voice desperate now. "Just once a week. Let me cook for you. You can leave any time you wish . . ."

Wang Ta forced his hands out of her grip and got up. "I have to go now, I'm sorry."

Miss Chao quickly got up and returned to her chair. She picked up her glass from the floor and took a long drink from it. "You are still ashamed of me," she said.

"I'm not ashamed of you," Wang Ta said. "I just don't love you. I don't think I shall ever be able to fall in love with you. I can't help it. I can't force myself to love . . ."

Miss Chao suddenly crushed her glass between her fingers. "All right, get out," she said, staring blankly; the unfinished drink dripped on the floor and blood began to ooze out of her fingers. Wang Ta hurried out of the apartment; he felt extremely unhappy. Helen Chao seemed to him terribly pitiful, but he simply couldn't love a woman because of pity, and in the meantime he hated himself for being so cruel. It was such a painful experience that he wished he had never met Helen Chao.

Back home he wanted to do some studying, but he couldn't. The painful event still bothered him, like something with a bad taste lingering in his mouth.

Having been raised in China, he was as sympathetic to pockmarked people, the victims of smallpox, as he was to those crippled by polio. His treatment of Helen Chao somehow made him feel as though he had kicked a cripple. He heard his father call Liu Ma to brew his herb medicine. A few minutes later he again heard Liu Ma shout to Liu Lung, her husband, telling him to buy sugared winter melon for the Old Master. He remembered that his father always ate something sweet to take the bitter taste off his tongue after he had drunk the herb juice. Perhaps he should do the same. He closed his book and went to a movie.

He went to a lot of movies in the following two weeks. Some of the movies were good "sugared winter melon." They not only helped remove the bad taste from his mouth, they sometimes even boosted his morale a little. One evening he saw a foreign movie called "The Little Kidnappers." He felt good as he came out of the theater, for the touching story provided an outlet for some of his pent-up emotions. It was one of the rare motion pictures that warmed his heart instead of trying to please his eyes with grandeur and resplendence in color. He walked into the street feeling like a man whose stuffed nose is suddenly cleared. He bought a copy of the evening paper, took a deep breath of the cool, fresh air and went into a corner restaurant to have a cup of coffee.

As he sipped the coffee and scanned the newspaper, a little item printed in a corner on the second page attracted his attention. Chinese Woman Found Drowned on Ocean Beach, the headline said.

". . . The body of an attractive Chinese woman was discovered yesterday morning by Miss Jean Parker, a legal secretary on her vacation. Miss Parker called police, who found the partially clad body on the beach, apparently washed ashore the night before. She was identified as Miss Helen Chao, 41, a seamstress at Universal Clothing Factory on Stockton Street. Her car was found later, parked on the Great Highway, near

Golden Gate Park. Her purse, which lay open on the front seat, carried her driver's license and other identification; her billfold was empty, lying on the floor. The police are uncertain whether she had been robbed and murdered, or whether she had drowned herself. There was no suicide note."

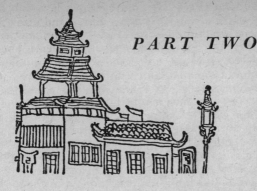

PART TWO

1

Wang Ta cashed his monthly hundred-dollar check at On On Drugstore and decided to spend some of it. He had no idea why his father had doubled his monthly allowance. Probably because the old man thought he had "reformed" and wanted to give him some kind of reward. If the extra money was really meant to be a reward for his merit or moral life, he thought, he had to throw it away as stolen money. His private life had been a mess, not only immoral, but also heavily burdened with guilt. Ever since Miss Chao's death he had been feeling like a murderer.

He wandered in North Beach but he avoided the brightly lighted spots. When passing Vessurro, the artists' bar which he and Miss Chao had frequented, he turned away quickly and crossed Columbus Street. A motorist honked and yelled at him, "That's jay-walkin', fella! What's the matter? Tired of livin'?"

He liked Vessurro and enjoyed looking at the pictures and the paintings on the wall done by unknown artists. He liked its atmosphere, which wasn't gloomy or heavily alcoholic like that in most others bars. Vessurro seemed to him a combination of college café and bar of the Bohemian type, patronized by Negro musicians and pale young men in tweed coats and unpressed gabardine trousers who looked like frustrated writers or artists; they drank beer and carried on intimate and sometimes animated conversations with extremely attractive girls. In a way it was also like a Chinese teahouse. The customer could buy a bottle of beer and spend the whole evening there sipping and talking and nursing an empty glass. It was an ideal spot to kill a lonely evening; but tonight Wang Ta couldn't bear looking at it. He wanted to go to a dark place, as if his soul couldn't stand scrutiny under a strong light.

He crossed Columbus and wandered in the dark section of Pacific and Montgomery. He walked past a bar and saw a short Filipino come out with a tall blonde and get into a waiting taxi. She was a pretty girl but drunk; she waved at him with a little handkerchief through the car window and called drunkenly, "Hi, Charlie." He wanted to get drunk too. He pushed in the swinging door and went into the dimly lighted bar. The jukebox was blaring cowboy music. He sat down at a small round table near an artificial palm tree and a blonde waitress came over smiling and greeting him cheerfully. He wondered why there were so many blondes in the bar. Sitting at the bar arguing with another Filipino was another one. "You keep your trap shut," she said. "I don't take that kind of bunk from nobody, I'll telling ya!"

"O.K., O.K.," the Filipino said.

"What would you like to have, sir?" said the blonde waitress in King's English with a faked British accent. Wang Ta ordered a whisky soda. Sitting at another round table nearby was a middle-aged American with thick brown hair and a red face. He was drinking beer and talking to nobody in particular. On his table were four beer bottles, three empty and one half-full. He poured himself another glass and watched the foam swell out of the glass. "Money talk, that's all," he said. "Good night, that's all."

"Next time you keep your goddam mouth shut," said the blonde at the bar.

"For Christ sake," said the Filipino with a heavy accent. "I apologized to you, didn't I?"

"All right, all right!" said the bartender. "Keep quiet. Let the lady alone."

"You are no more a cop than I'm Rita Hayworth, I'm telling ya," said the blonde. "If you're a cop, show me your goddam badge!"

"I was joking," said the Filipino. "I apologized, what more do you want me to do?"

"I said leave the lady alone," said the bartender.

The waitress came with Wang Ta's drink. "There are nice people here," she said apologetically. "See that girl over there? She is a poetess." Wang Ta glanced at a dark-haired Caucasian girl, a bit plump, sitting at the farther end of the bar. "She writes poetry. Really pretty poetry. A very smart girl. That'll be fifty cents, sir."

Wang Ta paid for the drink and tipped her a quarter.

"Money talk, that's all," said the man with the red face. "No pay, no nothing, that's all."

The waitress went to his table, collected the beer bottles and brought him a fresh bottle. She took a dollar bill from the table and made the change without a word. "No business, no pay, no nothing, that's all," the man said, pouring himself another glass from the fresh bottle. "That's all."

"Don't tell me you're a cop," the blonde was still scolding. "It's none of your goddam business what I do . . ."

"Hey, watch your language, lady," the bartender said. "There are gentlemen around!" There was some laughter and the blonde became angry. "I'm sitting here minding my own business," she yelled, "and that son-of-a-bitch here says he is a cop. Show me your badge, copper!"

"O.K., O.K.," said the Filipino. "I apologized, didn't I? What more can I do?"

"You can get your ass outa here," said the blonde, getting madder. "I don't take no bull from nobody, I'm telling ya! You a copper! You're no more a copper than you're Clark Gable—"

"Look, honey—"

"Don't honey me!" screamed the blonde.

"All right, all right! That's enough argument for today," the bartender said. "Let's have some peace and quiet here. I never had any trouble here and I don't want any now . . ."

"Oh, yeah?" said the man with the red face. A few men laughed and Red Nose raised a hand and added, as if to acknowledge big applause, "That's all, that's all!"

"That's the right atmosphere," the bartender said, slapping the counter with the palm of his hand. "Everybody happy! That's what I run this joint for! Sally, bring the gentleman over there another bottle of beer. It's on me!"

The door swung open and two Mexicans came in. Passing the bar they sized up the blonde. They went to a table in a corner and sat down. The dark one with thick hair and a Spanish mustache glanced at the poetess and jerked his head. The fat one said something in Spanish and they laughed. "Who is she?" he asked the waitress.

"Her name is Joan," the waitress said. "What'll it be?"

"Two highballs," the dark one said. "I'll buy her a drink."

"Who? Joan?"

"That's right."

After the waitress had left the two talked some more Spanish and laughed. When their drinks came, the dark one fished out his wallet from his hip pocket, took a stack of bills out of it, wet his fingers and peeled a twenty-dollar bill off the pile and slammed it on the table. The fat one said something funny and they laughed harder. The waitress took the money and went to make change. The dark Mexican returned his wallet

104

to his pocket with one hand and smoothed his long shiny hair with the palm of the other, while the fat one kept talking and laughing.

Wang Ta watched the two Mexicans and wished he could be as happy and carefree as they. He saw the bartender pour another drink for the poetess and point at the Mexicans, but the girl didn't even bother to look. The dark Mexican glanced at her and drummed the table with his fingers. The fat one proposed a toast in Spanish and downed half of his drink. "Ask her to come over," the dark one said to the waitress as she came with the change.

"She won't come," the waitress said.

The dark one flipped a dollar bill on the table after the waitress had made the change. "Buy her another drink."

"You can buy her ten drinks, but she won't come," the waitress said.

"Buy her another!"

"O.K.!" The waitress took the dollar bill and came to Wang Ta's table. "Would you like to have another drink, sir?" she asked, smiling. Wang Ta wondered why the waitress changed her accent and attitude whenever she talked to him. Did she think he was an F.B.I. agent or a movie talent scout or something? he thought. He ordered another whisky soda. "You know what?" the waitress whispered to him. "Joan is crippled. Automobile accident. You can buy her ten drinks, but she won't move. She just sits in that corner all night. She writes really pretty poems. Was on television just last week. You can talk to her if you wish. A real nice girl."

"That's all, that's all!" the man with the red face said suddenly. Some people laughed. A dark Spanish girl turned to him and asked, "What's up, pops?"

Red Face raised his hand and said to nobody in particular, "That's all!"

Everybody turned to look at him but the poetess. Wang Ta watched the girl and suddenly felt a strong sympathy for her. He wondered what was troubling her. She must have other troubles besides being crippled. As one unhappy person to another, he decided to make her acquaintance and have a little chat with her. He picked up his glass and went to the corner and sat on the stool beside her. "I understand you're a poetess," he said politely. "May I buy you a drink?"

She turned slightly. "Who told you?" she asked.

"The waitress," Wang Ta said. "She says you write beautiful poems."

"Oh," she said, taking a drink from her glass, her hand shaking slightly.

Wang Ta bought her a drink and asked, "What kind of poems do you write?"

"Oh, everything," she said. She lighted a cigarette and her hand shook more now.

"Have you had any poems published?" Wang Ta asked. "I'd like to read them."

"No." She kept puffing on her cigarette as if uncomfortable. There was a moment of silence between them. Wang Ta took a deep drink and said, "I'm sorry you had a car accident. When did it happen?"

The girl turned to him and glared. "Who told you?"

"The waitress. She said you are crippled. I'm sorry it happened."

"I don't need anybody's sympathy," she said, her voice angry. She crushed her cigarette nervously and said to the bartender, "Joe, tell Pat to quit being so big-hearted, I don't want sympathy from anybody!"

"What's the matter, Joan?" the waitress asked, coming over to her quickly. "What's wrong?"

"Just shut your mouth about me," she said angrily.

"What's the matter?" the waitress said. "He's nice, isn't he? You want somebody nice to talk to, don't you?"

Joan took a drink and put the glass down with a bang, spilling the drink. "I don't want you to broadcast all over the country that I'm crippled; it's nobody's goddam business . . ."

"O.K., O.K.," the waitress said hastily, "don't get so mad. I was just trying to help . . ."

"And I'm no poet," Joan said. "I don't write poetry.

106

Just keep your mouth shut about me; I don't want nobody's goddam . . ."

By this time the waitress had put a dime into the jukebox and loud music began to blare, drowning Joan's complaint. "I'm sorry I upset you," Wang Ta said. "Please have another drink." He left a half dollar on the bar and got off the stool. When he pushed the swing door open he heard Red Face shout above the music, "That's all, that's all!"

Outside the bar Wang Ta walked aimlessly for a moment. The incident depressed him. The nervousness of Joan reminded him of Helen Chao. Why people were so sensitive about their physical defects he did not know. Joan was a beautiful girl; she had an excellent profile with straight nose and full lips and a high forehead. He would have invited her to shows and to dinners if she had accepted people's kindness. Physical defects didn't bother him any more. He wouldn't even mind marrying a cripple if she was nice.

He turned on Clay Street and walked toward Kearny. When he was passing the police department in the old City Hall building, a policeman stopped him and greeted him in Cantonese. *"Ni ho, ni ho. Mei fei? Yat men yat chung."* The policeman showed him two tickets and asked him to buy. Wang Ta had no idea what they were but bought the tickets for two dollars. "Bring your best girl friend," the policeman said. *"Lei pei lu pa dem chung. Zai chian, zai chian."*

Wang Ta slipped the tickets into his pocket and walked past Kearny toward Grant Avenue. The traffic on the narrow street was as heavy as ever. On the sidewalks young lovers strolled arm in arm, window shopping; old couples admired the pagoda roofs and studied the menus pasted outside the restaurants; a balding husband, carrying an infant, followed his wife reluctantly into a gift shop. Their young daughter tagged along, looking at the display in the window and screaming with delight. The street was full of life, but Wang Ta was gloomy. Lively and bright places seemed to make his existence seem more destitute and futile.

He hurried home, threw himself on his bed in his room, trying to fight off the furious depression. He dug out the tickets the policeman had sold him. He studied them. "Policemen's Annual Ball," it said. "Dancing to the music of Richard Stern & Orchestra . . ." "Bring your best girl friend," the policeman had said. He stared at the ceiling and wanted to laugh. He didn't even have one girl friend, let alone the best. And the ball was to take place Friday evening. That's tomorrow, he thought. It would be short notice even if he had someone to invite. He tossed the tickets into the wastebasket and turned on the radio. A comedy show was reaching its climax—singing, laughing and cheering; he turned it off. Suddenly a terrible loneliness attacked him. He quickly got up from the bed, went to his desk, and wrote a letter to Chang:

". . . I think my staying in America is a waste of my father's money; besides, he probably does not have much of it now. . . . My existence here, it seems to me, is meaningless. The sense of futility, of uselessness and of being unwanted is about to break me down. . . . You may think I am out of my mind, but I am at this moment seriously considering going back to Mainland China . . ."

He felt slightly better after he had posted the letter the next morning. Two days later he received a reply from Chang: "I have thought of sending you a telegram but I changed my mind, for it might alarm your old man and he might demand a translation of it. Then I wanted to write you an airmail letter, but since the difference between airmail and ordinary mail from Los Angeles is only a matter of hours, I again decided I might as well save the three cents. At first glimpse, your problem seemed to be urgent, but now, while writing you this note, I think your problem is no more serious than that of an incorrigible street urchin who needs a good spanking. I am flying to San Francisco for the week end. Please wait for my phone call around four P.M. Saturday."

Wang Ta met Chang at the airport the following

Saturday afternoon. Chang looked even healthier and more spirited than before. He was still wearing the old tweed suit he had bought at a sale in Berkeley four years ago. "Look at my hands," he said as they drove to Chinatown in Wang Ta's car. "A few months' hard labor did it. The hands of the typical proletarian. The most outstanding change since I quit my intellectual life is the change of my hands." He spread his hands and looked at them admiringly. "The hands of strength and toughness help to bring food to my own mouth and potatoes to those of my fellow men. Ever since I became a grocery clerk, I've achieved a strong sense of being wanted and useful."

Wang Ta looked at Chang's hands and found they were roughened, with broken nails and healed scratches. "Do you think I should follow your steps?" he asked.

"For heaven's sake, no!" Chang said. "If I had been as lucky as you are, I wouldn't have become a laborer at all. What's wrong with studying medicine? Your father has the money, and you have the youth."

"Are you preaching?"

"Yes, I'm preaching. But I'm not going to continue it with a lot of abstract hogwash such as, 'Be happy, be contented! . . .' 'How to achieve peace of mind!' and so forth and so forth. I'm going to give you a little analysis of the world situation and let you draw your own conclusion. Are you still considering going back to China?"

"Yes."

"Good. It gives me a chance to talk. There are two camps in this world today: The Soviet camp and the American camp. Going back to China means joining the Soviet camp, have you realized that?"

"No," Wang Ta said. "I just want to lead a normal life, doing something and being useful. And I don't want to do things I don't want to do and I hate trying to be something I am not capable of being."

"Good," Chang said. "You're an honest man. But you must realize that in this country perhaps you are only refused the opportunity to do what you want to do; but in China you will be forced to do what you don't want to do. Let me quote some of Lenin's own words. 'As long as capitalism remains, we cannot live in peace,' he said. 'The basic rule is to exploit conflicting interests of capitalist states and system,' he said. 'In doing so, we have to use ruses, dodges, tricks, cunning, unlawful method, concealment and veiling of truth.' If you want to join their camp, you'll invariably be forced to do all these. As an honest man, you cannot happily plunge into jobs that are entirely against your nature. Even I, man not nearly as honest as you are, find the communist medicine a bit hard to swallow. This sounds like propaganda, but it's a fact we have to face; and you have to constantly bear in mind that communism and capitalism are like fire and water, they will never mix. As long as there is capitalism, communism will fight it. And you can assure yourself that capitalism isn't some back-yard weed that can be up-rooted easily."

"I don't think it is necessary for anyone to join the fight," Wang Ta said.

"It is absolutely necessary if you go back to China— Red China, I mean," Chang said. "Have you forgotten what Mao Tse-tung said a few years ago? 'Either you turn to the left, or turn to the right, there is no middle way,' he said."

"Have you honestly turned to the right?" Wang Ta asked.

"Would I preach if I didn't? Listen, besides moral reasons, there are practical reasons that you must turn to the right. First, you are like me, you won't fit in the communist picture. You are too old to convert; even if you could, they wouldn't trust you. Second, China—I mean Red China—is like an inflated bullfrog which is more of a bluff than a real great power. You and I who have studied political science and economics should know it. Manpower, especially manpower composed of starving men, is no immediate threat in this atomic age. Mao Tse-tung understands that; he will have to depend on Soviet Russia for everything else if he wants to wage an all-out war against America. This is as clear as a bride's mirror. Suppose the mirror isn't too clear to Mao Tse-tung; suppose he wants to get tough, will Soviet Russia go along with him? It is a question. If the only supply line—the trans-Siberian railroad—is bombed out, Red China will have nothing to feed the enormous war monster but human lives. But war is still possible. When the Kremlin is irritated and thinks that Mao Tse-tung is outgrowing his breeches, it might be happy to see him suffer a few broken ribs. Ah, I've been talking like a soap-box orator again. I'm hungry. Where shall we eat?"

"Have you tried Chi Chi?"

"Have I tried it! When I lived in San Francisco five years ago, I ate there so regularly that the proprietor started calling me by my first name and sending me Christmas cards in the New Year. He doesn't read English, I guess. My favorite dishes there are medicine pigtail soup and smoked duck feet steamed with pork. Let's go there. I would like to see Charlie again. See if he has stopped smiling. He never did since he bought that restaurant fifteen years ago. He wanted to make a million and retire to his village in China. Say, are you still considering going back to China?"

"I don't know," Wang Ta said. "Somehow you've swayed me a little."

"Good, so then I can stop talking politics for a while. I haven't talked politics for so long that I can talk about it day and night. You know what I've been talking about since I became a grocery clerk? Bowling. Now I'm a bowling expert. I'm the leader of the Black Dragon team, organized by my grocery colleagues. Don't despise bowling. Besides being good exercise, it's also good for the mind."

"What do you mean?"

"In another word, it's good for mental health. It must have prevented a lot of people from going crazy. If you get into an argument with your employer and have to accept your defeat for the sake of your job, you can always go to a bowling alley and let off your steam by smashing the pins and imagining they are your boss and his family, including his mother-in-law. When you go home, you feel happy and no longer hold grudges against the world. Most of my bowling friends agree with me. Now I've bought my private ball, and a canvas bag to carry it in. Perhaps you should also try."

"I've tried. All I get out of it is frustration."

"That's your trouble. You're afraid of hurting anything, even the pins in a bowling alley."

"I just can't enjoy the game. It has nothing to do with my soft heart or anything."

"I'm going to tell you a story," Chang said. "But right now I'm too hungry to tell it. Step on the gas, please. Heavens, I can smell the pigtail soup at Charlie's now!"

They drove to Chinatown and parked the car four blocks away from Chi Chi on Jackson Street. Parking was one of the biggest problems in Chinatown and Wang Ta had learned to take the first space in sight without worrying about a little walk. Chang was really hungry; he bought a package of peanuts and ate his way to Chi Chi. "I can't stand hunger," he said. "This is my real reason for staying in this country. You can give America at least one good credit—no one starves."

They climbed the stairs of the old red-lacquered wooden building in which Charlie had been running his typical Cantonese restaurant for fifteen years. Chang grabbed Charlie's hand and pumped it half a dozen times before the proprietor recognized him. "*Aiya!* Mr. Chang!" the little man cried happily. "It is you! For a moment I thought you a gangster!"

"I know how frightened you were," Chang said. "You actually stopped smiling for ten seconds. Have you made your million yet?"

"Just about," said Charlie, laughing. "In Chinese money, though. You look good. Like big shot. Where you been?"

"I've moved to Los Angeles. I take this special trip here to eat your medicine pigtail soup."

112

"You've come the wlong day," Charlie said. "Sea-weed soup for today. It is good. Come to this loom, please. The best loom—like it is leserved for you." He escorted them to one of the four little rooms facing the street and let down the white door curtain, then he busily brought them today's menu and served them tea. They ordered a squid fried with Chinese cabbage, a bitter melon fried with beef, a bean-cake fish, and smoked duck feet steamed with pork. The last item wasn't in the day's menu, but Charlie insisted on pre-paring the dish for them.

Wang Ta had come to the restaurant twice before and he liked the genuine Cantonese food. There was no decoration in the restaurant to please the tourists, and few tourists knew the restaurant's existence any-way. The red-lacquered walls were dingy with age; the customers sat on long wooden benches and ate their meals under bare lights. The cooks prepared the food in huge built-in boilers that resembled upturned um-brellas without handles. Except the ancient cash reg-ister which rang and rattled at the same time, every-thing in the restaurant was Chinese. It invariably re-minded Wang Ta of the small-town restaurants in China and made him homesick. "What about the story you wanted to tell?" he asked as he finished the sea-weed soup.

Chang attacked the squid with relish. "The story is about a pair of romantic Siamese twins," he said. "Probably they are the only living Siamese twins in China. The Liu brothers of Kiangsi Province. Prob-ably you have heard about them."

"I read about them in the papers years ago."

"Yes, at the age of sixty-five they still exhibit them-selves occasionally to raise money for their children's education. They look exactly alike. To avoid confu-sion, people have to remember their names with a little mental note such as, 'Liu Shun-ti, right, the elder; Liu Shun-kai, left, the younger.' When they were little, their parents tried several ways to separate them, in-cluding tying the 'meat tube' under their arms with a

113

guitar string to stop its blood circulation. They almost died. After that, no more attempts were made to separate them.

"Well, the twins made a lot of money exhibiting themselves. Both are married and have a lot of children. One day Liu Shun-kai, left, the younger, wanted to take a concubine. But Liu Shun-ti, right, the elder, objected.

"They had a quarrel, which soon developed into a fight. They banged each other with their heads until their father sent for a carpenter to make a partition for them. But the wooden partition proved to be a nuisance. A few months later, the twins agreed to get rid of it by promising their father peace. But Liu Shun-kai, left, the younger, still wanted a concubine . . ."

Chang took a fishbone out of his mouth, swallowed a large mouthful of rice without much chewing and went on, "Well, the problem had to be solved. Through friends' mediation and their friends' persuasion, Liu Shun-ti, right, the elder, finally okayed his brother's request." He gulped down a mouthful of tea and paused for a moment to indicate a short time lapse. "Three days after the younger took a concubine, the elder, for some reason or other, decided to take one too. It is said that the six of them—the twins, the wives, the concubines—lived happily together for some time, until one day one of the concubines decided to run away with another man and have some privacy."

Wang Ta chuckled. "What's the moral of the story? Are you preaching something?"

"Naturally," Chang said after gulping down a mouthful of tea. "When you told me you would never enjoy bowling, you sort of reminded me of Liu Shun-ti, the elder, who hated concubines at first."

"Are you trying to get business for some bowling alley?" Wang Ta asked, smiling.

"I'm trying to sell you a new attitude," Chang said. "A lot of people are too stubborn about their likes and dislikes. They never compromise. Take me, for instance. When I was a Ph.D., I was an intellectual.

I scorned a lot of things; I refused to associate with a lot of people. One summer, through my uncle's influence, I took a trip to Washington, D.C., and stayed with the Chinese ambassador. I went to New York with His Excellency's family and stayed at the Waldorf-Astoria. I dined with diplomats and danced with a European duchess at a party given by the governor of New York. I thought I belonged to that society. If I had known that I would become a grocery clerk today, I would have committed hara-kari." He put his chopsticks down, poured some octopus gravy into his rice and went on:

"But now I discovered a new world, like Liu Shun-ti, the elder, discovered the pleasure of a concubine. Now I've realized how dull some of the so-called intellectuals and aristocrats really are. On the other hand, I've found the simple working people delightful and much easier to get along with. And I found it much more so after I became one of them. And yet those are the people with whom I wouldn't dream of associating years ago. In those days, I had a deep-rooted idea that they were nothing but a bunch of harum-scarum, pigeon-brained dull lowbrows. Last week I met a laundress at a colleague's home. She beat me every time at bridge and crossword puzzles; her husband, a janitor, is the best living philosopher I've met. And yet they are simple, naïve, easy to understand; living among them you find life so much easier. Ah, I'd better stop talking about the simple working people, otherwise I'll go on and on until I begin to sound like a communist."

"I get your point," Wang Ta said. "I think it's a matter of adjustment."

"Exactly," Chang said. "By compromising, by being more objective, by trying to adjust yourself, you will find there is something nice about everything. Oh, heavens, now I sound like a schoolteacher. Let's finish the dinner and go some place. I have a few places in Chinatown I would like to visit again. They used to be my old hunting ground."

"Hunting ground?" Wang Ta looked up curiously. "Hunting what?"

"Hunting for moments of happiness and relaxation. I thought I was pretty lonely in those days. Say, you are not eating much, what's the matter?"

"I'm not too hungry."

"I'm not hungry any more," Chang said. "But I'll keep on eating. Next week I'll go back to American steaks again. I'm tired of steaks. But they are so cheap at wholesale price that it's a crime not to eat them."

They finished dinner, paid, said good-bye to Charlie and came down the rickety stairway. Gratified with Charlie's art of cooking, they agreed that someone should steal his recipes and write a cookbook. The traffic on Jackson Street was heavy; the whole block was blinking with colorful neon signs of the larger restaurants. The music of drum and gong of a Cantonese opera was in full blast; the singer's shrieking voice pierced the cool evening air, turning everybody's head toward the second floor of the prosperous Universal Restaurant where a wedding banquet was being given. "Well, some rich man's daughter is married," Chang said. "I have never attended any wedding banquet in Chinatown. I wonder if it's the same as in China."

"It's the same except that the bride is not a bit bashful," Wang Ta said. "I went to one with my father last year. Long before the banquet was over, the bride dragged the groom away, claiming that they had parked their honeymoon car illegally somewhere. The elders tolerated the lie and continued the banquet until after midnight. Where shall we go?"

"Just follow me," Chang said, walking toward Grant Avenue. "A place at the edge of Chinatown fascinated me some years ago. It's an artists' rendezvous. We can buy a bottle of beer, sit in a corner talking, and watching characters. There is no loud music and nobody gives a damn what you do or what you talk about. Once I saw a bearded man scratch his back with a bamboo scratcher for two hours without saying a word to his

116

lady friend, who finally went away with a man with a fortune bird. The fortune bird told her fortune, I presume, and advised her to change partners."

"You mean Vessurro?" Wang Ta asked.

"Yes. At the mouth of Grant. Like a fascinating island at the Yangtze estuary. Have you been there?"

"I would rather go somewhere else if you don't mind," Wang Ta said.

"You are a character," Chang said. "I regard all those who don't like that place as characters, and therefore there is more reason for you to go there."

"Not that I don't like Vessurro," Wang Ta said. "I have a private reason for not wanting to go there."

"Ah, it's getting interesting," Chang said. "Why? Did someone break your heart there?"

Wang Ta told Chang of Helen Chao, of their affair and of her death. Chang listened to it without interruption and remained quiet for a while even after Wang Ta had finished. "You know why you're often unhappy?" he finally said. "You don't tell enough. You shut everything within yourself and let it torture you unnecessarily for weeks and months. You should have told me of this secret long ago."

"I almost did in a letter. But I changed my mind. Confucius said, 'Family ugliness should not be exposed.' I regard it as an ugly part of my life. Miss Chao and I used to go to Vessurro and chat. Now each time I pass that place, it reminds me of her and I feel like a murderer."

"I'm going to tell you another story. But let me take you to another place first," Chang said, turning his back. "It's a ghostly place and it provides the right atmosphere." They went back to Jackson and turned into a dark little alley where Wang Ta had never been before. It was a narrow cleft in a dingy, two-story building. The doors were all shut and there was not a soul in the alley. "They say the hatchet men used to fight tong wars here," Chang said. "Many mystery novelists have used this place as the background for their murder scenes, but so far I haven't discovered any secret tunnels as some of them so vividly described in their books." He walked into a round door about eight feet in diameter. Wang Ta followed. An old red-lacquered ricksha was parked in a corner in the passageway. "They say this place was once the head-quarters of a famous underground gang. The door was made of steel; the walls were dungeon-thick. Now this place is a cocktail bar; this new moon-door, which has no door at all, symbolizes peace. I used to come here to spend a quiet evening all by myself. It reminds me of my home in the village. My grandfather's house vaguely resembles this building, with a moon-door leading to the bamboo garden. Come in, the owner of the bar was a movie actor once. He has a lot to tell about this historical alley."

They came in a second door and entered the dark templelike bar, with three large lanterns hanging from the red-lacquered ceiling. In the wall facing the bar was an altar of an unknown gilded god; flanking the god were shelves of antique vases and pottery. On either side of the bar was a glittering collection of snuff bottles of different shapes and colors. "Sit down," Chang said, indicating a round table beside the god. "Don't be afraid of the gilded gentleman. He might be one of the 'booze barons' of the Chinese mythology."

Wang Ta sat down in a rattan chair and glanced at the snuff bottles of silver and amber, at the shiny mother-of-pearl on vermilion Soochow lacquer, displayed along the walls like items in a museum. "The owner is not here tonight," Chang said, bringing two bottles of beer to the table from the bar. "You know why I like this place? It's quiet. No young punks come here to play the jukebox, so we can talk without shouting. And here is self-service, no waitress comes every five minutes to look at your empty glass." He sat down and poured the beer. "Do you still feel like a murderer?"

"In a way, yes," Wang Ta said. "I think I'll always feel like one. I still remember that night I read the news about Miss Chao's death. I was drinking coffee in a restaurant after a good movie. I was in an excellent frame of mind. But when I finished reading the news, I suddenly became a fugitive. The paper said, 'The police are uncertain whether she had been robbed and murdered . . .' I almost had a good mind to call up the police and tell them I was the murderer.''

"I think this is the root of your trouble," Chang said after swallowing a mouthful of beer. "Your intention of going back to Mainland China has also sprouted from this root. Let me tell you another story. It's about myself. Do you want to hear it?''

"Go ahead.''

"Years ago I had a girl friend in San Francisco. It's an ugly story, so I don't have to tell you her name. She was friendly, attractive and gay. We went out a lot; I met all of her girl friends. We had a wonderful time together. Every Sunday evening she gave a soft-drink party in her apartment, but never on Saturday. On Saturday she was always busy, washing, ironing, cleaning the house and so forth and so forth. One Saturday morning she called me. This was quite a surprise. She wanted me to take her and her girl friend for a ride in the country. Her girl friend was a patient at the Children's Hospital, suffering a mild case of polio. I was delighted. I even canceled another engagement to go out with them. For I always had a good time with my girl friend. She was so gay, quick with a joke.''

He paused, emptied his bottle into his glass and went on. "We drove to Half Moon Bay. We joked and talked and sang. On our way back, my girl friend suddenly became nervous. She repeatedly told me to step on the gas. It was getting late. I asked her why she was so anxious to get home. She said she had a lot of things to do, washing, ironing, cleaning the house and so forth. But I suspected she had a date. That was Saturday. She couldn't fool me. Suddenly I was terribly jealous.''

Chang took a drink, wiped his mouth and continued, "So, I purposely slowed down the car. My girl was furious. She began to say nasty things. That added gasoline to the fire. When entering San Francisco, I made a wrong turn and got lost. I drove around and around pretending that I couldn't find my way back. My girl friend ordered me to stop the car and let her out. She wanted to take a bus home. She wanted to get home so anxiously that she even ignored her girl friend, the polio case. I insisted that she should see her girl friend back to the hospital first. She was so furious that she beat me, pinched my ear and even grabbed the steering wheel to force me to stop. I almost smashed the car into a truck. That frightened her and finally she let the steering wheel alone; she clenched her hands so tight that her knuckles became white; she fidgeted beside me, growling and mumbling threats. In the meantime I was hopelessly lost in the intricate city of San Francisco."

Chang lighted a cigarette and blew out the smoke reminiscently. "You know," he went on, "her clenched fists really bothered me. They reminded me of a nymphomaniac in heat described by Somerset Maugham in one of his novels. She must be anticipating a great evening with her man, I thought, and the fire of jealousy burned in me. But the fire burning in her was more furious. She saw a yellow cab and she screamed. I quickly pulled the car to the curb and let her off. Of all women's weapons, including fingernails and teeth, screaming is the most dreadful. As an alien in this country, I didn't want to get myself into any record in which a woman's scream is involved. So I let her go and drove her friend back to the hospital. But, the green horns on my head were growing.

"After I returned the sick girl to her nurse, I took a short cut and sped to my girl friend's house. I parked the car in front of it and watched. It was already dark. The venetian blinds were down in her living room, but there was light inside, so I knew she had returned. I waited for about twenty minutes, wondering what she was doing inside. Suddenly a car appeared and slowed down, apparently looking for a parking space.

It turned the corner; in about three minutes a man appeared, wearing a spring coat and hat. I couldn't see clearly how he looked. He went up the steps and rang my girl friend's doorbell. The door was flung open and immediately it swallowed the man up. I sat in my car and watched the window and let my imagination torture me. And it didn't take much imagination to tell what was going on. Some ten minutes later the light was out."

Chang took a deep drink from his glass, puffed on his cigarette and blew out the smoke heavily. "That week I was a dead man," he went on. "I was a walking corpse—eating, breathing, but dead inside. Before the week was over I revived. And because I was a devil, I wanted to do something destructive. It was Saturday. I walked into a National Dollar Store and did something I would never have the courage to do again. I walked up to a saleslady and asked for a pair of woman's underwear. I didn't look at her face. Although a devil I was still a bit embarrassed. She asked what size and I said any size. She must have thought I was someone just out of a mental hospital from the back door. Nevertheless she sold me a pair of medium-sized pink drawers. They were about right. I wrapped them up in a scarf which my girl friend had left in my car last week, then I went home and waited for my big show.

"Well, evening came. Ten minutes before seven I drove to my girl friend's house. I parked the car half a block away and waited. Her lover was late. He didn't show up until eight that Saturday. When he was about to go up the steps, I rushed to him. 'Are you visiting Miss So and So?' I asked. He looked at me and hesitated. 'Yes, why?' he asked. 'She forgot something in my apartment last night,' I said, handing him the bundle. 'I'm on my way to catch a plane, I won't have time to see her. And please tell her I won't be in tomorrow. Thanks a lot.' When I finished my line, I rushed to my car and drove away fast. I don't know what happened. After that I didn't care any more. A gentleman might not try to find out what was in that scarf. But that man didn't look like a gentleman to me. He was the sneaky type. Might be a married man from out of town. Anyway, I tossed my bomb; whether the bomb exploded or not, I didn't know."

"It was a dirty joke you played on that girl," Wang Ta said.

"A cruel joke," Chang said. "She must have cared for that man a great deal, you know. Well, I was a fool. I thought I really loved her. As Maupassant has said, if a man loves a woman too much, his vision is distorted, and he becomes silly and brutal at the same time. I was brutal, I became destructive, like a maniac. That girl was just friendly to me. She never said she loved me, and yet I took it for granted that she was mine. And I played that stupid joke on her. When I think of it now, I really want to deliver a vicious kick in my own pants. I think Miss Helen Chao made exactly the same mistake. She became destructive; the only difference is that she destroyed herself."

"Our case is different," Wang Ta said. "I had an illicit relationship with her."

"I have not yet met a man who, under the influence of alcohol, could resist the seduction of a woman," Chang said, chopping the table with the edge of his hand to emphasize every word. "You know, I think she actually was a victim of this peculiar situation— the shortage of Chinese women. Because of this shortage, she automatically priced herself high, or overestimated her own value. Consequently she was only interested in customers like you, young, handsome, well-educated and so forth and so forth. And she took it for granted that you should marry her. She simply couldn't face the fact that you didn't love her. Just as I didn't face the fact that my girl was in love with some other man, and that for some reason or other she had to keep it a secret, possibly pending the man's divorce from his wife. I think a lot of destruction has been done in this world for the sole reason that so many of us are afraid of facing facts. Now I begin to sound like a missionary. Do you want another beer?"

"No. Beer makes me dizzy."

"Let's take a walk on Grant Avenue," Chang said. "Grant Avenue after dark is quite a sight. I hope someday I'll have the time to write a book, a book packed with romance and action and mystery, entitled, *Chinatown After Dark*. I bet I can write such a book, since I've tossed my Ph.D. degree into the gutter." He finished his beer and rose. "Let's go."

They came out of the alley and walked toward Grant Avenue through Washington Street. Before they reached Grant they heard a shot. "Well," Wang Ta said, laughing, "it seems that someone is writing the first chapter of your book now."

"That's a firecracker," Chang said. "Do you realize that it's only two weeks away from the Chinese New Year?"

Wang Ta looked at the full moon in the cloudless sky. "The middle of January. That's right. In two weeks, the Year of the Horse will be here. Will you come?"

"I never miss the Chinese New Year in San Francisco. I love the parade, the firecrackers, the dragon, the New Year dance, the gambling and so forth and so forth. You know, during the Chinese New Year you really get some Chinese spirit here—the *ma ma fu fu* spirit. Even the police are somewhat indulgent, and tend to relax some of the restrictions. Take parking, for instance, you can park your car right under a NO PARKING AT ANY TIME sign without getting a ticket. And firecrackers. The law has banned firecrackers; but during the Chinese New Year the law closes one eye and says, 'It's illegal to sell and buy firecrackers.' It doesn't say anything about firing firecrackers. So everybody tosses firecrackers around. That's the good old *ma ma fu fu* spirit, and the city has really grasped it . . ."

As they were talking and walking south on Grant, they were startled by two more shots. A lot of people stopped and turned in the direction from which the shots came. Suddenly a man dashed out of Sacramento Street and ran up the hill toward Powell on the west side. Presently two other men dashed past Grant, one of them firing a gun toward the sky and ordering the fleeing man to stop. Chang and Wang Ta quickened their steps; when they reached Sacramento a police car roared by, its siren screaming.

"That's not firecrackers," Wang Ta said. "That's the first chapter of your *Chinatown After Dark!*"

"Look," Chang said. He quickly turned east on Sacramento. About a block down there was an ambulance, its red light blinking. A small crowd was nearby, talking and gesticulating. Wang Ta and Chang hurried to the scene, and saw a man being carried into the ambulance. "O.K. let's go," a policeman said, opening his patrol car parked beside the ambulance. Two men helped a whining woman into the car.

"I'll be darned," Chang said in English. "Isn't that Miss Tung?"

"That's Linda Tung all right," Wang Ta said.

"Who else is an eyewitness?" the policeman asked.

"We'll go with you," a well-dressed young Chinese said, dragging a girl in a light-blue evening dress into the car with him.

The ambulance started and turned north on Kearny. The police car followed. Soon their wailing sirens faded in the distance. "What has happened?" Chang asked an onlooker.

The man shrugged his shoulders. "Somebody shot somebody for a girl," he said. "You'll read about it in the papers."

The crowd began to disperse. "Another case of destruction," Chang said. "That's what you get by mixing up with a girl like Linda Tung." They started back for Grant, and Chang added, "it could have been you, you know."

Wang Ta was quiet for a moment. "Which one?" he finally asked, refusing to be depressed by the scene, "the escaped shooter or the one in the ambulance?"

"The one in the ambulance, naturally," Chang said.

"You know, you are probably the rare type of man who does not become destructive by loving too much. You just become unhappy, that's all."

"I'm not so sure of that," Wang Ta said. "Sometimes I really want to explode and shoot somebody. Where shall we go next?"

"The shooting spoiled the evening," Chang said. "I think I'll just go to a hotel and go to bed. I can't look at blood and I hate violence."

"And yet you want to write a book called *Chinatown After Dark*," Wang Ta said.

"I want to write about its romance, its uniqueness, its quaintness and serenity. Brutality only distorts the picture of Chinatown. I think this shooting is again a result of this peculiar situation—not enough women to go around. In Shanghai, girls like Linda Tung are a dime a dozen, to use an American expression. Nobody would lift a finger for her, let alone shoot."

"It seems to me you blame everything on the scarcity of women."

"I do. Your case is a good example. A fellow like you should have married a long time ago and stayed home enjoying your three children. And yet here you are, pacing the street at this ungodly hour and lamenting your unhappiness. You know, the more I think of this situation, the more I believe it has caused all the tragedies in Chinatown. Believe it or not, Helen Chao was killed by a double-barreled gun."

Wang Ta looked at him and scowled. "What do you mean?" he asked.

"First barrel, she overestimated herself because of this peculiar situation, as I said before; second barrel, because of this situation a good-looking man like you had to fool around with an ugly duckling like Helen Chao—"

"Let's change the subject," Wang Ta interrupted hastily. "We've finished talking about her."

"I'm going to a hotel," Chang said. "The shooting spoiled my mood. I don't even want to talk now."

After Wang Ta walked Chang to the Court Hotel

on Bush Street he returned home through Stockton Street. It was a pretty long walk. He reviewed what Chang had said and found there was some horse sense in his cynicism. It was unusual to find a person who was both cynical and optimistic. Undoubtedly Chang was such a strange character. Perhaps his attitude was a special product of this peculiar situation; perhaps it was a correct attitude, or even the only attitude a Chinese refugee should take in dealing with this situation, if he wanted to be moderately happy. When he reached home he felt somewhat better, as though he had found a temporary relief for a painful disease.

2

For convenience in writing checks, Old Master Wang had been learning English. Each day he would practice writing "one, two, three . . ." up to a hundred for an hour or so with the same enthusiasm and precision that he practiced calligraphy. Madam Tang had bought him a ball-point pen, which he held a bit awkwardly like an American holding a pair of chopsticks for the first time.

Nevertheless Old Master Wang was determined to learn how to write the numbers up to ten thousand, which was the amount of money he intended to keep in his checking account constantly. He found it a great pleasure writing checks; it seemed to give him great authority and make him feel important; besides, it was gratifying to know that the recipient of the check and the people in the bank had to read his writing.

It was a quiet evening. After a good dinner by himself, and having enjoyed his coughing, he practiced writing until his fingers were seized with cramps. He put his pen aside, massaged his fingers and cracked them, and in the meantime enjoyed looking at the result of his labor on the fine bond paper, with a chuckle. What would his wife think of his newly acquired ability, had she been alive? he thought. She had always admired his calligraphy. Now this strange language was really something for her to admire; he wondered whether his writing of it lacked strength and character. One of these days, when he was more familiar with the language, he thought, he would write a couplet scroll in English and see how it looked on the wall. It was enough writing for today. He put his writing away and called Liu Ma to bring his ginseng soup and the Chinese newspapers.

Liu Ma came in promptly as if she had been waiting outside his door. Her fat face was red with excitement and her thin lips were tightly pursed as though she were holding something explosive in her mouth and ready to release it. "Old Master," she said, laying the newspapers on the desk in front of Wang Chi-yang, "please read this piece of news with this picture printed here."

It was a girl's picture, with a duck-egg-shaped face and long dark wavy hair and earrings resembling a seven-tiered pagoda. Another she-devil, Wang Chi-yang thought, and with a slight scowl he read the news. "Chinatown Gun Battle," the headline said. "Last night two men quarreled over a woman and one of them was shot. The woman, Linda Tung, a divorcee, went to a dance at a businessman's club on Sacramento Street with a man who she claimed was her brother. While dancing cheek to cheek with her 'brother,' Miss Tung ignored one of her ex-boy friends who greeted her. The ex-boy friend, Dick Wei, a seaman, patted her on her bare shoulder and asked her whether she had heard his greeting. Miss Tung opened her eyes and fluttered her eyelashes. Wei, not satisfied with the cold reception, touched her shoulder again and announced his desire to cut in. A quarrel ensued. Her partner, who was later identified as George Sun, an insurance salesman, invited Wei to step out. Both men went out of the club. While Sun was taking his coat off Wei simplified the whole matter by pulling a gun on his rival. Sun, in a moment of unusual bravery, defied the gun and lunged at Wei and immediately received a bullet in his stomach. Wei was arrested on Powell Street and booked for suspicion of attempted murder with a deadly weapon. Sun was sent to Tung Hwa Hospital where his condition was reported as serious."

The moment Old Master Wang finished the news, he looked up and said, "The news of a she-devil. I usually do not waste my time reading this type of nonsense. Why do you want me to read it?"

Without a word Liu Ma dug out a picture from her pocket and laid it in front of her master. Wang Chiyang looked at it with a deep scowl. "This is the picture of this she-devil. Where did you get it?"

"In Young Master Wang Ta's room," Liu Ma said importantly. "I found it in his desk drawer."

"Tell the young master to come immediately."

"He is out. He went out after dinner."

"The incorrigible dog," Wang Chi-yang mumbled angrily. He tossed the picture on the table and asked, "Does he go out every night?"

"I do not know, Old Master," Liu Ma said. "But each time I pass his room in the evening, it has no light."

"Has he brought bad women to this house?"

"I do not know," Liu Ma said. Then she leaned forward and confided, "Liu Lung told me he heard noises one night. I shall ask him what kind of noises he heard."

"Where is Young Master Wang San?" Wang Chi-yang asked. "Where is everybody tonight?"

"Young Master Wang San went to see a motion picture with Madam Tang. They have not returned yet. The cook has a visitor . . ."

"I am not interested in the cook," Wang Chi-yang interrupted. "Ask Madam Tang to see me when she comes in. And take this ginseng soup away. I do not want any tonight."

"Do you want me to beat your shoulders, Old Master?"

"No!"

After Liu Ma had left, Wang Chi-yang walked around in his room, hating Wang Ta's wild life. He must discipline him; but he didn't know how. If he cut down his monthly allowance, people would think him stingy, and the boy could get the money from his aunt; if he scolded him, his words would go in one ear and promptly come out of the other. And he couldn't beat a grownup man's palm with the bamboo stick with which he used to discipline Wang San. Suddenly he missed his late wife and felt somewhat helpless without her. She had been a good woman, a fine disciplinarian, always keeping the house in good order. After she had died, everything seemed to go wrong. The sons became wild and disobedient, the servants became lazy and untrustworthy, even the whole Chinese nation went to communism. Now this new house, which was no larger than the old house in China, seemed empty and forlorn, and the warmth of a home was gone forever.

He went to the living room, which was the only room comparable to the middle hall in his old house in China. He had always liked to walk in the middle hall in the old house and smoke his water pipe on the kang, which was as wide as a double bed and had a low tea-table placed in the center, with paper spills, watermelon seeds, tea and sweetmeats within his easy reach. On each side of the tea-table was an embroidered pillow made by his wife, and he used to take a nap on the kang after each meal. There were the god of longevity with his enormous forehead and long ear-lobes, the plates heaped with fresh fruits, the gold clock, the incense burner, the moon-window looking out on his bamboo garden. . . . What did he have in the living room of this foreign house? Nothing but straight-backed chairs. The room had a deserted look that was almost ghostly. He quickly returned to his bedroom, took out a piece of paper and started listing the things he must buy. He must redecorate the living room for the Year of the Horse, which was approaching; he must drive the evil spirits out of this foreign house with the old spirit and warmth of the old house created by his late wife. . . .

Around ten o'clock Madam Tang came into his room. "Liu Ma told me that you wanted to see me," she said, sitting in one of the rattan chairs. "Is there anything wrong?"

Wang Chi-yang was having a spasm of coughing. "Have you read the Chinese newspapers?" he asked, clearing his throat and groaning.

"Yes, I have," Madam Tang said, then she looked at him, narrowing her eyes with a scowl. "Your coughing is getting worse. You should go to see a Western doctor if the herb doctor cannot cure it. You should do something about it . . ."

"At this moment I am not worrying about my cough," Wang Chi-yang interrupted. "My cough will be better if my sons are not busy ruining themselves. The newspapers said a man killed another man for an evil woman; have you read it?"

"The man is not killed," Madam Tang said. "I know him. He is in the hospital. This type of thing happens frequently in foreign society, but this is the first case in Chinatown in fifteen years."

"Do you know Wang Ta is involved with this evil woman?"

Madam Tang looked shocked. "No, I did not know," she said. "Did the policeman come?"

"No, but Liu Ma found a photograph of this woman in Wang Ta's desk drawer."

Madam Tang stared at her brother-in-law for a moment and then shook her head despairingly. "My sister's husband, having her picture does not mean that Wang Ta is involved with her. For a moment you frightened me unnecessarily. This woman wants to be a singing star of some kind, she has been passing her photographs around like a bill-passer on a street corner. I do not believe that Wang Ta would associate with a woman like her. She is an ex-dancing girl who has married at least a dozen times, legally or otherwise."

"Wang Ta associated with that pockmarked woman whose corpse was found in the ocean," Wang Chi-yang said. "Why is it that he always has something to do with a woman who is either involved in a killing or dies a violent death?"

After a quick glance at the door, Madam Tang leaned forward and warned, "My sister's husband, I hope that nobody had overheard you. You talk as if Wang Ta were a gangster chief who specializes in killing women. Miss Chao committed suicide. The foreign newspapers said that the police have confirmed it. Do not ever talk like this again!"

"My wife's sister," Wang Chi-yang said after a sigh, "Wang Ta was born in the Year of the Sheep. He should be a man of peaceful nature. But now I begin to suspect there is an evil spirit in this house that has been leading him astray, leading him to people involved in blood and death . . ."

"That is superstition!" Madam Tang said firmly. But Old Master Wang ignored her; he rose to his feet, paced the floor and went on. "The old spirit created by your sister is gone. The new house is never like the old. Perhaps that is why the evil spirit invaded this house. Today I made a decision. I intend to redecorate the living room like the middle hall in the old house; everything will be rearranged just as it was by your sister in the old house. Do you know where I can buy a kang in Chinatown?"

"I know a merchant who might have a kang for sale," Madam Tang said, her voice softened. "You are right, my sister's husband. Since my sister died, things are not the same any more. Do you still have her gold clock?"

"Yes, I have brought it to America with me. And I also have the portrait of the god of longevity. All I

131

need is the kang. With the old atmosphere restored in the house, perhaps the Year of the Horse will be different."

"It will be," Madam Tang said. "Nothing evil would have happened if you had remembered my sister sooner. Perhaps you would not even cough so badly. I am glad that you realize it now."

After Madam Tang had left to look for a kang in Chinatown, Wang Chi-yang opened another of his locked trunks and took out the portrait of the god of longevity and the gold clock, which his wife had treasured more than anything else in the old house. Both items, in his opinion, would have the power to ward off any evil spirit in the middle hall, the passageway to all rooms. Then he prepared his best ink on his large ink slab and wrote a few couplet scrolls with his largest brush. The poems were the same as the ones written originally in the scrolls in the old house. With everything prepared, he called Liu Ma into his room and told her of his intentions.

The next day Liu Ma and Liu Lung started redecorating the living room and rearranged the furniture. A black-lacquered teakwood kang with its low tea-table arrived in the afternoon. It was placed against the wall facing the entrance. Flanking the kang were the couplet scrolls. The portrait of the god of longevity was hung above a teakwood table against the wall on the right, with an incense bowl and two plates of peaches arranged in a triangle on the table as offerings. The gold clock was placed in front of the incense bowl. According to the old arrangement all these would have been on the left side, but in this foreign house there was a fireplace in the left wall which, in Old Master Wang's opinion, served no purpose other than provide the evil spirits with another entrance. So he decided that the god of longevity should be hung on the opposite wall so that the celestial member could keep an eye on the "hole in the wall." Chairs and ebony tea-stands filled the vacant spots along the walls, with a few pots of orchids placed in the corners of the room.

Hanging over the doors were embroidered silk curtains Liu Ma had brought from the old house. Liu Ma had brought everything movable except the half-dozen brass cuspidors. Madam Tang said it was hard to buy cuspidors in this country, so the room would have to do without them.

In the meantime the cook was busy cleaning his kitchen for the New Year. He washed everything and scrubbed the floor. He took down the paper-and-cloth image of Tsao Wang, the kitchen god that had hung all year above the stove; he smeared the god's wide mouth with honey and burned him so that he would ascend to heaven to report the family conduct with sweet words. Then he pasted a new image above the stove. Something had bothered him for years; the foreign kitchen had no cockroaches, the servants of the kitchen god. In the Year of the Horse something must be done about it. He reported this to Old Master Wang and the old master in turn told it to Madam Tang, asking for her help. Madam Tang hated cockroaches, but since it was not her kitchen she promised to get a few of them from the cook at any of the daily newspapers, which had the oldest kitchens in Chinatown.

On the twenty-ninth of the twelfth moon the house of Wang was thoroughly cleaned. Two large cockroaches had been let loose in the kitchen; smoked pork and guts were hung on the kitchen wall to indicate the prosperity of the house; two live fish were swimming in a tub and a fat hen was cackling under the cutting board, one of her feet tied to the kitchen table. Sea slugs, bird's-nest, shark's-fin and other dried delicacies were being soaked in fresh water in huge bowls. The cook was sharpening his kitchen knife, ready to prepare the New Year dinner with all his skill and ability.

Liu Ma and Liu Lung brought out their best clothes from the bottom of their trunks, washed all their old clothes and sunned their beddings. Old Master Wang sent for a Cantonese barber and every male in the house had his hair cut, and the barber received his pay wrapped up in lucky red paper. Old Master Wang had prepared more than a dozen red packages of money, some containing five dollars and some containing ten. He was to distribute the good-luck money among his servants and his sons and the children of friends who might drop in to wish him a Happy New Year.

On the thirtieth everything was prepared. The main event of the day was the New Year's Eve dinner. In China it would have been a banquet of at least twenty tables; guests and relatives would play mah-jongg and gamble until dawn, when a long string of firecrackers would be set off at the front gate to herald the arrival of the New Year. In this country the Wangs didn't have any relatives except Madam Tang, so the banquet was only a "one table" affair. But it was an elaborate table, with all the delicacies cooked in chicken broth, decorated with mushrooms and bamboo shoots cut into flowers. The fifteen-course dinner contained two soups and the cook's specialty—the eight-treasure rice, a sweet dish that resembled a bejeweled artificial hill built in a huge Kiangsi bowl, with red dates, lotus seeds and sweetmeats of assorted colors buried in the rice in an intricate design.

At the New Year dinner table everybody forgot his sorrows and worries. Old Master Wang, sitting on the noblest seat facing the entrance, actually smiled, but not as much as to lose his dignity. Madam Tang, taking the secondary seat on his right, kept heaping food in her nephews' bowls. Wang Ta ate slowly and sparingly and grinned occasionally to show that he was following the tradition, ready to start the coming New Year with a clean body and a clean conscience. Wang San, having seen a Robin Hood picture the previous night, was eating an enormous chicken leg with his hand, a gesture at table that would ordinarily have irritated the elders, but today nobody was to be irritated. Wang San knew it and he was taking full advantage of it.

"I hope that every one of you have cleared all your

debts," Wang Chi-yang addressed his sons benevolently. Clearing one's debt before the New Year was so important that Wang Chi-yang had paid all his household bills in advance. Wang San, again taking advantage of the situation, declared that he had ordered a bicycle and two baseball bats.

"Why two baseball bats?" Madam Tang asked.

"Everyone at the school has a spare one, my aunt," Wang San said.

Old Master Wang had no idea what a baseball bat was and he wasn't too interested in finding out. "How much do all these items cost?" he asked.

"Seventy-five dollars," Wang San said.

"Give your aunt the merchant's address and we shall send him a check for that amount," Wang Chi-yang said.

Wang San thanked his father and suddenly he finished his dinner. He sneaked out of the house to order the bicycle and baseball bats, regretting that he hadn't said a hundred dollars.

"How about you, Wang Ta?" Madam Tang asked.

"I have no debt," Wang Ta said, "except I owe you five hundred and thirty dollars, my aunt. But I shall not be able to pay you back this year."

"I shall give your aunt a check for that amount," Wang Chi-yang said hastily.

"Thank you, father," Wang Ta said. "If you and Aunt Tang do not mind, I would like to pay this debt myself . . ."

Wang Chi-yang suddenly looked up at his son as if displeased. "With what are you going to pay . . ."

"Ahem, ahem," Madam Tang coughed. "How about your car, Wang Ta? Does it still run?"

"Yes, it still runs," Wang Ta said. "It is a good car."

They looked at each other and forgot about money matters; they talked on pleasant subjects and expressed agreeable opinions which left no room for argument. When they finished dinner the servants sat at the table and continued the banquet until half the food was devoured. It was a successful New Year dinner and everybody was in a good mood, an indication of a good, prosperous New Year.

Next morning the whole house was awakened by a fifteen-foot-long string of firecrackers set off by Liu Lung at the front gate to welcome the Year of the Horse. In the middle hall incense sticks were lighted and offerings of food and fruits were made to the ancestors under the Old Master's supervision. At ten o'clock, after an elaborate breakfast of porridge and many cold dishes of smoked meat and guts of pork and fowl, the congratulatory ceremony began.

Madam Tang, who had come early, bowed to Old Master Wang, who returned the bow politely with his hands clasped in front of him, smiling slightly. Then Wang Ta and Wang San gave each of the elders three bows, and the elders returned the salutation by nodding their heads. When this was over, both father and aunt dug out some red packages from the pockets of their new satin gowns and handed them to Wang Ta and Wang San, who accepted the money with pretended modesty as required by custom and good breeding.

The servants wouldn't settle the ceremony with bows. They insisted that Old Master Wang and Madam Tang sit down in two ancestral chairs which Liu Lung had placed in the middle of the hall, facing the entrance. After they were seated, the servants, headed by the cook, kowtowed to them one by one. Old Master Wang was pleased. The servants were good and loyal; they wouldn't change the old habit even in a foreign land. He accepted the kowtows smiling, waving his hand and saying, "Don't dirty your clothes, don't dirty your clothes."

Madam Tang sat in her chair and protested like a sixteen-year-old girl being pestered by some men whom she didn't dislike. She turned her head away, half-smiling and half-scowling, fluttered one of her hands and kept saying, "Go away, that's enough. Go away!"

Having accepted the servants' kowtows, Old Master

Wang and Madam Tang once more dug their hands into their pockets. Each of them brought out three more red packages and distributed them among the servants, who protested, "No, no, you are too kind, Old Master, Madam Tang; please don't give us the money, we don't deserve it!" And they pocketed the money eagerly, still protesting.

"Wang Ta, Wang San," Madam Tang said to her nephews, "today I am giving a New Year dinner at Hung Wa Low Restaurant. You two shall go there at six o'clock. Do not be late, or we shall miss the New Year parade on Grant Avenue at eight thirty, do you hear?"

"Yes, my aunt," Wang San said, eager to go out. The red packages containing ten dollars each were getting restless in his pocket. "I shall be there, my aunt." Then he added in English, "Oh, brother, New Year parade! May I go now?"

"You can go," Madam Tang said.

Wang Ta also started for the door. "Thank you very much for the lucky money, father, Aunt Tang," he said. "I shall be at the restaurant on time."

After the sons were gone and the servants had withdrawn to their quarters, Wang Chi-yang heaved a sigh and said to his wife's sister, "I am glad that at least one son has not forgotten his Chinese and still has some manners."

"Wang San has reached a difficult age," Madam Tang said. "I shall not worry too much about him. He will know better when he reaches Wang Ta's age."

"Wang Ta is approaching thirty," Wang Chi-yang said. "According to Confucius, a man nearing thirty should have established himself."

"Confucius lived more than four thousand years ago," Madam Tang said. "The standard is different now. In this modern world there are men and women who are over forty and still going to school . . ."

"Yes, yes," Wang Chi-yang said hastily, "But Wang Ta is still single. That has been worrying me. Oh, I forgot to tell you, my wife's sister, I have negotiated a wife for him through a go-between in Hong Kong at the recommendation of an herb doctor. Day before yesterday I received the girl's picture. She is not bad-looking, and was born in the Year of the Rabbit. I shall not tell Wang Ta of the arrangement until I have your opinion of the girl." He took a small photo from his pocket and handed it to Madam Tang, who looked at it for a moment, her face expressionless.

"What do you think of her?"

"I like the face," Madam Tang said. "How about her limbs and weight? Do you have a complete physical description of her?"

"No physical defects," Wang Chi-yang said. "That is guaranteed. She is slightly plump, as indicated by her face. That is desirable, since plumpness is a sign of fertility."

Madam Tang looked at the picture for another moment and she smiled. "I like the girl. She has level eyes and thick lips, an indication of honesty. How is her background?"

"She is the daughter of a schoolteacher who died in the Hong Kong fire three years ago."

Madam Tang nodded her head. "I shall keep the picture and ask a noted physiognomist to give it a careful analysis. If she becomes Wang Ta's wife, she will one day share my properties, and I must be assured of her virtues."

"You are right, my wife's sister," Wang Chi-yang said. "But right now we have a problem. If the girl is as good as the go-between has guaranteed, how shall we get her over to this country? The herb doctor says if Wang Ta is not a citizen of this country, it poses a great problem."

"I shall talk to Miss Shaw about it," Madam Tang said. "Miss Shaw is my citizenship teacher. We shall have her advice. You will meet her tonight. I have invited her to my New Year dinner."

She looked at the picture again, then with a nod of her head she quickly put it into her handbag. "I like the girl," she added casually, trying to hide her excitement. "I hope the picture is a recent one. A restaurant owner in Chinatown got a picture bride from Hong Kong who cheated by fifteen years."

"I do not believe this one will cheat," Wang Chi-yang said. "The picture looks new, and the go-between is reputable, recommended by an herb doctor who has become my close friend."

"I would like to meet this herb doctor," Madam Tang said. "Let us invite him to my New Year banquet. Please write an invitation and tell Liu Lung to deliver it. As your close friend, he might drop in for a cup of wine even if he has other engagements."

Wang Chi-yang agreed with her. He hurried to his room to write the invitation, while Madam Tang walked around in the middle hall, fanning herself with her handkerchief. She was getting more excited as she saw the possibility of Wang Ta's marriage to a girl whose innocent looks had met her approval. Being childless herself, she was anxious to see her sister's family grow. And since her money was eventually going to fertilize this family tree, she felt it was part of her responsibility to see that no undesirable weeds and creepers become entangled with the tree and absorb its fertilizer. When she thought of it she suddenly became very busy and important. "Liu Lung, Liu Ma," she called. "Come here, all of you, and tell the cook to come, too!"

When the servants gathered in the middle hall, she fished out a twenty-dollar bill from her purse and handed it to Liu Ma. "Today I am giving a banquet at a restaurant. There will be no more work for you today. You three can also eat at a restaurant and then go watch the parade. Here is some money for you to spend."

Liu Ma took the money with a broad smile. She thanked Madam Tang and ordered her husband and the cook to extend their thanks too.

"My sister's husband, have you finished writing the invitation?"

Old Master Wang hurried out of his room with the

invitation, which Madam Tang took and hastily handed to Liu Lung. "Deliver this immediately. Tell the herb doctor to be sure to honor us with his presence."

"Enh?"

"Oh, I am busy," she said, snatching the invitation from the deaf servant's hand and handing it to the cook.

"Lao Fong, you go and deliver it. The address is on the envelope. My sister's husband, I shall see you at Hung Wa Low at six."

"Are you going so soon?" Wang Chi-yang asked.

Madam Tang wanted to see the physiognomist and have the girl's face analyzed immediately, but she didn't want to look too anxious

"Yes," she said. "I am going home to take a nap."

Old Master Wang smiled. He sat down on the kang and enjoyed another spasm of coughing.

3

The ear-rending firecrackers exploded throughout Chinatown, which has an unofficial boundary starting from Kearny at the east to Larkin, nine blocks to the west, and from Bush at the south to Broadway, with "colonies" extended to North Beach, the Italian section. But it was on Grant Avenue and Stockton Street, the business center of Chinatown, that the firecrackers really roared on New Year's Day.

From six o'clock on in the morning Grant Avenue smelled of powder, food, and wine. Many shops were closed, but there were music and laughter floating on the gentle breeze from San Francisco Bay. The Stars and Stripes, the red and blue and bright sun flag of Nationalist China, fluttered among colorful banners and lanterns. The sidewalks became a flower mart;

140

pink and white azaleas, camellias, narcissus, orchid plants, water lilies, plum and peach blossoms were everywhere, their earthen pots wrapped up in lucky red and gold.

Old Man Li and his nineteen-year-old daughter, May Li, walked on Grant Avenue with their meager luggage carried on their backs, their faces turning in all directions, fascinated. They had just arrived in San Francisco from Los Angeles by Greyhound bus. Old Man Li carried in his bosom two important items: a letter of introduction, and his great ambition to open the only Peking restaurant in San Francisco's Chinatown. He and his daughter had been in this country for three months: they had come with General White, a retired army general who had lived in China for more than twenty years, and would have died there, as he had hoped, if the Communists had not driven him out. Li had followed the general from China to Formosa, and eventually to Los Angeles, where the general had established his new home. When the general had died at the venerable age of seventy-eight, Li was so broken-hearted that for three weeks he fought the desire to follow him further.

Li had regarded the general more as a lifelong friend than a benefactor. The general had employed him fifteen years ago when Li was singing flower songs with his wife at the famed Heavenly Bridge in Peking and running a small restaurant at night. The general had frequented the open-air market shopping for antiques and eating Li's hot bread with sesame oil and eggs fried with black fungus; he liked the dish so much that he finally hired Li to cook for him at an eye-popping salary of ten U.S. dollars a month, almost three times as much as the monthly profit of the small restaurant. During his fifteen years' association with General White, Li had enjoyed a comfortable life, although his wife, always uncomfortable if not working, had died of hard work. Now he was in the largest Chinatown in America, tired but excited, ready to go back to his old business.

He halted at the corner of Grant and Pine and wiped the perspiration on his forehead with a forefinger.

"*Shew*, we have walked a distance of five *li* from the bus station," he said in Mandarin. "Are you tired, May Li?"

"A little," the girl said. She was dressed in a Chinese gown of light blue and wearing a pigtail wound round her head, her pretty face without make-up glowing with health.

"Shall we go visit Mr. Poon now, father?"

"Oh, do not be foolish. Nobody visits people so early. This is New Year's Day, people sleep in the morning with a full stomach of food and wine and do not wish to be disturbed. We shall have our breakfast and rest our legs for a while." He wiped his forehead once more and looked around.

"Here is a teahouse, father," May Li said, pointing at a red signboard saying "Lotus Room."

"Good," Old Man Li said. When he looked at the stairway he frowned. "No, May Li, I shall not climb this with my luggage on my back."

"Let me carry it up for you, father," May Li said.

"No, you are carrying enough of your own."

"I can carry a lot more." She held her father's canvas bag until Li finally yielded it to her, shaking his head. "You are just like your mother, May Li. Forty years ago when she was your age she could carry a hundred catties of flour and walk seventy *li* a day. She was strong as a cow, and just as amiable . . ."

"What shall we eat, father?" May Li asked.

"We shall see," Old Man Li said, trudging up the stairway. "We shall have some New Year dishes. But we must be careful in our selection. The owner of this place might be greedy, otherwise he would not have built a restaurant upstairs. He knows that people will eat more after this climbing, *shew!*"

When he reached the top of the stairs he promptly changed his opinion of the owner. The spacious dining hall with red-lacquered lattice windows was clean and impressive, almost filled with customers. Only a reputable place could be so prosperous, he thought. The smiling manager greeted them and directed them to a vacant table near one of the windows and handed them two copies of the menu with special New Year dishes attached to them. Old Man Li held the menu tensely, swallowing and resisting, his eyes roving among the expensive items. He wanted to eat everything, but he felt his economical nature held him back like an iron chain restraining a dog. He quickly closed the menu and rubbed his neck. "May Li, I shall let you order."

"Shall we eat some New Year dishes?" she asked.

Old Man Li swallowed. "Sure, sure. But it is close to lunch time now. We shall not eat too much."

May Li ordered a dollar's worth of chow mein and a New Year dish—the taro pudding. When the food came, Old Man Li picked one of the three puddings with his fingers and shoved the rest toward May Li. "It is all yours, May Li."

"No, you eat, too, father," May Li said, shoving the dish back.

"You eat it," Old Man Li said, trying to keep his eyes off the pudding. "My stomach is getting withered; it does not need much food now. A few mouthfuls of social drinks will satisfy it." He fished out a flask from a pocket and took a drink from it. "Shew, it is good. Eat your pudding, May Li. Don't wait until it is cold."

While May Li was eating the taro pudding sparingly, Old Man Li poured tea and served the chow mein. "Are you happy in America, May Li?" he asked.

"Yes, father."

"That is good, that is good. Do you know what I am going to do in America besides opening the best Peking restaurant? I am going to find a fashionable man for you. He will be a scholar and have the ambition to be an ambassador."

He took another drink from his flask and sighed. "May Li, if I had married another woman, I would

143

have learned how to read and write, and I might have become a scholar or a government official myself. But I married the wrong woman."

"What had my mother to do with all your ill luck, father?"

"Plenty. You know, if your mother had nagged me a little, I would have gone to a school. But she was too nice, too nice. Killed herself with hard work, poor woman."

"Oh, you always think of mother and feel sad."

"Good people always die first," Old Man Li said, shaking his head. "General White was a good man. Now he has also left us and gone to heaven."

"We shall make friends, father," May Li said. "We shall meet new people in San Francisco."

"I hope Mr. Poon is a good man."

"He must be, otherwise, the consul general would not recommend him to help us."

"I wonder what the consul general said of us in his letter of introduction," Old Man Li said, bringing out a letter from his breast pocket. He turned the letter in his hands and said, "We are not supposed to read people's letters, May Li. It is a sin to read people's letters."

"You are not going to read this one, are you, father?"

"Of course not . . . but, but you know I don't read much . . . perhaps it is harmless for me to take a glance at it. It is just like a blind man walking into a bathroom while a woman is taking a bath. He cannot see, so no harm is done."

"There is no harm, I guess," May Li said.

Old Man Li blew the envelope open and peered into it. Then he gingerly fished the letter out and turned it in his hands for a moment. "Oh, you take a glance at it, May Li," he said, handing the letter to May Li. "Since it is not sealed, perhaps Mr. Poon does not mind people glancing at it."

"I guess not," May Li said. She unfolded the letter and her eyebrows knitted. "It is written in foreign language, father."

"*Shew,* give it back to me. It is a sin to read people's letters." He quickly took the letter, folded it, replaced it in the envelope and pocketed it. "Finish your chow mein, May Li. We shall walk around in Chinatown and get acquainted with the place first."

"I like Grant Avenue," May Li said. "Shall we open our restaurant on Grant Avenue?"

"Yes, if there is a place big enough. We shall open the largest restaurant in Chinatown, serving Northern food and wine. Maybe we have some entertainment, too. Do you remember what General White said about your flower drum songs?"

"He never talked to me about my singing," May Li said.

"You sing just like your mother. That is why the general did not tell you; he did not want you to become conceited. Do you know what he said before he died? He winked at me and said, 'Li, that daughter of yours will fly high if she is discovered. Her flower drum songs will make people eat off her little hands one of these days.' That is what General White said, and it gave me the idea of opening a restaurant. When we have the restaurant, May Li, you will do nothing but sing and dance for the customers."

"And make them eat off my hands?" May Li asked, laughing.

"Well, you can make suggestions if the customers ask for your opinion of the food. It is much better than building a restaurant upstairs and make them eat more that way. Have you finished?"

"Yes."

"Good. Let us go and acquaint ourselves with the place first."

They left the teahouse and walked northward on Grant. "*Shew,* the luggage is heavy," Old Man Li said. "Let us find a hotel first."

"Maybe we should visit Mr. Poon first, father," May Li said.

"No. We are strangers. We should not visit him on

145

New Year's Day. We shall go to see him tomorrow afternoon. Let us go to a hotel."

"Let me carry your bag."

"No, I am not that old."

"I can save energy for both of us if I carry your bag, father."

"How?"

"Put your bag down."

Old Man Li put his bag down. May Li tied it with hers and slung it over her left shoulder. "You see? I even have my hands free now."

"Just like your mother," Old Man Li said, shaking his head. "Balancing a hundred catties of flour on her shoulder she climbed the West Mountain. Well, I guess I still could carry my own luggage and walk fifty *li* without rest if General White did not spoil me. For fifteen years I was the laziest cook in China . . ."

"Here is a hotel, father," May Li said, halting in front of a hotel beside a large restaurant, with a wide marble doorway leading to the second floor. Old Man Li looked at the impressive doorway and hesitated.

"This is a first-class hotel, May Li," he said. "Before we open our restaurant, maybe we should stay in a second-rate hotel. You know some Cantonese talk, maybe you should ask a passer-by to direct us to an inexpensive hotel nearby."

"All right, father."

They walked another block north. At the intersection of Grant and Sacramento, May Li stopped an old man and asked him in Cantonese where the cheap hotels were. The old man sized them up and jerked his head toward the east. "All on Kearny Street. A block from here. Hotel rooms a dollar a day if you do not mind bedbugs."

Old Man Li understood a little Cantonese. He quickly turned east on Sacramento and motioned May Li to follow.

"A dollar a day is good enough," he said. "In China hotel rooms cost only three dollars a month. Times have changed. We can be a little luxurious these days."

As they walked toward Kearny firecrackers began to explode everywhere. Old Man Li straightened up and sighed. "Just like the old days in China, May Li. General White would enjoy this if he had not died." He stopped under a long string of exploding firecrackers hung from the balcony of a two-story building, and inhaled deeply the powder smell. He stood there with his eyes closed and a smile on his face as though enjoying a cold shower on a hot day, whereas the tourists shunned the explosion, and a few ladies ran past him with fingers stuffed in their ears, screaming and laughing.

After the last firecracker had exploded Old Man Li opened his eyes, squared his shoulders and said, "Now, all my ill luck of the past year is blasted away. Our restaurant will be a great success in the Year of the Horse." He dusted some firecracker fragments off his shoulders and picked his ears with his forefingers. "*Shew*, it was noisy! Let us go find a hotel."

They found a small hotel on Kearny and climbed the rickety stairway to the clerk's desk on the second floor. A Cantonese showed them two dark rooms smelling of stale tobacco. Old Man Li tested the squealing double bed in each room and nodded his head. "Good, they are soft. We shall take these two rooms. May Li, let us take a nap first. The beds are good, and they cost a dollar a day, we must not waste them."

After a nap they had a light lunch of pork noodles at a small restaurant next door. Then they wandered around getting acquainted with the topography of Chinatown. The firecrackers were still exploding away; people roamed on the streets, wishing each other *"kung he fa choy"*; housewives went from one food store to another, selecting the choicest fowl, the freshest fish and fruit and the tenderest vegetables, for the feasting was to last two weeks; children, dressed in their best, searched for unexploded firecrackers and flocked to the stalls that sold sweetmeats and New Year candies; merchants decorated their stores with new couplet scrolls and potted flowers wound about with red ribbons on

147

which joyful greetings gleamed in gold characters; music was everwhere—Cantonese opera, the eerie folk songs of the South, the modern Chinese music of tango and rumba.

Old Man Li and May Li walked back and forth on Grant Avenue enjoying the sight and smell of the New Year. They walked until evening when Chinatown was all aglow. Family associations, framed in thousands of lights, shone like bejeweled palaces; stores and large business establishments were radiant with neon signs and New Year lanterns. The restaurants were packed. Old Man Li inhaled the smell of food and decided to break his budget for the first time in fifteen years.

"Let us have a good meal at a first-class restaurant, May Li. Are you hungry?"

"Yes, I can eat a water buffalo."

"Good, we shall eat a four-course dinner tonight. A full stomach on New Year's Day insures a good New Year."

They dropped in at Hung Wa Low and got a little booth after half an hour's waiting. They ordered a four-course family dinner and Old Man Li cleansed his stomach with two mouthfuls of his "social drink" before the dishes were brought in. Outside, people began to line up along the street. When Old Man Li and May Li finished their dinner the sidewalks were already packed, with children sitting on the curbs, elderly ladies resting quietly on grocery boxes, others standing behind them, three or four deep, craning their necks to look over others' heads; young lovers threaded through the crowd hand in hand, talking and laughing.

Old Man Li was surprised by the crowd. "What is this? Has some house caught fire?"

"The parade; father, didn't the man at the consulate tell you about it?"

"That's right, that's right. I have forgotten it. Good, May Li, let us watch it. *Shew,* what a crowd!"

He took May Li's arm and joined the waiting spectators. Presently two motorcycle policemen roared by. People turned their heads to the south end of the vacated Grant Avenue. Music was heard now; firecrackers exploded sporadically, drowning a wild applause as many cars bearing important men began to glide down the street. The main body of the parade followed. Band after band strutted along the route, first the members of the armed forces; then the gaudily dressed drum corps of the Chinatown middle schools, with their pretty leaders prancing and smiling and blowing their whistles; then the costumed children and the flag-waving student bodies; then the illuminated floats on which the Chinatown Queen and her princesses in embroidered Chinese gowns smiled, waved their hands and tossed fresh flowers at the applauding spectators; and finally the block-long ferocious dragon, dancing to the special music of drums and gongs, prancing, leaping and twisting through the street amidst exploding firecrackers, its glaring eyes ogling, its wide mouth gaping as if drunk on New Year's wine.

May Li was busy clapping her hands, Old Man Li, dazzled by the sight, suddenly felt nostalgic and wiped a bit of moisture from the corners of his eyes. When the parade was over the crowd started moving toward the north like a torrent. On the reviewing stand a show was on, a pretty Cantonese opera singer was singing to the accompaniment of the band of *fu chin*, the two-string violin, and the *moom* guitar. Old Man Li watched the show for a while and an idea came to his mind.

"May Li," he said excitedly, "we shall give a show, too. I am going to the hotel to get your flower drum and gong and we shall sing a few flower songs for them . . ."

"Oh, no, father," May Li protested hastily.

"Why not?" Old Man Li said. "This is a good chance to find out how good you are. You are not afraid, are you?"

May Li swallowed. "No, but . . ."

"Good," Old Man Li interrupted, "when we open our restaurant in Chinatown, you are going to sing and dance for these people anyway. You wait here. I am

149

going to get the instrument. Wait here, don't move!" Quickly he shouldered his way out of the crowd and hurried to the hotel.

Fifteen minutes later he returned with a small flower drum with a strap and some red ribbons attached to it, and a shiny gong the size of a dinner plate. After he had handed the drum to May Li he started beating his gong.

"Make room, honorable ladies and gentlemen," he said in Cantonese with a heavy accent. "Please make room, my daughter and I are going to give a show, a flower drum show from the North, please make room, thank you!"

The crowd quickly opened up, clapping their hands. Old Man Li walked around in the circle made by the spectators and beat his gong. "Well, my little slave," he said professionally, "what are we going to sing today?"

May Li pranced after her father. "The Flower Drum Song," she said in an operatic tone, her left arm extended in an operatic gesture.

"What are we going to play today?"

"The flower drum and the flower gong."

"Yes, the flower drum and the flower gong." He beat his gong three times and asked, "Well, my little slave, what flower songs are you going to sing?"

"The Song of Feng-yong."

"What else?"

"The Song of Poor Little Chiu Hsiong."

Old Man Li beat his gong again and said to his audience, "Kindhearted and distinguished gentlemen, both of us can play and sing. When this little slave sings . . ."

"The song will be like a song."

"When I sing . . ."

"The noise will be like the broken gong."

"*Ai*, my little slave," Old Man Li said. "Do you not know modesty? Have I not taught you the teachings of Confucius?"

"Yes, my teacher, for ten years, when I was young."

"Then you should have read his great books and learned his eight virtues."

"How could I have? Even you, my teacher, often hold his books upside down."

"Kind-hearted ladies and distinguished gentlemen," Old Man Li said apologetically. "This little slave is spoiled. Do you know where I picked her up? I picked her up . . ."

"Be careful, my teacher, this is our first visit to this friendly town!"

"All right, all right, our sage has well said: 'Family ugliness cannot be exposed.' As you said, little slave, this town is friendly and the people are nice . . ."

"And our show is good, so we must not keep the nice people waiting long!"

"All right, we shall start the singing as soon as forty more people come, forty more people."

"No, my teacher, four more people. When four more people come we shall sing our song."

"All right, four more people. Be patient, noble audience, patience is the tonic of life."

"Patience can turn gray hair black, weak to strong!"

"Ah, a venerable lady has come," Old Man Li said. "Please make room for the venerable lady. Please make room! Ah, three more gentlemen! Little slave, we have four more now, what shall we do?"

"We shall beat the instrument and start the show!"

Old Man Li jumped to the center of the circle and beat his gong three times. "My little slave, do not forget your bows!"

May Li stopped prancing and bowed to the audience three times. "Kind-hearted ladies and distinguished gentlemen, my humblest bows to you."

"Kind-hearted ladies and distinguished gentlemen," Old Man Li said, "if her song is good . . ."

"Give me a little applause when I am through," May Li said, bowing again.

"If her song is bad . . ."

"Give me applause too."

Hastily Old Man Li beat his gong and May Li beat her drum, *ch'iang t'ung t'ung ch'iang, ch'iang t'ung t'ung ch'iang, ch'iang t'ung, t'ung ch'iang t'ung t'ung ch'iang.* . . . When the overture was over Old Man Li stopped beating his gong and May Li started singing to the accompaniment of her drum:

> *Say Feng-yong, sing Feng-yong,*
> *Feng-yong was once a wealthy town,*
> *But was cursed by the birth*
> *Of our emp'ror Chu-Yan-chong.*
> *Rich men took to lowly trade,*
> *Poor men's sons were sold out of town;*
> *I have no more children to sell,*
> *With my flow'r drum I beg around.*

When she finished singing, Old Man Li joined in with his gong and they beat the instruments as before, *ch'iang t'ung t'ung ch'ang, ch'iang t'ung t'ung ch'ing, ch'ang t'ung t'ung ch'iang t'ung t'ung ch'iang t'ung t'ung ch'ang.*

"Well, my little slave," Old Man Li said.

"Yes, my teacher."

"So, you are from the wealthy city of Feng-yong."

"Yes, my teacher, but I was sold out of town."

"Poor girl, have you no relative?"

"I have hundreds of them, fat and thin, old and young."

"When you were rich . . ."

"They followed me like bloodhounds."

"When you were poor . . ."

"Like the wind, they were all gone."

"Poor girl, you need someone to feed you."

"Right now, I can eat a Cantonese sausage a mile long."

"*Shew!* No wonder nobody wants the little slave. Well, I am worse, right now I can eat a water buffalo, together with its old horn."

"Food does not fall from heaven, gold does not grow on the ground."

152

"Well said, my little slave. What do you suppose we do?"

"With our drum and gong, we shall sing our best song!"

They beat the instrument again in the same rhythm. When it was over, Old Man Li and May Li started singing together:

> *Feng-yong drum, Fen-yen gong,*
> *With drum and gong we'll sing a song.*
> *What shall we sing?*
> *We only know the Feng-yong Song.*
> *Feng-la Feng-yang flow'r drum.*
> *Ai-ya-ai-hu-ya.*
> *Drrr-lang-dang p'iao-yi-p'iao.*

Then May Li sang:

> *Sad is my fate, oh how sad!*
> *I married a man with a flow'r drum.*
> *Stupid is he,*
> *Oh, how stupid and dumb.*
> *All day long he beats his singsong drum,*
> *Beats his singsong drum.*
> *Ai-ya-ai-hu-ya.*
> *Drrr-lang-dang p'iao-yi-p'iao.*

Then Old Man Li sang:

> *Sad is my fate, oh how sad!*
> *To spend my life with such an ugly mate.*
> *Of all the women you ever did meet,*
> *My wife has the largest pair of feet.*
> *Largest pair of feet.*
> *Ai-ya-ai-hu-ya.*
> *Drrr-lang-dang p'iao-yi-p'iao.*

Old Man Li and May Li sang together:

> *Drrr-lang-dang p'iao-yi-p'iao,*
> *Drrr-lang-dang p'iao-yi-p'iao,*
> *Drrr-p'iao, drrr p'iao, drrr-p'iao-p'iao,*
> *Drr-p'iao, drr-p'iao, drr-p'iao-p'iao-yi-p'iao.*

When they finished singing, Old Man Li laid his gong on the ground and bowed to the audience. "Kind-hearted ladies and distinguished gentlemen, if the song has pleased your honorable ears, please give this little slave an applause."

As the spectators applauded, May Li smiled and curt-sied. Old Man Li picked up his gong, and using it as a plate he went around and began to collect coins. "Generous ladies and honorable gentlemen, if you really liked the song, please give this little slave a little appreciation fund, give whatever you like, just a little appreciation fund . . ."

Many people didn't understand his Cantonese, but they knew what he wanted and all dug into their pockets and in a few minutes his gong was full of nickels and dimes; some appreciative tourists even tossed dollar bills into his gong.

Back in the hotel Old Man Li counted the money. Seven dollars and thirty-five cents. Never in his life had he made so much money in one hour. He wrapped up the money with red paper and gave it to May Li, who was just as excited as her father about the unexpected gain. "This is the lucky money of the Year of the Horse," said Old Man Li. "Keep it in your inner pocket and never spend it. The people of San Fran-cisco are generous, May Li. It is a good sign. With your flower songs and my cooking, we are going to have a great future in this town. Let us sleep late tomorrow, and go visit Mr. Poon as soon as we finish our lunch."

After lunch the next day they went to Jackson Street to visit Mr. Poon. They rang the doorbell of the two-story house and a fat woman answered the door. "We have come to see Mr. Poon of Peking," Old Man Li said politely in Cantonese with a heavy Mandarin accent.

"There is no Mr. Poon in this house," the fat woman said in Mandarin with a heavy Hunan accent.

Old Man Li looked at the number and scratched his neck. "The house number is right," he said.

"There is no Mr. Poon living here," the woman said, shutting the door.

They rang the bell again and the woman flung the door open and said heatedly, "I said there is no Mr. Poon in this house!"

"But the number . . ." Before Old Man Li finished the woman slammed the door shut. "*Shew*, what an ill-tempered old hag! May Li, you read the house number once more and see if it is right. Maybe I am old . . ."

"It is the right number, father," May Li said, checking the address on the envelope. "Maybe Mr. Consul General wrote the wrong address."

"Is this Jackson Street?"

"Yes. The street sign says it is. The foreign word on the sign is the same word on the envelope; look, father."

"Well, all foreign words look alike to me. Maybe we should ask somebody. Strange, I don't see a male or female on the whole street. Where are all the people? Put down your luggage, May Li, let us rest our legs for a while. *Shew*, I have never met anyone so impolite. She is not a Cantonese. *Shew*, what an ill-tempered woman!"

They put down their luggage, sat down on the steps and rested for a moment. A car passed by. Old Man Li shot up and shouted at it but it didn't stop. "Maybe we should give a show here," he said, sitting down again.

"Nobody will see our show on this street," May Li said. "It is so quiet and lonesome here."

"Lonesome? No place will be lonesome when I beat my good gong." Old Man Li brought his gong out of his bag. "May Li, powder your face a little, let's give a show." He got up and started beating his small gong. A few housewives pushed their windows up and stuck their heads out to see what was going on. "Father, I see someone now," May Li said excitedly.

"What did I tell you," Old Man Li said, beating his gong more violently. "People always appear when they hear my good gong. Take out my whip and beard, May Li, and have your flower drum ready! Quickly!"

May Li took out the things as told and then joined her father with her flower drum, beating it in their usual rhythm, *ch'iang t'ung t'ung ch'iang, ch'iang t'ung t'ung ch'iang, ch'iang t'ung t'ung ch'iang t'ung t'ung ch'iang t'ung t'ung ch'iang. . . .*

Suddenly the fat woman flung the door open and said, "Who are making so much noise in front of this house? Why, are you two still here?"

"We have just played a little music here," Old Man Li said. "It is music, not noise, woman."

"This is Old Master Wang's house, no monkey players are allowed to disturb his afternoon nap. Go away, go away!"

"We are not monkey players," May Li said heatedly. "We are strangers in Chinatown. We shall go when we are ready, you do not have to show so many of your teeth and growl."

Liu Ma stepped out of the front door and shook a finger at May Li. "If you do not scramble out of here immediately, you will see what is going to happen to you, you beggar maid!"

May Li sat down on her bag with a snort. "Father, we are going to stay right here. I want to see what is going to happen to us."

"What is going to happen to you? You will be arrested. You will be thrown into jail! You will die and rot, and your bones will be thrown to the hills to poison the wild dogs! Your soul will wander in a foreign land and never return to China . . ."

"Thank you, thank you," Old Man Li interrupted. "We have our future all well planned by ourselves, you do not have to bother with it, woman. Your job at the moment is to inform your old master that if he does not like music and song, he may stuff his ears with cotton and cover his head with three wet blankets . . ."

"Ah, may thunder strike you to death for insulting the Old Master in front of his own house!" Liu Ma said. "If you were in China, you would have been thrown into jail long time ago . . ."

Wang Ta was returning from school. He came up the steps hurriedly and asked, "What is going on here?"

"This old man has just insulted the Old Master," Liu Ma said, "and that beggar maid . . ."

"We are singers," May Li said. "We have just played a little music—"

"They are monkey players," Liu Ma shouted. "They have just made a lot of noise here to disturb the Old Master's afternoon nap . . ."

"Let this young lady talk," Wang Ta interrupted. Then he turned to May Li and asked, "What were you about to say?"

"I was about to say that the Old Master in this house has certainly hired the right woman to guard his door. I have traveled from China to America and I have never heard any dog that could bark as loud as she does!"

Liu Ma barked, "Oh, you beggar maid, may a thousand thunderbolts strike you to ashes . . ."

"Stop this shouting," Wang Ta said. "You are disturbing the Old Master's nap yourself."

"All right!" Liu Ma said. "I am going to tell the Old Master. You will see what is going to happen to you, you miserable beggars, hummph!" She hurried into the house and slammed the door.

"Father, let us go," May Li said, putting her drum into her bag.

Wang Ta was somewhat amused by the scene. He said with a chuckle, "Don't be afraid, that woman is only a maidservant. She thinks she is still in Hunan Province in China, where the Old Master can do anything. Did you say you are a singer?"

"Yes," May Li said, "we are flower song singers . . ."

"I am also a cook," Old Man Li said hastily. "I cooked for General White for fifteen years . . ."

"What flower songs can you sing?" Wang Ta asked May Li.

"I can sing songs of filial piety, songs of loyal officials, songs of gods and ghosts, songs of love and misery . . ."

"We are high-class singers," Old Man Li said. "We do not sing vulgar songs like 'A Woman in Love with Her Pillow,' or 'The Young Widow Sighs in Front of Two Pairs of Chopsticks.' General White liked our singing."

"Oh, mister," May Li asked, "do you know where Mr. Poon of Peking lives?"

Wang Ta frowned slightly. "Mr. Poon of Peking? No, but I shall look it up in the telephone directory and find out his address for you. What is his full name?"

"We have his address," May Li said. "He lives in this house."

"Oh, I know whom you mean!" Wang Ta said. "No wonder the name is familiar! He was the owner of this house before. He sold it and moved to Hawaii four years ago. Have you known him long?"

"We have not met him," Old Man Li said. "The consul general in Los Angeles, a good friend of General White, wrote this letter of introduction for us. He said Mr. Poon could help us open a Peking restaurant in San Francisco." He hastily dug out the letter and showed it to Wang Ta.

"So you are a real good Peking cook," Wang Ta said after reading the letter.

"My daughter and I plan to open the only Peking restaurant in Chinatown," Old Man Li said, "with singing and dancing . . ."

"Oh, father," May Li interrupted, "no use talking about it now. Mr. Poon is not here to help us, and we don't know anybody else in this town."

Old Man Li shrugged his shoulders. "Guess you are right, May Li. Maybe we will have to change our plans. But the Year of the Horse will be a good year for us, May Li. We have nothing to worry about. Let us go back to the hotel." He turned to Wang Ta and asked,

"Mister, could you tell us where to find a small hotel with reasonable price and no bedbugs?"

Wang Ta looked at May Li. "Well, there might be cheap hotels without bedbugs but they have drunkards instead. Why don't you live in a nice rooming house? Wait, I shall find a place for you to stay temporarily."

"Please don't recommend us to any expensive place, mister," Old Man Li said.

"It will cost you nothing, Mr. Li," Wang Ta said with a chuckle.

"Charity house?" Old Man Li said hastily. "No, mister, I stayed in a charity house once; I paid nothing but I lost my pants."

"Follow me, Mr. Li, you will not lose anything in this house." Wang Ta opened the front door with his key.

"What?" Old Man Li said, stepping back from the door. "This house?"

"Why not?" Wang Ta said, holding the door open for them. "This is my house. The Old Master is my father."

"Oh, no, oh, no," Old Man Li said, waving his hand.

"At least you can leave your luggage here, Mr. Li," Wang Ta said, smiling, "while we go and look for a rooming house for you."

"Come, father," May Li said happily, dragging her father toward the door, "please don't be afraid. We are guests of the Young Master!"

4

Today was the third day of the Year of the Horse. Old Master Wang decided to stay in bed for an extra hour in the morning to recuperate from the New Year celebration. He enjoyed the morning cough and the mem-

159

ory of the celebration. He was completely satisfied with the New Year's Day, which had passed without a single bad omen. He hoped that by next year he would have a daughter-in-law and a grandchild and another addition the year after. He hoped that from the Year of the Horse the family would really start growing. With the same excitement as that of a merchant calculating and anticipating his profit, Old Master Wang, lying in his enormous bed, estimated the growth of the House of Wang for the next five years.

His hope was fortified by the opinion of Miss Shaw, Madam Tang's citizenship teacher. According to Miss Shaw, there were two ways to get Wang Ta's picture bride to America; one was to apply for an immigration quota, the other was to wait for Wang Ta to become a citizen. Both ways took a little time, Miss Shaw had said at Madam Tang's banquet, but she had hastily added a few lucky words befitting a New Year occasion, something like "May God bless the couple."

Old Master Wang was satisfied with Miss Shaw's opinion; besides, his late wife, heaven bless her soul, would also help. Her spirit would undoubtedly influence everybody concerned and help the Wang family grow. He thought of this and felt a contentment that was almost happiness. He changed his position in the large bed and coughed for a few moments, grunting and groaning with pleasure, and wondering whether he should get up. Then he heard Liu Ma's voice scolding someone. He didn't want to interrupt her, for her scolding seemed to be the only disciplinary measure in the house besides his bamboo stick, which could only be used to whip Wang San, now. He listened to Liu Ma's scolding with an approving nod, but it was not until he found out she was only tongue-lashing her stone-deaf husband that he decided it was a complete waste of breath.

"Liu Ma," he called, "Liu Ma . . ."

Liu Ma, who was mopping the furniture and scolding Liu Lung in the middle hall, heard Old Master Wang's call and hurried into his room to prepare his toilet articles. Washing his face was one of the Old Master's major events in the morning and he demanded a careful preparation for it: the water in the washbasin must have the right temperature, the soap must be on the exact spot so that he could reach for it without looking, the towel must be perfumed, the dental cream squeezed and lying properly on the tooth brush, which in turn must be placed properly on a glass of lukewarm water—all this must be done for him and Liu Ma saw to it that the Old Master depended only on her for them.

When preparing for the Old Master's toilet, Liu Ma contemplated the most effective way to impart the news of the two unwelcome guests whom Wang Ta had invited into the house. She disliked both of them, especially the young wench with the red cheeks, who had unceremoniously compared her to a fierce watchdog yesterday at the front door. The more she thought of the girl, the angrier she became. She decided not to tell the Old Master of the visitors while he was washing; she needed more time to tell the news and must have his complete attention.

When she returned to the middle hall, Liu Lung, her husband, was still there sweeping the floor energetically. She wasn't in a good mood the whole morning on account of the guests, and automatically she resumed her scolding, "Liu Lung, you are already not fit to be a husband, cannot you try to make yourself a good servant?"

Liu Lung put a hand behind his ear and asked, "En—n?"

"Do you not know how to sweep a floor properly?" she shouted into his ear, snatching the broom from his hand. "Sweep it slowly and gently, not like a windmill, hula hula blowing the dust all over the house!"

"O—oh," Liu Lung said with a nod.

"All right, try again," she said, thrusting the broom back into his hands.

While Liu Lung resumed his sweeping in the same manner, Liu Ma watched him with mounting anger.

She watched him with her lips tightly pursed and arms akimbo until she couldn't stand it any more. "I said sweep the floor slowly and gently!" she cried, stamping one of her feet. "Look at the table. I have just mopped it clean, now it is covered with dust an inch thick. Each time you sweep the floor, I must mop everything twice. Is not my work heavy enough? Must you give me more trouble?"

Liu Lung handed the broom to his wife and said, "You sweep the floor, I mop the table."

Liu Ma snatched the broom from his hand. "Oh, why must God punish me by throwing me at a waste bag like you?"

"En—n?"

"I said you were a good for nothing idiot, a deaf and dumb old turtle!"

"Oh," Liu Lung said, "I heard that before." He picked up the rag which his wife had thrown at him and started mopping the table calmly.

"Oh, I am miserable," Liu Ma said, sweeping the floor angrily. "Men are worse one after another. You are the worst I have met." She gathered up the dust into a heap and swept it under the kang. Then she put the broom away and came back to let more steam out of her system. "Liu Lung, I ask you, how much money did you spend on drinking?"

"How much? Nothing."

"You lie. Your breath smells like a brewery!"

"I did not drink. I had only one little sip from that old man's flask."

"What old man?"

"En—n?"

"I said what old man?" Liu Ma cried.

"Oh, Old Man Li, the old man who moved in last night."

The information was like a wasp sting on a spot that was already sore. "Oh, you good-for-nothing idiot," Liu Ma said, trying not to raise her voice lest the whole house could hear her, "you disgrace me! If I find you talking to that old dirty beggar again, you can go away and sleep somewhere else, never come near me again!"

"En—n?"

"I said, you keep away from me!" Liu Ma cried. "You go sleep in the basement with the rats!"

Liu Lung's dull face suddenly brightened. "Always?" he asked hopefully.

It was too much of an effort to quarrel with her husband, Liu Ma decided. Whenever she quarreled with him she always got angrier and he got happier, and consequently she never seemed to be able to win the quarrel. "Oh, you deaf and dumb old turtle," she concluded despairingly, "I waste my breath shouting at you!"

She sat down in a chair and had a cigarette, then she heard a spasm of coughing. She threw a rag at Liu Lung and ordered, "The Old Master has finished his toilet. Go bring his ginseng soup. Take the rags and bucket with you."

Wang Chi-yang came to the middle hall, coughing. He decided to drink his ginseng soup on the kang every morning from now on as he always had in the old house in China. It would please his late wife's spirit, he thought, if he gradually went back to his old life pattern, resuming all his old habits as though nothing had changed. He sat on the left side of the kang heavily and coughed. He was still tired, having had a heavy day yesterday. The two Chinatown banquets had given him some indigestion and the Cantonese opera at night had exhausted him. In a way he was glad that the New Year came only once a year.

"Liu Lung is bringing your ginseng soup, Old Master," Liu Ma said, ready to report the bad news of the two unexpected visitors.

"Come and beat my shoulders," Wang Chi-yang said, turning slightly on the kang.

Liu Ma went to his left side and started beating his shoulders with her palms in a fast, flowery rhythm, waiting for him to inquire about the general welfare of the household. "Hm, humph," the Old Master grunted with pleasure, "what day is today of the week?"

"Saturday, Old Master."

"Hm, humph. Where is Young Master Wang San this morning?"

Liu Ma was in such a bad mood that even Wang San, her occasional ally, seemed to be a pebble in her shoe. "He is in the street playing with the urchins as usual. I worry about him, Old Master."

"Liu Ma," Old Master Wang said, "you have been working for the Wang family for more than twenty years. Since the last mistress passed away, you are the only woman I can trust in this house. From now on you take some care of Wang San. Tomorrow you shut him in his room and make him read the books of Confucius. Tell him if he goes to play with street urchins again, I shall lame his legs." He coughed a little more and Liu Ma beat his shoulders a little faster. "Is the breakfast ready?"

"Not yet," Liu Ma said. "The cook is getting lazy. He had a visitor last night . . ."

"Tell him the breakfast must be ready as soon as I have had my ginseng soup. As the late mistress always said, 'Spring is the best time of the year; morning is the best time of the day.' From now on I want everybody in this house to get up early, like the old times in China. If anybody misses his breakfast, tell him to tighten his belt and wait for lunch. Make this clear especially to the young masters."

Suddenly Liu Ma stopped beating. It was the right moment for the bad news, she thought. She leaned close to Wang Chi-yang's ear and said confidentially, "Old Master, do you know what Young Master Wang Ta did this morning? He was out of bed, washed and all dressed up before sunrise. And he already had his breakfast with the servants!"

Wang Chi-yang scowled slightly. "Why? Has he finally decided to start a new life? Where is he this morning?"

"He has been with his new friends the whole morning," Liu Ma said emphatically.

"Hm, humph," Old Master Wang said with a nod of approval, "I am glad he has finally associated with some people who are out of bed by this time on a Saturday. Who are these people?"

"Two beggars, sir."

"What?"

"A dirty old man and his ugly daughter. Young Master Wang Ta invited them into this house yesterday. I wanted to tell you yesterday but you went out after your afternoon nap and did not come home until after midnight."

"Did they pass the night here?"

"They slept in the guest rooms upstairs. I am afraid they have brought fleas and bedbugs into this house."

"Wash the beddings when they are gone," Wang Chi-yang said. "What beggars? I have never seen any beggars in Chinatown."

"They are from China. They speak Mandarin. The girl's mouth is full of foul language."

"Oh, the rebellious dog," Wang Chi-yang said, shaking his head with a deep sigh. "Since he began to follow the religion of that man nailed on a cross, this has become a charity house. Last year he invited three penniless students to live here for five weeks, now two beggars. I do not mind students; they are refugees from good families. But beggars! Liu Ma, when they leave the house, keep an eye on them. See if their pockets are bulging."

"Ease your mind, Old Master," Liu Ma said, resuming the beating. "Nobody can take a bit of dust out of this house if I have my eyes on him!"

Wang Chi-yang's cough was subsiding. He could have enjoyed a day of relaxation after the strenuous New Year celebration, but now the information about the beggars began to bother him. "It is enough beating," he said. "Tell Young Master Wang Ta to come."

"He went out with his new friends, Old Master. They went out immediately after they had breakfast with us. Heavens! How that beggar maid can eat!"

"Tell Wang Ta to see me as soon as he comes back," Wang Chi-yang said, rising from the kang. "Tell Liu Lung to bring my ginseng soup to my room."

"Yes, Old Master."

Old Master Wang retired to his room. After he had his ginseng soup, his breakfast and pipe, he was in no mood to practice his calligraphy and English writing. He wondered where Wang Ta had picked up the beggars. The boy should have asked his permission before he brought strangers into the house. After his wife's death, his sons had become more uncontrollable. He hoped that the girl in Hong Kong would be someone like his late wife, who always had a few clever methods in dealing with men. In dealing with him, he recalled that her 'boycott method' had been one of her most effective weapons. It was not so strict as to make him desire a concubine, yet strict enough to make him behave the way she had wanted. When he thought of it now he couldn't help nodding to himself with approval. He wondered whether the method had cut down the number of his progeny. If it had, he thought, he was glad of it. Children raised in this modern world were not exactly a blessing. Perhaps Wang Ta could make up the loss by producing a few more.

Before lunch he went back to the middle hall to sit on the kang for a while. The kang and the decorations helped him recall the good old days in the old house in China. From now on perhaps he should make it a habit—a half hour's meditation on the kang before lunch. Just as he had closed his eyes and his mind had wandered back to the ancient home in Hunan Province, he heard Liu Ma greet his sister-in-law.

"How are you, Madam Tang?"

"Not good, not bad," Madam Tang said. "Good morning, my sister's husband."

With a bit of irritation, Old Master Wang opened his eyes. "Good morning, my wife's sister."

Madam Tang looked as busy as ever. She seated herself on the other side of the kang heavily and said, "I have a few important things to discuss with you today. Have you had lunch yet?"

"Not yet," Wang Chi-yang said.

"Good. Liu Ma, tell the taxi man not to wait. I decided to have lunch here."

Liu Ma was laying the table for lunch in the dining hall. She answered her and hurried out.

"I have good news, my sister's husband," Madam Tang said, inserting a cigarette in an ivory holder. "I had the girl's picture carefully analyzed. Mr. Foon, the leading physiognomist in Chinatown, has assured me that the girl has five blessings behind her future, but not the blessing of longevity. The girl has a short chin, it means she will die young; besides, I have inquired about her chances of coming to America. To apply for an immigration quota, it takes about ten years; to wait for Wang Ta to become a citizen, it takes five years, and by the time he is permitted to bring his wife over, it will take another five years. Again ten years. By the time she arrives in this country, it is about time for her to die . . ."

"My wife's sister," Wang Chi-yang interrupted irritably, "is this the good news you have brought me?"

"I am telling the good news in a moment," Madam Tang said. She put her cigarette down, fished out the girl's photo from her handbag and returned it to Wang Chi-yang. "Please send the pictures back. Tell the herb doctor that the match can not be made because of the immigration difficulties. You can pay him a hundred dollars for all the trouble he has taken to arrange this match, if you wish . . ."

"We can not act so hastily," Wang Chi-yang said. "The herb doctor himself is a physiognomist. If the girl is destined to die young, he would have told me . . ."

"My sister's husband," Madam Tang said, "whether she will die young or live a long life is not a problem of great importance. Can you wait for ten years for Wang

Ta to take a wife? He will be forty and you will be over seventy. Perhaps you will never have the opportunity to see a grandson."

"There must be some way," Wang Chi-yang said, "some other way to bring the girl to this foreign land."

"Yes, there is another way—an illegal way," Madam Tang said. "You can hire an American citizen to do the job. The hired man can go to Hong Kong, marry the girl in name, bring her over and divorce her. It will cost a great deal of money; besides, you never can trust a hired man in such matters. It will be like asking a stranger to bring a package of candy to relatives across the ocean; if the stranger delivers it at all, nobody can guarantee that he has not opened it and stolen a piece or two. And above all, it is illegal. Do you want a daughter-in-law who is . . ."

"My wife's sister," Wang Chi-yang said hastily, "it is out of the question. Marriage is sacred; it is out of the question. What is the good news?"

Madam Tang puffed on her cigarette a few times. "Do you remember Mr. Loo?"

"The Shanghai Loo or the Cantonese Loo?"

"The Shanghai Loo, the one who was once the mayor of Hang Chow."

Wang Chi-yang remembered the man. He was a friend of Madam Tang's husband and had worked for the Japanese during the war. He didn't think too much of him. "Yes," he said, "a man distinguished for his Japanese mustache."

"He has shaved it."

"Hm, humph, he still has his Japanese wife, I presume. What is the good news about?"

"Mr. Loo has asked me to bring you an oral invitation—shark's-fin dinner at his home at seven o'clock next Friday."

"Hm, I wonder why he has become so hospitable?"

"That is what I have come to talk to you about, my sister's husband," Madam Tang said enthusiastically. "His three daughters have all grown up. How could he marry them off to good families if he does not invite select people to eat more dinners?"

"Do you mean he intends to dispose of one of his daughters at my house?" Wang Chi-yang asked, with a scowl.

"Perhaps two," Madam Tang said emphatically, "if he knows that your second son, Wang San, is growing fast. But never mind, he will be disillusioned when he sees the boy. But for Wang Ta, I know the old man has taken a fancy to him. He inquires about him each time I go to his house. My sister's husband, cannot you see this is as clear as a mirror?"

Wang Chi-yang disapproved of interracial marriage and he abhorred the idea of taking into his family a girl who was half Japanese. He said hastily, "I do not know his daughters well . . ."

"The second one is excellent," Madam Tang said, her enthusiasm mounting, "even the ex-governor of Hopei takes a fancy to her, but that stupid son of his wants to choose his own wife. Now General Liu, that ex-warlord from Szechuan, has begun to make friends with the family, but his son is a good-for-nothing play-boy. If the girl falls into his hands, it would be like a fresh flower falling into a garbage can. My sister's husband, if we want the girl we will have to act soon, or General Liu will be ahead of us."

"I am sorry, my wife's sister," Wang Chi-yang said. "I can not accept the dinner invitation."

"What?" Madam Tang asked, looking shocked.

Wang Chi-yang poured himself a cup of tea from his Kiangsi teapot. "I can accept the invitation as a friend, but to talk matrimonial business over his dinner, no. I do not know any of Mr. Loo's daughters."

"My sister's husband," Madam Tang said irritably, "every man of your age has a strong desire to tickle a plump little baby which is his own grandchild. You do not seem to be interested in this pleasure. This is most strange!"

"To be frank with you, my wife's sister," Old Master Wang said, blowing and sipping his tea in an effort to reduce the heat of the argument, "I do not wish to have foreign blood in my family."

"Japanese blood is most fashionable these days," Madam Tang said. "Many white Americans have taken Japanese wives and are calling them 'baby dolls,' a most affectionate way of addressing a wife in this country. Besides, this girl is only half Japanese; she is intelligent, filial, quiet, and not so pretty; she makes an ideal daughter-in-law!"

"I can not decide, I can not decide."

"Liu Ma," Madam Tang called, rising, "go call a taxi."

"Yes, Madam Tang," Liu Ma answered from the dining room, "but the lunch is ready . . ."

"The talk is over. I decided not to have lunch in a house where everything is so old-fashioned. Go call the taxi."

"Yes, madam."

"My sister's husband," she turned back to her brother-in-law and said heatedly, "you are going to regret it. Someday you will be in deep remorse for having not grabbed that girl!"

Old Master Wang blew and sipped his tea. "I can not decide, I can not decide."

Madam Tang left the house in anger. It was the first time she had lost an argument. She could induce Wang Ta to marry the girl, but losing an argument was something else; it bothered her extremely. Going downtown in a taxi, she decided to return to her brother-in-law's house in the evening and continue the verbal war until she won.

5

To Old Man Li, the guest room in the house of Wang was luxurious. The bed was so soft and wide, the bedding so neat and clean that he was sure no bedbugs could have existed in them. Compared to the small smelly hotel room for which he had paid a dollar a day, this was indeed a heaven. It was a miracle that he and May Li had stayed in such a large house for one night, all for free. Although the fat, glaring woman was somewhat unpleasant, yet the experience on the whole was a pleasant one. He liked the young master of the house and Liu Lung, the deaf servant, who seemed to treat him like a long-lost brother. The Year of the Horse had a good start.

But he would hate to take advantage of the situation and stay another night. It wouldn't be right. When Wang Ta suggested after breakfast that they go look for a rooming house for them, Old Man Li somehow felt both sorry and relieved. He hoped that he could find a place nearby so that he could associate with such a nice family. He had not met the Old Master yet, but he was sure that only a nice old gentleman could have produced a Young Master so generous and friendly.

The house-hunting wasn't too successful. The places they visited were either too far away or too expensive. May Li didn't seem to mind it; she enjoyed the ride in Wang Ta's car so much that she innocently admitted that she liked house-hunting every day and hoped that tomorrow would be the same. Old Man Li was embarrassed by her frankness; he apologized to Wang Ta and told him repeatedly that she was only a country lass. Wang Ta liked frank girls; they immediately put him at ease. He liked May Li's company and he, too, secretly enjoyed the fruitless hunting.

Before dinner they returned, happily frustrated. The moment Liu Ma saw them she said to Wang Ta gravely, her eyes glancing at Old Man Li and May Li ominously, "The Old Master wants to see you, Young Master."

Wang Ta went to his father's room, where he seldom went unless necessary. He found his aunt there having a heated argument with his father, but the moment they saw him they stopped. Both seemed to be in a bad

171

mood. He smiled and greeted his aunt. "How are you, my aunt?"

"Not good, not bad," Madam Tang said.

"Have you sent for me, father?" Wang Ta asked.

"How dare you bring strangers into this house without asking for my permission?" Old Master Wang said. "Who are they?"

"They are innocent people, father, too poor to rent a hotel room to pass a cold night."

"Very good," Madam Tang said with a nod of approval, then she turned to her brother-in-law and added: "He has a philanthropic nature, inherited from my sister, who was born with a charitable heart."

Old Master Wang grunted. He turned to Wang Ta and said, "I asked you who are these people?"

"They are artists, father. They sing and act."

"What?" Madam Tang asked, slightly shocked. "Have some actors passed a night here?"

"Yes. They would have frozen to death in some public park if I had not invited them in."

Madam Tang didn't have a high opinion of actors, especially actors who didn't even have a bed to sleep in. She pointed a finger at her nephew and asked, "You mean you picked them up in a public park?"

"No, my aunt," Wang Ta said hastily. "They were looking for the ex-landlord of this house. They did not know he had moved to Hawaii four years ago. They had no place to go so I invited them in . . ."

"You should have asked for my permission first," Wang Chi-yang said. "The world is full of bad people nowadays!"

"Oh, father, how could a frail old man and a young girl do any harm?"

"What?" Madam Tang said, more shocked. "A young girl?"

"Yes, my aunt. She is the old man's daughter. They have a letter of recommendation from the consul general at Los Angeles."

"Where are they from?" Old Master Wang asked.

"They are from Mainland China, speaking Mandarin. They have no money, no friends . . ."

"How old is the girl?" Madam Tang asked.

"Perhaps seventeen, perhaps older."

"Bad age," Madam Tang said.

"They want to open a night club in Chinatown," Wang Ta said. "The old man can also cook."

"Ridiculous," Madam Tang said. "They want to open a night club and yet they do not even have the money to rent a hotel bed."

"Well, that is their worry, my aunt."

"How old is the old man?" Madam Tang asked.

"Perhaps sixty-five, I don't know."

"Is he deaf?"

"He can hear a needle drop in a haystack."

"My sister's husband," Madam Tang said, "since this old man is going to starve, why don't you hire him to take Liu Lung's place? I also need a little slave to water my garden; I may use the girl if she is clean."

"I have enough servants already," Wang Chi-yang said.

"Liu Lung is so deaf that even if an atomic bomb exploded in his ear he would not hear it," Madam Tang said. "You can still keep him on a charity basis; this old man . . . what is his name, Wang Ta?"

"Old Man Li."

"Yes, this old man is a refugee from Mainland China. It is always cheap to hire refugees as servants. If you do not want the old man, my sister's husband, I shall take both of them."

"Wang Ta," said Old Master Wang, "tell them to come in. I shall take a look at the old man before I can make the decision."

Wang Ta had expected a scolding from both his father and his aunt; now that the interview turned out so differently he was quite surprised. He was afraid that Old Man Li and May Li might not like the idea of working as servants, but when he went to them and told them of the job offering they jumped at it.

Wang Ta brought them to his father's room and introduced them to his father and his aunt. Old Man Li rubbed his hands humbly and bowed low. "Old Mr. Wang," he said, using the choicest words at his command, "your distinguished name has been rumbling in my ears like a great thunder since I set foot in this honorable Chinatown. It is indeed a great honor and privilege to see you. May Li, bow to Old Mr. Wang for his kindness and generosity."

May Li bowed to Wang Chi-yang. "Ten thousand benedictions to you, sir."

Wang Chi-yang was pleased. It was a long time since he had received from people such old-fashioned courtesy. He waved his hand and grunted, "Hm, humph, no ceremony, no ceremony." He asked Old Man Li a few questions about his past and examined the letter of recommendation from the consul general, then he decided to use them. "Old Man Li, you look like an honest man and you are from Mainland China, speaking an understandable dialect. I intend to give you a job; are you interested?"

Old Man Li bowed again. "Oh, where else can I have a greater pleasure? I only hope that my humble flesh and bones could render their services satisfactorily in this great house."

"I would like to work here, too, Old Mr. Wang," May Li said. "Really, you don't look so dignified and horrible as we expected."

Wang Chi-yang gaped; Madam Tang quickly put her handkerchief over her mouth to hide any sign of mirth; Wang Ta turned his eyes to the ceiling, wiping the sweat on his hands inside his trouser pockets. Old Man Li coughed in great embarrassment. "Old Mr. Wang," he said apologetically, "she is only a country lass, she does not know the city people's good manners. May Li, bow to Madam Tang."

May Li bowed. "Ten thousand benedictions to the madam."

"Hm," Madam Tang said, sizing her up carefully, "you look neat and clean outside."

"Thank you, madam," May Li said.

"Old Man Li," Old Master Wang said, "I want you to understand that I employ you not because I need more servants. You are old, you cannot help much in the housework. I only hire you on a charitable basis, do you understand?"

"Surely, surely," Old Man Li said hastily. "That is a sign of your great heart, Old Mr. Wang."

"Your daily routine here will be cleaning the back yard, sweeping the porch and watering the flowers. Little errands like mailing a letter or buying cigarettes for guests will be your extra work."

"Well, that would be just like a vacation to me," Old Man Li said cheerfully. "I only hope that my humble flesh and bones could be of more use to you, Old Mr. Wang. Ha, ha."

"Although the work here is light," Old Master Wang said sternly, "diligence, honesty and obedience are strictly observed in this house."

"Oh, you don't have to remind me of virtue and morals, Old Mr. Wang. Confucius has already taught me all that. And I am not an ungrateful old bone. To-morrow, if you find a dead leaf in the back yard or a single bit of dust on the porch, you may curse my ancestors up to five generations, and I will not say a word back!"

"As for you, young girl," Madam Tang said to May Li, "good discipline is the first rule in my house. No loud laughter, no noisy talk are allowed."

"Yes, madam."

"Second, cleanliness. I do not want you to bring any of your own belongings with you. Old clean clothes will be provided in my house."

"Madam, am I not going to work in this house?"

"No! Third, woman's virtue. No indecency is permitted either in conduct or in conversation."

"But, madam," May Li interrupted, "I want to work in this house."

"Do not talk back!" Madam Tang said hotly.

"Oh, Mr. Wang," May Li said, turning to Wang Ta, "can't I work here with my father?"

"My aunt," Wang Ta said, "perhaps this girl does not want to be separated from her father. Could you not get somebody else to help with your garden?"

"Do not think I can not get help," Madam Tang said, rising from the kang. "Many Chinatown girls are anxious to work for me. My sister's husband, think over Old Mr. Loo's dinner invitation. I shall see you tomorrow."

Wang Chi-yang was secretly pleased with May Li for refusing to work for his sister-in-law. He said politely, "Are you not going to have dinner with us?"

"No," Madam Tang said, starting for the door, "I am busy."

After Madam Tang was gone, Wang Chi-yang coughed with dignity and said, "Old Man Li, you can settle down in this house and start working tomorrow. Liu Ma, give some work for this girl to do tomorrow."

Liu Ma, who had been watching the hiring with apprehension, cast May Li a poisonous glance and said emphatically, "I will, Old Master."

After dinner Wang Chi-yang retired to his room. Wang·Ta invited Old Man Li and May Li to the middle hall for a social evening. Liu Lung was serving them tea. "Well, work starts tomorrow," Wang Ta said to his guests, "you might as well sit down on the kang and make yourselves comfortable while you are still my guests today. Liu Lung, you may take a rest too, and calm your breath with a cigarette." He offered a cigarette to the deaf servant, who accepted it with a smile and went to a corner to smoke it; Old Man Li and May Li sat down on the kang, sipping tea.

"This is certainly the most fashionable house I have set foot in," May Li said, looking around curiously. "Mr. Wang, are all these writings on the wall poetry?"

"Yes," Wang Ta said. "My father's calligraphy. Everybody admires it but nobody understands it. Smoke, Old Man Li?"

"Yes, yes," Old Man Li said eagerly.

Wang Ta offered him a cigarette and struck a match for him. Old Man Li held the cigarette between his thumb and forefinger and put it between his outstretched lips gingerly. "To be frank, Mr. Wang," he said, exhaling the smoke through his nostrils, "I am not used to this foreign stuff. I brought my water pipe from China but one of General White's lady relatives stole it as a souvenir. Guess I must learn how to smoke a cigarette from now on."

"Do you smoke, May Li?" Wang Ta asked.

"Oh, yes!" May Li said hastily.

"Don't encourage her to smoke, Mr. Wang," Old Man Li said. "She smoked my water pipe once and she coughed a whole day."

"What was wrong?" Wang Ta asked. "Did some smoke get into your windpipe?"

"No, some water," May Li said.

"This is dry," Wang Ta said. "It is safe." He offered her a cigarette and all laughed.

They talked and laughed for a while, then Old Man Li became serious and coughed. "Mr. Wang," he said, "there will be a lot of joyful days working in this great house. But there is something—well—well . . ."

"What is it?" Wang Ta asked.

"Well, it is something quite embarrassing," Old Man Li said. "This is—you know—this is different from just raising my bamboo plate to people . . ."

"I know what my father wants to say," May Li interrupted briskly, "he wants to know how much you are going to pay him."

Old Man Li coughed with embarrassment. "Well, well, it is like this, Mr. Wang. We'd like to open a Peking restaurant in Chinatown, with singing and dancing and serving the best Peking duck, but it takes money to open such a restaurant. I just want to figure —well—just to figure out how much we can save . . ."

"Old Man Li," Wang Ta said, "my father is not a stingy man; probably he will pay you as much as he pays Liu Lung. Liu Lung, how much money do you make here every month?" He made a gesture with both hands to help Liu Lung understand his question.

"How much money do I make?" Liu Lung said behind the thick cigarette smoke that he was producing by vigorous puffing. "I make nothing."

"What?" Wang Ta asked, somewhat surprised. "Does not my father pay you any salary at all?"

"Salary?" Liu Lung said. "Surely he pays me. He pays me in the morning; my wife takes it away in the night, so I make nothing."

"Liu Lung," Wang Ta said with a scowl, "each time I see you, I decide that celibacy is my chosen future. Old Man Li, don't worry about your salary, in time you will save enough money to open your business in Chinatown. When I work—I don't know when, but I think I eventually will—I shall invest in your business and back you."

"Do you hear that, May Li?" Old Man Li said cheerfully. "You work hard here, May Li. When we leave this great house to start our own business, we shall leave with a good reputation."

Liu Lung vaguely understood what they had been talking about. He put a hand behind his ear and asked, "You work here, too, Old Man Li?"

"Can not say work, Liu Lung," Old Man Li shouted. "Just attempt to cheat a bowl of rice out of the kind-hearted masters in this house, that is all, ha, ha!"

"Good, good, you work here too, good!" Liu Lung said. He hurried to Old Man Li, lifted up his Chinese gown and showed him a flask that was hanging on his belt. "You see this? I bought it this morning." With a smile he quickly hid it again. "I show you the back yard, en—n?"

"Sure, sure," Old Man Li said with an understanding nod. "Mr. Wang, excuse me, I am going to get acquainted with this great house a little. Come, Liu Lung." They went to the back yard through the kitchen, laughing and patting each other on the shoulders. Wang Ta and May Li looked at them indulgently, then turned to each other and smiled.

"Do you like this room?" Wang Ta asked. "It is an

178

exact copy of the middle hall of the old house in China. Everything is arranged just as my mother wanted it in the old house, the decorations, the pictures, everything. Do you like the pictures?"

"I like that man," May Li said, pointing at the god of longevity on the wall. "He has a funny face. He looks as if someone is tickling him." She went to the picture, looked at it, and laughed.

Wang Ta followed her to the picture. "Be careful what you say. He is not a man."

"Not a man? How could a woman look like that?"

"He is an immortal," Wang Ta said. "One of the high officials in the celestial world. He controls people's ages."

"You mean he is the god of longevity?"

"Yes."

May Li bowed to the picture and murmured in reverence, "Oh, god, forgive my ignorance."

"You don't have to be so ceremonious to him, May Li," Wang Ta said, laughing. "He is a business god. He will not give you a long life unless you bribe him with big juicy peaches." He took a peach from the offering plate on the table, wiped it with his hand, murmured an "excuse me" and then bit into the peach.

May Li looked horrified. "No!"

"When I was at home in China, I often borrowed peaches from him," Wang Ta said. "He won't mind." He took another peach from the plate and offered it to May Li. "Come, have one on him, too. He won't mind."

May Li took the peach gingerly. "Don't—don't you believe in the god of longevity?"

"Sure," Wang Ta said, eating the peach heartily. "My father always offered him the best fruits in the market. In China I ate them all. All this extra nourishment might have added a few years to my life. Do you like this clock? It belonged to my mother."

May Li looked at the gold clock on the table, her eyes widening with admiration. "It is beautiful. Is it an offering to the god, too?"

179

Wang Ta laughed. "Oh, no! A clock ticks time away and hastens people to their graves. How could the god of longevity appreciate such a gift? He must be disgusted with it. But my mother was not so thoughtful; she put it here for years, probably to remind the god of his duty."

"Where is your mother?" May Li asked.

"She died a few years ago. Sometimes it makes me wonder if she really offended the god of longevity."

May Li looked at the god and then at the clock. "Are you not going to remove it?"

"Well, this clock is our family treasure," Wang Ta said. "Perhaps my father thinks this is the only safe place for it. Who dares to steal a gold clock right from under the nose of a god?"

"Is this a gold clock?"

"Yes. You may wind it. Probably it will be your daily routine from now on."

May Li touched the clock respectfully with a finger. "A gold clock! I never touched gold in all my life."

"You are treating it too carefully, May Li. Let me show you how to wind this clock." Wang Ta tossed the peach core onto the offering plate, picked up the clock and wound it carelessly. The ancient clock answered the rough treatment with a rattling sound and stopped. Wang Ta shook it a few times and then listened to it.

"Has it stopped?" May Li asked fearfully.

"Dead as a rock," Wang Ta said. He put the clock back on the table. "I shall repair it tomorrow. Doctoring sick men is my major study, repairing clocks is my sideline. Come, let me take you to a movie in Chinatown." He took her hand and led her to the door.

"Mr. Wang," May Li said, still looking at the picture, "why don't you believe in the god of longevity?"

"Oh, forget that funny face," Wang Ta said. "I study modern medicine in the university. If I am good, I shall be a god of longevity myself. If I am bad, no god of longevity can stop me from shortening people's lives. Come, let me take you to a movie."

6

During the past three weeks, May Li found life in the House of Wang very agreeable. Everybody in the house ate Chinese food, spoke Chinese and did everything in typical Chinese ways except Wang San, who talked the foreign tongue and tossed an olive-shaped leather ball around that annoyed her a little. Yes, life here was just like that in China. Chinatown supplied everything the family needed except Old Mr. Wang's water pipe tobacco, which had to be ordered in Hong Kong.

She liked the Chinatown movies. She understood the Cantonese dialect and could follow their stories easily. The foreign movies were colorful and exciting but she seldom understood them. When she was seeing an American movie, she always missed the point of the funny talk. Each time the audience laughed, she often felt as though she had an itch but couldn't reach it. She should have learned the foreign talk from General White a long time ago, but the general had enjoyed speaking Chinese so much that he had never spoken a word of English to her. All she had learned from him was how to drink ice-cold water and cow's milk.

When she thought of General White, she missed him. The old general was different from Old Mr. Wang; he had often laughed and joked and eaten his meals heartily; whereas Old Mr. Wang was always serious and stern-looking and had only a small appetite, and besides, he never drank cold water or cow's milk. General White had liked to play Chinese checkers and take long walks; Old Mr. Wang liked to practice his writing and take long afternoon naps. General White had enjoyed talking; Old Mr. Wang seemed to enjoy coughing. One was so gay and the other so stern. She liked a gay old man better. She wondered who was older, General White or Old Mr. Wang. If Old Mr. Wang was older, she thought, it was apparent that the god of longevity liked a stern old man better.

The work in the House of Wang was just as light as that in the general's house. Although Liu Ma often made her do things over again, still there wasn't enough work to keep her happily busy. She loved to work. When she had nothing to do, she would come to the middle hall and shine Old Mr. Wang's water pipe.

It was a leisurely afternoon. Wang Ta and Wang San had not yet returned from their schools. Everybody else in the house was taking an afternoon nap. She came to the middle hall and shined Old Mr. Wang's water pipe, humming merrily her favorite tune, the Feng-yong Flower Drum song.

Old Man Li, who enjoyed life in the House of Wang just as much as did his daughter, came into the middle hall with a pail of water and a ladle. His face was beaming with happiness.

"Oh, father," May Li said, "did you not take a nap like everybody else?"

"Well," Old Man Li said, "I do not have long to live, why should I waste it in bed? I like to do a little housework to enjoy myself. Why don't you take a nap?"

"I tried, but I could not fall asleep. I don't know why the people in this house can sleep so easily. Like Old Mr. Wang, he starts snoring even before he reaches his bed."

"Well, we are different," Old Man Li said, watering the orchids. "We were born different from the rich people. God makes the rich people enjoy the bed and makes us enjoy the food."

"Old Mr. Wang certainly does not eat much," May Li said, shining the water pipe energetically. "Did you see him eat his dinner? When he sees the delicacies, he always scowls. He always seems unhappy at the dinner table. You are never unhappy in your bed, are you, father?"

"Well, not if the bed has no bedbugs. May Li, our sage has well said: 'Content people are the happy

182

ones.' " He stopped watering the orchids and asked seriously, "Are you happy here, May Li?"

"Yes, I am!" May Li said.

"That is good!"

"I am happy except when I see Liu Ma, that old hag."

"Don't have trouble with her," Old Man Li said hastily; "our ancient physiognomist has well said, 'A woman whose cheekbones are high and lips are sharp has a heart as poisonous as a rattlesnake.' I noticed that Liu Ma has such features. What did she do to you?"

"She always glares at me and snorts."

"Well, as long as she does not use her teeth and fingernails on you, don't mind her."

"Her tongue is sharp, father. Yesterday when I was here shining Old Mr. Wang's water pipe, she came and nagged me. She said, 'Who the turtle's eggs do you think you are, sitting on the kang?' I said, 'Why can't I sit on the kang?' She said, 'That is the Old Master's seat!' I said, 'The Old Master is not here.' She said, 'No servants are allowed to sit on the kang!' I said, 'I have sat on the kang many times with the young master, why did he not know this rule?' . . ."

"That is right, that is right," Old Man Li said. "What did she say to that?"

"She said, 'Hum!' "

"Well, you won the argument. But don't have trouble with her any more, May Li. I am sure the ancient physiognomist won't be wrong about her cheekbones. Be good to her. Our sage has well said, 'Don't sail against a storm,' understand?"

"I shall try."

"Is Mr. Wang good to you?"

"Oh, yes," May Li said, her eyes gleaming suddenly. "He is going to teach me how to read and write the foreign language."

"Is he? Ha, ha! Good! You study hard. It is a great thing to be able to read and write, no matter in what language, especially if you have a lover or a rotten relative who keeps writing to you. *Shew!* I would have been more respected in China if I could read those classical letters from that crooked cousin of mine. Each time I asked somebody to read them to me, they thought I was crooked too, *shew!*"

May Li fished out a fountain pen from under her blouse and showed it to her father. "Mr. Wang also gave me this foreign pen. He said it has a small ink-stand hidden in it."

Old Man Li examined the pen gingerly. "Ah, it is good of him to give you an expensive thing like this. You keep it carefully in your inside pocket and don't use it too often." He returned the pen to May Li. "What does Mr. Wang study in the foreign university?"

"He studies how to be a doctor. Father, you should see how he writes that foreign language. He writes it so fast that you would think he is not writing, but drawing little worms on a piece of paper."

"I know, I know," Old Man Li said. "This foreign language is strange. It looks different in writing. The foreign sailors often have the language tattooed on their arms. Ah, what a mess! Some of the words look like women's legs to me!"

May Li saw Wang Ta come in and she jumped up to her feet. "Mr. Wang," she called excitedly.

"Hello," Wang Ta said, throwing a stack of books in a chair and himself in another. "Am I tired!" He was tired, having rushed home from school. Ever since he had known May Li he had been rushing most of the time. Every day he was anxious to come home. Life wasn't dull any more, and he was a changed man.

"You are back early today," Old Man Li said. "Seems to me it is not too hard to study to be a doctor."

"Short days, but long years, Old Man Li," Wang Ta said, smiling.

"Are you not going to take an afternoon nap, Mr. Wang?" May Li asked.

"I already had my nap in my class."

"Well," old Man Li said, "I certainly wouldn't mind

studying to be a western doctor. But if I was ill, I certainly would not like to see one, *shew!*"

Wang Ta laughed. "When I get my diploma, Old Man Li, I certainly won't advise you to see me if you are ill. What have you been doing this afternoon, May Li?"

May Li handed him the Old Master's water pipe. "Look!"

"What? A new water pipe?"

"No, I shined it. I changed the water, too."

"No wonder it even smells clean. You know, this pipe is as old as my brother Wang San. I must say this is the first time it has enjoyed a real shine since it came out of the factory. May Li, you are going to win my father's favor faster than anybody else in this house."

"I like your father," May Li said. "He looks so stern, but he never scolds anybody."

"He beats my brother, though," Wang Ta said.

"Are you his favorite son, Mr. Wang?" May Li asked.

"I have tried to be, but not too successfully. Whenever I ask him for something, he often has his mouth loaded with 'no's' and fires it at me like a machine gun. Old Man Li, my father is pleased with your work, too. He said the back yard is cleaner, the flowers look fresher and grow larger since you came."

"Mr. Wang," Old Man Li said, highly pleased, "flowers are just like human beings. You treat them well and they grow better and look fresher. Even those bloodthirsty dogs in China, they growl and show their teeth to everybody, but once you throw a bone at them, ha! They will wag their tails to you thereafter. It is true of everything."

"It is not true of every human being, though," Wang Ta said. "There are a lot of people who take advantage of a man's kindness and make a fool of him."

"I call them bedbugs," Old Man Li said. "They always explode under their benefactor's body when they have sucked too much blood."

"Father," May Li said, making a face, "you mention bedbugs every day—it is nauseating."

"Well," Old Man Li said, "I have been their benefactor for more than sixty years, how can I forget them?"

Wang Ta laughed. Old Man Li was pleased. He glanced at the young people and thought it was about time to leave them alone. "Well," he said, taking up the water pail, "the flowers in the back yard are waiting for my water."

"You certainly love the flowers, Old Man Li," Wang Ta said.

"You will too, Mr. Wang," Old Man Li said with a wink, "when you become my age and cannot find anything better to love." He cast May Li a quick glance and hurried out of the middle hall, laughing.

"Let us sit on the kang," Wang Ta said, coming to the kang.

"Are servants allowed to sit on the kang, Mr. Wang?" May Li asked.

"In this house you are allowed to do anything except call me mister all the time."

"I shall call you Young Master Wang Ta then," May Li said, sitting down on the other side of the kang.

"Don't you ever use that feudalistic title on me!" Wang Ta said. "It stings my eardrums. I hate it so much that I don't even mind trading it for Liu Lung's title."

"What is Liu Lung's title?"

"Deaf and Dumb Old Turtle."

May Li laughed. "What shall I call you then?"

"Call me Ta. Nobody in this house calls me Ta. That is why the atmosphere in this house is like that in an icehouse, and everybody here is like a hunk of frozen beef."

"All right, I shall call you Ta," May Li said softly.

Wang Ta looked at her and smiled, then he moved to her side of the kang. "Well, the barrier is gone. Do you like to work here, May Li?"

"Yes, Ta."

"You would like it much better if this was the old house in China. It was heavenly in the springtime. The

186

garden was full of flowers, bees and butterflies; the young bamboo shoots grew a foot a day . . . wonder what happened to the old house now . . ." He turned to the wall behind the kang and pointed at it. "See that space over there? That was a huge moon-window facing the garden. Through it you could see the great big bamboos." He lowered his head slightly and pretended to look up through an imaginary window. "Did you notice that basket, the basket that hangs on top of that tall bamboo?"

May Li was puzzled for a moment, then she smiled and pretended to look too. "Yes, I see it. How could anybody hang a basket that high?"

"I did. When I hung the basket on the bamboo, it was only ten feet high. Look at it now; it has reached the sky. I used to sit here and watch the bamboos grow, especially the one with my basket carried on its top. Sometimes I felt sad when I saw the basket go so high— it finally went way beyond my reach. Somehow the basket became a symbol of my life's goal, and yet time was taking it farther away from me. In those days I was a pretty sad fellow. In fact, I always was . . . until I met you."

He turned to look into May Li's eyes. May Li lowered her head, blushing slightly. He quickly turned back to the wall and pointed at it again. "Do you see that?"

May Li pretended to look. "No. What is it?"

"The bamboo that was cut down."

"Oh, yes. Why was it cut down?"

"My brother, Wang San, was responsible for its execution. He imitated my ingenious doing by hanging a basket on it. He was only seven then, but he was a clever boy. He put two eggs in his basket. Do you know what happened? Two wild pigeons came; they made their home in the basket and hatched the eggs. They were chicken eggs. When the pigeons found their babies growing so large, they were frightened away. My father discovered it and was frightened too. He thought the evil spirit must have invaded the garden. Who has ever heard of chickens raised on top of a bamboo? He had the bamboo cut down, invited two Taoist priests home to send the evil spirit away, and then buried the chickens with a big funeral. Those two eggs cost him exactly two hundred thousand yuans, the value of a cow."

May Li laughed. "Why? Didn't anybody tell him the truth?"

"I did. But it did not help much. He still believed in evil spirits. But Liu Lung and I had a good chicken dinner. He dug the birds out of their expensive graves and fried them in pure lard. Oh, heavens, they were delicious! We ate them in the hills so Liu Ma couldn't find us."

"Didn't you invite your brother to share them?" May Li asked. "They were his chickens."

"Yes, but Wang San had too many worries. My father almost lamed his legs for raising chickens on top of a bamboo." He took out a bamboo stick from behind the kang and waved it in the air. "Do you know what this is? This is called the 'Terror of Wang San.' When my brother sees it, he trembles from his feet to his head. Give me your hand, let me show you how my father used to terrorize my brother."

May Li stretched out her right hand. Wang Ta held it with his left hand and pretended to beat it with the bamboo stick. "Ten strokes for stealing, fifteen strokes for failing to recite the Four Books of Confucius."

"How many strokes did he receive for raising chickens in the sky?" May Li asked, laughing.

"Twenty heavy strokes," Wang Ta said, "not on his palm, but here." He gave her round little bottom a gentle stroke with the stick. Both laughed. Wang Ta put the stick away, but his hand still held hers. They looked at each other for a moment and suddenly May Li lowered her face, blushing. "I must go now," she said, "Old Mr. Wang may come here to smoke his pipe."

"Don't worry," Wang Ta said. "He usually sleeps the whole afternoon, and sometimes it takes an extra hour for him to wake up." He pulled her close. "You are very pretty, May Li."

May Li smiled and blushed profusely. "I must go now, really."

"Has any man held your hand before, May Li?" Wang Ta asked.

"Yes."

"Well, who was this scoundrel?"

"A Russian adviser."

"A Russian adviser! Where did you meet this romantic Communist?"

"In a nightmare," May Li said. "When I was in Formosa I dreamed I saw a motion picture in which the Russian adviser was a real monster."

"Did you see a real Russian in a Russian picture?"

"No, I never saw a Russian picture. My father said back home everybody is seeing Russian pictures now. Did you see one?"

"Yes, I saw one in San Francisco. In that picture everybody is a hero. He works twenty hours a day, seven days a week. He salutes his comrades tirelessly. When orders come, he raises his arm and flag with a battle cry, dashes to the battlefield and dies. Have you seen many American pictures?"

"No," May Li lied. "I never saw an American picture."

"Next time I shall take you to an American picture. They are different from the Cantonese pictures we have seen in Chinatown. In an American movie, everybody has a beautiful car; in every car there is a beautiful woman. And the heroes don't die so often, as the Chinese heroes do. Sometimes they do die; if they don't, they always end up the whole thing with a long kiss. You know what a long kiss is, don't you?"

"No," May Li lied again.

"Well," Wang Ta said laughing, "perhaps you are the only person on American soil who does not know what a kiss is. Well, let me explain it to you. A kiss is—it is—a touch or press of the lips—on the lips or the cheeks or—well, it is much easier to do than to explain.

189

Anyway, press your lips anywhere you choose, but with a feeling of strong personal attachment induced by sympathetic understanding—or by ties of kinship—or by ardent affection or . . ." He paused, looked at her intently. "Do you understand?"

"No," May Li said.

"I know you don't," Wang Ta said. "Well, I shall explain it in a simpler way. Physically a kiss is a—is a—let's say it is an action, loved by everybody in the Western countries, especially in America. Do you know what action is?"

"No," May Li said.

"Oh, you are hopeless. All right, I shall show it to you. Close your eyes."

May Li closed her eyes. Wang Ta raised her chin a little and went on, "Yes, raise your head and relax your lips . . . that's right . . . just like a little crack on a pomegranate. That's right." Then he held her with both his hands and planted a gentle kiss on her lips.

May Li opened her eyes quickly and asked, "Is this a kiss?"

"Yes," Wang Ta said, smiling, "but compared with the kisses you see in an American movie, this is only half-done."

"Only half-done?"

"Yes, only half-done. Let me take you to an American movie. They will show you how it is well-done. Come on."

"Now?"

"Yes, now. We'll be back in time for dinner." He took her hand and dragged her out.

7

Madam Tang had not been quite successful in arguing with her brother-in-law that he should accept Mr. Loo's dinner invitation, let alone persuade him to accept one of Mr. Loo's daughters as a prospective daughter-in-law. She wondered why the old man had become so stubborn. She had successfully made him deposit all of his cash in the bank and tricked him into buying a suit of Western clothes which he loathed, but inducing him to eat Mr. Loo's dinner seemed to be almost impossible. Her failure in this errand bothered her a great deal. Besides suffering a personal defeat, she would also lose face in front of Mr. Loo, and above all, it would be a great shame if Mr. Loo's second daughter should fall into the hands of that good-for-nothing playboy son of that Szechuan ex-warlord. The girl was just right for Wang Ta.

When she thought of all this she almost hated her brother-in-law for being so stubborn. It puzzled her a little why Wang Chi-yang was getting more hard-boiled. She analyzed the situation and decided that it had something to do with the rearrangement of the furniture in that middle hall. Her sister's old spirit was back in the house. It must have boosted Wang Chi-yang's courage and stubbornness. If she wanted to influence the old man perhaps she should change her tactics from now on. She knew that Wang Chi-yang was an upright old turtle despite all his weaknesses. He was never greedy, and had always been indifferent to fortune and fame. But he had a great respect for scholastic achievement. All through his life he had admired nobody but great scholars and poets.

Then she remembered that Mr. Loo had written some poems during those jobless days when he had been supported by his three daughters. She understood that he was still writing poems occasionally after four hours' humiliating work at a restaurant as a cashier. She wondered how many poems the ex-mayor of Hang Chow had written. If there were enough for a book, perhaps she could do something about them.

She picked up her phone and called Mr. Loo at his house. "Yes, I have written thousands of them," Mr. Loo told her, "but my wife has been using my poems to wrap her flower seeds and has burned some to build fires in the fireplace."

"Please write more and salvage those which your wife has not yet burned," Madam Tang said. "I can find a publisher for you. I know a Chinatown newspaper publisher who is interested in publishing a collection of Chinese poems. Please have the manuscript ready."

After Madam Tang had finished talking to Mr. Loo she sent for a Yellow cab, and within twenty minutes she was in the heart of Chinatown talking to one of the newspaper publishers. The publisher wasn't interested in publishing any collection of poems but his paper was doing some printing business on the side. For three hundred dollars he could print a thousand copies of anything of pamphlet size. Madam Tang had no time to study the project in greater detail; she dug out her checkbook and signed a check for five hundred dollars. "Please pay Mr. Loo two hundred for his poems," Madam Tang said, handing the publisher the check. "Tell him it is your money, please, and send somebody to pick up the poems and have them printed within a week. Here is Mr. Loo's address."

The publisher accepted the check with a dubious scowl but it was business for the firm and he didn't want to be too inquisitive about the strange deal. It might be a birthday present for Mr. Loo or some such thing, he thought.

The taxi was waiting. Madam Tang got back into it and told the driver Wang Chi-yang's address. She was fighting a war and she couldn't afford losing precious time. When she entered the middle hall in the House of Wang, Liu Ma seemed to be very pleased to see her; she looked as though she had great news to report. "How are you, Madam Tang?"

"Not good, not bad," Madam Tang said. "Has the Old Master gotten out of his bed?"

"Not yet," Liu Ma said, "but he will soon. I heard him cough a moment ago."

"Tell him I have come to see him," Madam Tang said.

"Yes, madam," Liu Ma said, starting for Wang Chi-yang's bedroom, but at the door she halted. She must first tell Madam Tang of what she had seen. If she told the Old Master first, the story might be different when the Old Master repeated it. The story was something roof-shaking and she didn't want anybody but herself to tell it to Madam Tang. She hurried back to Madam Tang and whispered emphatically, "Madam, do you know what I saw this afternoon?"

"How could I know?" Madam Tang said. "What is it?"

"I saw them hold hands!"

"Who hold hands?" Madam Tang asked, slightly irritated.

"The Young Master and that beggar maid."

"What!"

"May five thunderbolts strike me dead if I lie, madam. I saw Young Master Wang Ta hold the girl's hand and the girl hold his, right in this room!" She leaned closer to Madam Tang, lowered her voice further and added, "If you had come an hour earlier, madam, you would have seen something else too."

"I was busy," Madam Tang said. "What else did you see?"

"I saw them doing this!" Liu Ma said. Finding it difficult to describe what she had seen while hiding behind a door, she enacted the scene with her two hands representing the two lovers. She put her two fists together and went on. "The Young Master told the girl to close her eyes and raise her head, then he held her

193

in his arms and pressed his head on hers like this!"
She exaggerated the kiss by rubbing her fists together.

"What is this?" Madam Tang asked, scowling.

"I don't know, madam," Liu Ma said. "Young Master Wang Ta said it was only half-done."

"Half-done?" Madam Tang asked. "What half-done?"

"I don't know. They went out an hour ago. But I am sure they are hiding somewhere doing the other half now!"

"Incredible, incredible!" Madam Tang said, fanning herself with a handkerchief. "Ask the Old Master to come out quickly!"

"Yes, madam," Liu Ma said. Having started for Wang Chi-yang's door she suddenly halted and whispered again. "Madam, I am sure that beggar maid knows some sorcery. She must have bewitched the Young Master."

"Oh, nonsense. Ask the Old Master to come!"

"It is true, madam. That old man looks just as dangerous. Sometimes I suspect that he attempts to seduce me too, but I told him that he was an old frog wishing to eat the flesh of a flying swan . . ."

"Tell the Old Master to come here!" Madam Tang interrupted her angrily, waving her handkerchief in disgust.

Wang Chi-yang had been lying in his huge bed, resting and enjoying a moment's mild coughing. When he heard his sister-in-law's angry voice in the middle hall, he closed his eyes and waited for the relative's unavoidable intrusion into his world of peace and quiet. Presently he heard Liu Ma come in.

"Old Master," Liu Ma called hesitantly beside his bed.

Old Master Wang opened his eyes and asked, "What is it?"

"Madam Tang is here to see you," Liu Ma said. "She has something important to tell you." She came closer to the mosquito net and whispered, "Old Master, do you know what I saw . . ."

194

"You can tell me what you saw while you beat my shoulders tonight," Wang Chi-yang said. "Tell Madam Tang that I shall see her in the middle hall in a few moments."

"Yes, Old Master."

Wang Chi-yang struggled out of the mosquito net, seated himself in a rattan chair, wiped his face with both hands and grunted and groaned for a moment, then he got up and went to the bathroom to wash his hands and rinse his mouth. He wondered what his sister-in-law had to tell him. He hoped that she hadn't come to talk about Mr. Loo's dinner invitation again. Never in his life had he been so persistently urged by someone to eat someone else's dinner. The more his sister-in-law urged him, the more reluctant he became to eat that dinner. It seemed to him that eating Mr. Loo's dinner would be like accepting a bribe and surrendering his principles. No, he thought, he can not yield an inch in this matter. If she brings up the subject again, he must tell her once and for all that he will not accept Mr. Loo's invitation.

He took his time washing his hands and rinsing his mouth, then spent another ten minutes trimming his mustache. Until he entered the middle hall, Madam Tang had been fanning herself impatiently with her little handkerchief as though she had been sitting on a hot stove for half an hour. "My sister's husband," she said, leaping to her feet. "Something terrible has happened!"

Wang Chi-yang coughed, sat down on the kang and picked up his water pipe. "What is it?" he asked quietly.

"My sister's husband," Madam Tang said, waving her handkerchief at him, "do not tell me that I did not warn you when you employed that old man and his daughter. I have just come to this house with good news, but now this good news is all shadowed by a great misfortune that old man and his daughter have brought into your house!"

"Hm, humph," Old Master Wang said, filling his

pipe with tobacco. He rather liked Old Man Li and his daughter. He couldn't see why his sister-in-law was so peevish while talking about them. "Hm, I do not see anything wrong with the old man and his daughter. What have they done?"

"That girl and Wang Ta were making love," Madam Tang said. "Right in this room!"

"Nonsense, nonsense."

"It is true! Liu Ma saw it with her own eyes! They were holding hands and—and—Liu Ma, show the Old Master what they did in this room!"

"Yes, madam. They were doing this, Old Master!" With her hands Liu Ma enacted the kissing scene, which Old Master Wang watched with a deep scowl.

"All right, you may go now," Madam Tang said.

"Yes, madam."

After Liu Ma had left, Madam Tang turned to Wang Chi-yang and said gravely, "My sister's husband, I presume that you understand what Liu Ma's gestures mean. Please let me remind you, if they can do that in the daytime, can you imagine what they can do at night? This is most unfortunate!"

"The unfilial dog," Wang Chi-yang mumbled, controlling his anger.

"Just imagine your own son," Madam Tang said, "making love to a maidservant. What will Chinatown think of this family if this horrible scandal spreads?"

"I told you. Wang Ta has been under bad influence ever since he started associating with women of bad reputation. Now he has started seducing innocent girls."

"How do you know it is not that lewd wench who has been seducing Wang Ta?"

"That girl is a hard-working country lass," Wang Chi-yang said. "If it is a matter of seduction, Wang Ta is undoubtedly the initiator!"

"Let us not argue about who started it," Madam Tang said. "Right now you are facing a danger which could cut you barren of descendants. Who is going to

196

marry their daughters into this house if the family is stained by such a scandalous affair?"

"I know, I know," Old Master Wang said, looking worried.

"I just told you that I have come with good news. Mr. Loo has just had his poems published by one of the leading publishers in Chinatown. The publisher said Mr. Loo is one of the most outstanding Chinese poets he has had the honor to associate with in recent years. Many scholars have read his poems and all agreed with him. And Mr. Loo has been kind enough to promise me a few copies of the poems and has asked me to present you with a copy. Wang Ta had an excellent chance to marry the daughter of such a great scholar; now everything is ruined."

"My wife's sister," Wang Chi-yang said, his stubbornness deflating like a balloon, "I begin to believe that under the modern influence, the young people can never keep themselves clean and pure as we did. Their virtues are low. In order to avoid any further defamatory catastrophe, I admit that it is wise to have Wang Ta married as soon as possible."

"What did I tell you?" Madam Tang said triumphantly. "Was I not busy making a match for him? Your indifferent attitude has been very discouraging, but my concern for Wang Ta's future has never been thwarted!"

"Let us get down to business, my wife's sister," Old Master Wang said. "Do you think that Mr. Loo will consider marrying off his second daughter first?"

"Why not?" Madam Tang retorted. "Must all his other daughters become old maids if the eldest can not find a husband? Mr. Loo is a wise man; he knows better!"

"But," Wang Chi-yang said pensively, "girls should be married in the right order. Mr. Loo, being a poet and scholar, might object to this disorderly marriage." Suddenly he looked at his sister-in-law anxiously and asked, "My wife's sister, if he insists on the correct

197

order, is his oldest daughter good enough to be considered?"

"No!" Madam Tang said firmly. "The oldest one has studied art in Paris and is already twenty-six years old. Who knows if she is still a virgin? The third daughter is too pretty and too foxy. That type of woman never makes a good wife. She can win her husband to her side and fight his own parents. Only the second daughter is ideal, as I told you before . . ."

"Please go to see Mr. Loo tomorrow and tell him that I have the desire to see Wang Ta properly married before he inherits my property. See if he would honor us by marrying his second daughter to our family."

"Tomorrow will be too late," Madam Tang said. "I am going to talk to him today. But first we shall find a go-between, find somebody whose prestige is high in Chinatown. The president of the Six Companies will be an ideal man. Or Dr. Ling, the history professor at the University of California . . ."

"We shall ask Dr. Ling to be the go-between," Wang Chi-yang said hastily. "I have always wanted to meet him."

"All right. I know him," Madam Tang said. "Then we shall buy two fat geese as the engagement present. After Dr. Ling has proposed the match formally, I shall go to Mr. Loo's house with the geese. All this should be done within a week."

"Hm, humph," Old Master Wang said, smoothing his mustache pensively, "don't you think, my wife's sister, don't you think this is a little too hasty?"

"My sister's husband, think of the danger! If that maidservant boasts of her romance in Chinatown, the whole thing will be ruined. I shall never have a day of peace unless Wang Ta is officially engaged to some decent girl from a good family. The more I think of it, the more urgent it seems." She grabbed her handbag and rose from the kang. "My sister's husband, let us go to see Dr. Ling."

Old Master Wang also rose, nodding his head. "Have

your way, have your way." He went to the door and called Liu Lung.

"Do not call Liu Lung," Madam Tang said hastily. "Can't you remember that he is deaf?"

"Old Man Li," Wang Chi-yang called.

"That old man is a bad omen," Madam Tang said. "Come on, my sister's husband, let us go to the street and get a taxi ourselves."

"Have your way," Wang Chi-yang said, putting on his black satin cap that had hung on a nail beside the kang.

Just as they were about to leave the house, Liu Lung and Old Man Li hurried in. "Did you call us, Old Mr. Wang?" Old Man Li asked.

"Never mind," Wang Chi-yang said. "We are going out."

Madam Tang turned to Liu Lung and shouted, "Liu Lung, when you see your wife, tell her not to talk, do you hear?"

"En—n?"

"I said tell your wife to keep her mouth shut!" she shouted.

"Ah?"

"Oh, my sister's husband, why is this man getting more deaf every day! Oh, we are busy. Let us go."

After Madam Tang and Old Master Wang had left the house, Liu Lung turned to Old Man Li with a puzzled look. "What did she want?" he asked.

"She wanted your wife to keep her large mouth shut!" Old Man Li shouted into his ear.

"Oh," Liu Lung said, nodding his head. "That is good, but hard."

Both laughed. "Well," Old Man Li said, "I wonder what has happened in this house today. Everybody looks so busy and excited. Where is your wife, Liu Lung?"

"My wife? I don't know. Maybe she is taking a nap. That is the only time she keeps her mouth shut."

"Quite true, Liu Lung," Old Man Li said, laughing, "quite true! Do you take afternoon naps, too?"

"Me? Sleep beside my wife in the daytime? Pah! Is not the night long enough?"

"You are right, Liu Lung," Old Man Li said, laughing harder. "I sympathize with you. *Shew*, she is quite a wife! Well, everybody is out, it is a good time to enjoy a moment of peace and quiet. We might as well sit down here and have a drink together. What do you say, Liu Lung?"

"En—n?"

Old Man Li fished out his flask from his pocket and patted it affectionately. "Our common hobby, get it?" he shouted.

"Oh, oh!" Liu Lung said, smiling. "Sure, sure!"

Both went to the kang and sat down. Liu Lung loosened his flask from his belt while Old Man Li dug out a parcel of peanuts from his pocket. He put it on the low table on the kang and invited Liu Lung to share it. They drank and ate the peanuts and looked very happy. "You know, Liu Lung," Old Man Li said, "a man must have some hobby if he wants to live his life happily."

"En—n?"

"I say, if you want to be happy, you must find something to love. Like children, they love candy; like young fellows, they love women; like middle-aged people, they love money; like old men, they love peace and quiet and a drink of this." He patted his flask again. "That is hobby, get it?"

"I see, I see," Liu Lung said, nodding his head incessantly, then with a broad smile he confided, "Old Man Li, at my age, I love everything but candy!"

"You are right," said Old Man Li laughing. "You are right Liu Lung. That is a very frank talk!" He leaned closer to Liu Lung and also confided, "Tell you the truth, Liu Lung, if I had two more good teeth, even candy would not be too disagreeable in my mouth, get it?" Both leaned back and roared with laughter. "Come, come, have another drink." They toasted each other and drank from their flasks deeply.

Liu Ma burst into the middle hall with a snort. She

planted herself in front of the petrified men and glared at them for a moment, her arms akimbo. "What are you two doing here?" she demanded.

In consternation, the two men tried to hide their flasks awkwardly. "Oh, oh," Old Man Li said, "we are enjoying a little joke together, that is all, that is all."

"You lie!" Liu Ma said. "I smell the stench of bad liquor. Liu Lung did you drink again? Speak up, you scoundrel! Did you touch somebody else's dirty liquor again?"

Liu Lung looked miserable.

"Do not wrong him, Liu Ma," Old Man Li said, "he is self-supporting."

"What? Did you buy liquor yourself, you drunkard?" Liu Ma asked her husband. "Give me the liquor. Give it to me, I said!"

Liu Lung handed his flask to his wife timidly. "Here."

"Hum!" Liu Ma said, snatching the flask from his hand. "You hide it from me, eh? Where did you get the money to buy it?"

"I go sleep in the basement, en—n?" Liu Lung said.

"Oh, scramble out!" Liu Ma said furiously. "Scramble out of here! Never come near me again!"

Liu Lung quickly got up from the kang and fled the room. Liu Ma turned to Old Man Li and demanded, "Where is your daughter, old man?"

"I have been looking for her myself," Old Man Li said. "Wonder where she has gone."

"Where has she gone?" Liu Ma said with a snort. "She has eloped with the Young Master. I have been looking for them everywhere and I cannot even find their shadows. Let me warn you, old man, if they do not return by evening, the Old Master will charge you with kidnapping the Young Master!"

"I kidnap the Young Master? Oh, heaven has eyes! What makes you talk like a crazy woman?"

"If you did not, your daughter did!" Liu Ma said. "They have disappeared, that is true! She has seduced him, she has bewitched him, that is true!"

"I am going to find them," Old Man Li said, starting for the front door. "I shall show you what kind of girl my daughter is. If she is a kidnapper, I shall ask your Old Master to throw me into the foreign jail. I shall let my flesh and bones rot in jail until the maggots begin to starve!" He stormed out of the door angrily.

Liu Ma threw herself on the kang, nursing her rage, then she put her husband's flask to her mouth and took a long drink from it. Suddenly an idea came to her mind. Slowly her eyes traveled toward the gold clock on the table. . . .

8

Wang Ta regretted that he had taken May Li to his school before they went to the movie. He had thought of educating her a little by showing her what he had been studying, but after May Li had seen a few limbs and other sections of the human body soaked in a tank, she couldn't enjoy the movie. All through the first feature, she covered her mouth with her handkerchief and made little noises that annoyed Wang Ta. He went out and bought a pack of chewing gum and gave it to her. "Chew one of these," he advised. "It will help."

The chewing gum didn't help. Before the show was over they left the theater, and May Li made motions in the street as though she were seasick. In desperation, Wang Ta went into a grocery store and bought a package of chili peppers, tore it open, and handed a small red-hot pepper to her; May Li chewed it and soon tears started welling out of her eyes. "Feel better?"

"Yes," she said, sucking air into her mouth to cool her burned tongue.

"Now, try this," Wang Ta said, giving her the chewing gum.

When they got into the car, May Li was normal again. "I am hungry," she said.

"Since you did not enjoy the movie," Wang Ta said, "I shall compensate for it by taking you to a foreign dinner and then to a foreign place to watch dancing." He drove her to Van Ness Avenue and wondered whether he should take her to the Chicken House or to the Steak House. Both were his favorite restaurants. Thinking that cutting a bloody steak might remind her of the dismembered body she had seen at his school, he decided to take her to the Chicken House.

May Li liked the foreign meal except the ice cream, which she ate with her brows knitted and she made faces when she swallowed. "What is the matter?" Wang Ta asked. "Don't you like ice cream?"

"Too cold," she said, shivering.

"Well, your tongue has suffered enough today," Wang Ta said, rising. "Let's go somewhere and see a good live show."

"I think I should go back now," May Li said. "Your father might have work for me to do."

"Get this straight, May Li," Wang Ta said. "This is America. You only work eight hours a day, and there is no more work after dinner. When did you start working this morning?"

"Six."

"We came out at two-thirty. You worked eight and a half hours already. According to law, you should charge my father an hour overtime, with double pay. Come, I shall take you to the Italian Village to see a night-club show. Have you ever been to a night club?"

"No. What is a night club?"

"You will see."

After Wang Ta had paid the bill, he discovered that he had only two dollars left. Instead of taking her to the Italian Village where two dollars was only enough for tips, he took her to William Tell in a dark section on Clay Street. He had been to the place with Chang a few times before and each time they had seldom spent more than two dollars. He liked its friendly and cosmopolitan atmosphere and always had plenty of exercise dancing in that spacious hall.

He and May Li went through the bar and entered the dance hall that somehow always reminded him of a drained swimming pool. A waitress escorted them to a table covered with white-and-red-checked cloth and Wang Ta ordered a beer and a Coke. A three-piece band—an accordion, a piano and a drum—was producing some continental music louder than could a ten-man band. People who talked different languages or English with an accent started arriving. Three colorfully dressed couples were waltzing; they looked like Dutch in their native costumes and yet they waltzed like Viennese, whirling around in the hall swiftly and gracefully, their heads tilted slightly to one side.

"Is this a show?" May Li asked, watching the dancing couples excitedly.

"No," Wang Ta said. "They are customers like us."

"They are different from the foreigners we see on the street," May Li said.

"They are foreign foreigners," Wang Ta said.

Sitting at a small round table beside them was a little man with deep well-like eyes and a balding head. He was wiping his enormous forehead with a large handkerchief and at the same time scanning the horizon trying to select his next dancing partner. At another table nearby were a group of people talking French and laughing loudly; a red-faced Frenchman with a beard was doing most of the talking, gesticulating wildly with his hands and his handsome eyes rolling; a slim young girl beside him looked at him with dreamy eyes, her hand on his muscular thigh.

"Look," May Li said excitedly, pointing at the dance floor where the dancers were racing around now, leaping, turning, stamping, their hands stretching over their heads at one moment and resting on their hips at another; sometimes the girls' skirts flew up and spread like an umbrella, baring their shapely legs. The music was louder and faster, with a heavy and delightful beat. May Li watched the dance, fascinated.

Presently more people joined the dance and the dance floor became a battlefield of violent action of rhythm and cheer. When the music was over, the little man at the next table returned, sweating and wiping his enormous forehead; the French people were still talking and laughing, ignoring the people on the dance floor completely; the slim girl with the dreamy eyes was now nesting in the bearded Frenchman's arms, her head resting on his shoulder, and both her hands had moved to his muscular thigh. A whiff of strong perfume came from the next table. Wang Ta sniffed and noticed that the little man with the enormous forehead was wetting a forefinger with perfume from a little jar. He dabbed the perfume behind his ears and in the meantime scanned the horizon trying to pick his next dancing partner.

Suddenly there was a familiar voice shouting Wang Ta's name. He looked and saw Chang and a girl emerging from the crowd on the dance floor. They came toward his table hurriedly. Wang Ta greeted Chang as he shot up to his feet, almost upsetting the table. "What wind has blown you here?" he yelled at Chang in Mandarin. "Why didn't you let me know that you have come?"

Chang arrived at the table with the girl, who was young and pretty, with large sparkling eyes and dark complexion. "First, let me introduce my wife," Chang said in English. "This is my wife Dolores. Born in Mexico City."

Wang Ta introduced May Li to them and invited them to sit down. Then he ordered more drinks. "You certainly like to surprise people," he said. "Why didn't you tell me that you are married?"

"Just got married a week ago," Chang said. "Too busy enjoying my honeymoon to write."

"When did you come to San Francisco?" Wang Ta asked.

"This afternoon. Flew in from Reno. Called you three times after I arrived—once at the airport, once in our hotel, and once at the Far East Restaurant while waiting for our dinner. Nobody in your house knew where you've disappeared to. I've thought of looking for you at the police station." He glanced at May Li and laughed. "Now I don't blame you for not staying at home, and I don't have to ask you how life is treating you, your eyes are telling me everything."

"You look well, too," Wang Ta said. "Life must have been treating you very well."

"Couldn't be better." Chang slid a hand through his wife's long black wavy hair, held the back of her neck and shook it gently. "Here's the proof."

The Mexican girl gave Chang's arm an affectionate squeeze and laughed, "You talk wonderful," she said. "*Wo ai chi.*"

"She means 'I love you,' but it sounds like 'I am gluttonous.'" Chang said, laughing. "She has been learning Chinese. The Spanish accent makes our language sound more musical, but a bit harder to understand."

"How long are you going to stay here?" Wang Ta asked.

"Going back tomorrow morning. That's why I've kept calling you. Lucky we met here."

"It's heaven's will that we should see each other tonight," Wang Ta said cheerfully. "If I had five more dollars in my pocket, we would have missed each other. Why go back so soon? What's wrong with San Francisco?"

"Business appointment," Chang said. "I'm buying a grocery store. A small business, but I'm going to build it up. Excellent location, near the Mexican colony. Don't forget, I'm now a grocery expert, with a Ph.D degree. In ten years I'll have a supermarket, in twenty years I'll have a grocery chain, and in thirty years . . . well, in thirty years I'll be an old goat about seventy-five." He shook his wife's neck and laughed.

The Mexican girl squeezed his arm and said, "In thirty years you be a tired man with a young wife, no?"

"You mean a retired man with a young wife."

"No. I mean tired."

"All right, tired," Chang said, laughing. "If you insist on simplifying the English language, I am with you."

"*Wo ai chi,*" his wife said, squeezing his arm.

The little man at the next table came over, clicked his heels and bowed stiffly to May Li and asked her for a dance. Wang Ta told May Li what the man wanted and urged her to dance. "That's a German," Chang said in Chinese after May Li had left the table. "Perfectly harmless. Here all you have to avoid is a Frenchman."

No sooner had he made the remark than a Frenchman came from the other table and asked Chang's wife for a dance. Wang Ta had never laughed so hard and Chang shrugged his shoulders. "I have nothing to complain about," Chang said. "It shows that our girls are hot commodities here. If you sit here with your wife or girl friend for two hours without a soul paying her any attention, somehow your pride is hurt." He gulped down a mouthful of beer and wiped his mouth with the back of his hand, which, to Wang Ta's surprise, had become more rough and coarse. "Why don't you go into the grocery business with me? This is a business country. I firmly believe that our real future can only be built in business."

"I have no capital," Wang Ta said.

"Your honesty is your capital. I need a partner like you."

"A month ago I would have jumped at this offer," Wang Ta said. "But not now. Thank you just the same."

"Why? Have you decided to stick it out with your medical study?"

"Yes. I begin to find it interesting," Wang Ta said, smiling.

Chang studied him. "You certainly are changed. And you've learned how to laugh, too. I never heard you laugh like that before. It's a change for the better, I must say. And I think I know why." He jerked his head toward the dance floor. "Where did you meet her?"

Wang Ta told him the story, briefly, of how he had met May Li and her father. "She is a life-saving shot in my arm," Wang Ta added; "she seems to be a kind of incentive, giving me a new interest in life. Recently I was surprised at the change myself, but I am awfully glad of it. Tell me how you got married."

"I gratefully attribute my marriage to two things," Chang said; "first, the unfriendly attitude of the Immigration Service; secondly, the bad habit of a neighbor. A riddle, isn't it? Let me explain." He downed another mouthful of beer and lighted a cigarette. "Some Immigration investigators or inspectors," he went on, "completely ignorant of our problems, seem to have the tendency to think that all bachelor aliens over forty are homosexuals. In order to have my immigration status adjusted, I decided to prove to them that I'm a normal human being, just as anxious to get married as they are to get rid of the 'undesirables.' So I decided to marry anyone who would marry me, no questions asked. A complete unconditional surrender. You know, the case was getting pretty urgent. I wanted to have my own business and settle down; in order to achieve that you must first have the Immigration officers' blessing, otherwise you're building your castle on sand. To us aliens, they are the High Lamas in this land."

He paused, took a drink and went on. "Then suddenly my neighbor's bad habit came to my aid. He was a carpenter, but had the luxurious bad habit of not talking to his wife. When warm, he read the paper and the funnies over and over; when cold he stood for hours over the floor heater in the living room, his legs apart, his hands behind his back, rocking and enjoying having the lower part of his body thoroughly baked . . ."

"He still could talk to his wife, couldn't he?" Wang Ta asked.

"No. He said conversation with his wife interrupts

the sensation. I tried to make him give up one of the pleasures and devote a little time to his wife, but no, he worked hard, he wanted his pleasures. So his wife, to revenge herself, spent all her waking hours on the telephone, talking to anybody, just anybody who had given her a phone number. It irritated me infinitely."

"I don't see how that would irritate you. Are the walls too thin?"

"No. It happened that her phone was my party line. I never had a chance to make a call or receive a call except after midnight. Finally, I pleaded with the phone company to have my party line changed. The phone company obliged. This new party line was never busy. I was completely satisfied, wondering who shared it; maybe somebody who has been vacationing somewhere, or maybe a traveling salesman, away from his abode nine days out of ten. One day I was talking to a friend on the phone, suddenly a third voice interrupted me—a young girl's sweet voice with a Spanish accent—asking me politely if I would be kind enough to hang up and let her make an emergency call. Her mother was seriously ill. Well, I was very neighborly. I made the emergency call for her, and one thing led to another, and within a week we became close friends, and you know the rest of the story."

"That's fate," Wang Ta said.

"You may call it fate," Chang said. "We have a word for it in China—*yuan*. Remember the old saying? If you have the right *yuan*, you come a thousand miles to meet the right girl; if you don't have the right *yuan*, you won't know each other even if you come face to face with each other. But sometimes providence uses the most intriguing, the most unpredictable method to bring people together. I think my *yuan* was a pretty strange one. But an excellent one, for now I realize that I've married the best girl in the world—cheerful, hard-working, affectionate, and above all, treating her mother extremely well. That's Chinese, you know. I still believe that filial piety is a necessary virtue, especially in a woman. If a woman can't love her own

209

mother, how can you expect her to love anybody else?" He jerked his head toward the dance floor. "How about her, do you expect to marry her?"

"I haven't thought of it yet," Wang Ta said. "It all depends on my *yuan*."

"And hers, too," Chang said. "Like you and Linda Tung and Helen Chao, you just didn't have the right *yuan*. By the way, do you know where Linda Tung is?"

"No. I've never thought of her again after I stopped being her 'brother.' "

"She has free-lanced to Los Angeles," Chang said. "Apparently San Francisco Chinatown has expelled her. I met her at a friend's house there. She looks different now. The great change is that she never looks at you when you talk to her. She always gives you the profile."

"Why? Ashamed of herself?"

"No, just the opposite. My friend said that some painter told her she had a profile like that of a Greek beauty. Ever since that comment, she has been giving people her 'Greek' profile."

Wang Ta laughed. "Does she know what Greek means?"

"Apparently not. Her nose needs at least five more ounces of meat to look Greek. Anyway, she is pretty popular at the moment, and has acquired a couple of new 'brothers.' "

"They have my sympathy," Wang Ta said, laughing.

They talked and had more beer until Chang's wife and May Li were escorted back to the table by their dancing partners. Both girls were perspiring. May Li had enjoyed the dance; it was an exciting experience to her. "How do you like your partner?" Wang Ta asked her.

"He smells good," May Li said.

"I know," Wang Ta said, laughing. "If you were a little shorter, you would breathe behind his ear and get knocked out by that perfume."

"Is the Frenchman a wolf?" Chang asked his wife.

210

"He no wolf," Dolores said. "He gentleman. He dance good, too."

"That's worse than a wolf," Chang said.

They ordered more drinks, talked and laughed and danced until midnight. When they were saying good-bye in the street, Chang put a hand on Wang Ta's shoulder and said seriously, "In case you change your mind, remember that my offer still stands."

"I'll remember it," Wang Ta said. "But I doubt that I'll ever change my mind."

"Well, good luck."

After they had parted, Wang Ta took May Li's hand and walked toward the car quietly, breathing the fresh, cool morning air. Inside the car he took May Li's hand again. "Are you happy?" he asked.

"Yes, very happy," May Li said.

"You know, when I think of how we met, I believe that it is the *yuan* that has brought us together. It started with General White's death."

"Why?"

"Well, if General White hadn't died, your father wouldn't have thought of opening a restaurant in San Francisco Chinatown; if he hadn't thought of opening a restaurant, he wouldn't have gone to see the consul general, and the consul general wouldn't have written that letter of recommendation to Mr. Poon of Peking, and consequently you wouldn't have come to our door and we wouldn't have met at all. So you see, everything was cleverly prearranged by heaven. It is *yuan*."

"Yes, it is *yuan*," May Li said softly.

Wang Ta took her into his arms and kissed her. "And this is a kiss—well-done," he said.

May Li took a deep breath, put her head on Wang Ta's shoulder and said, "I like it well-done."

9

It was after midnight when Liu Ma returned to her room. From under her blouse she brought out the gold clock and then glanced at her husband who was snoring noisily in their double bed. She put the clock down, went to the bed and sat down. She must let her husband know that their security was being threatened by Old Man Li and his daughter. If she and Liu Lung lost their jobs, they certainly would become beggars in this strange country where they had no friends or relatives. She must do everything to remove the threat and have Liu Lung take active part in her scheme.

"Liu Lung," she called softly, shaking his shoulder.

Liu Lung stopped snoring, snorted and swallowed, then he rubbed his eyes, smacked his lips and grunted drowsily. "En—n, en—n?" he asked.

"Listen," Liu Ma whispered heavily into his ear, "listen carefully! I have something for you to do. It is important."

Liu Lung winced and picked his ear with a forefinger. "Do what?" he asked after a loud yawn.

"We are going to get rid of that old beggar and his daughter!"

"Why?" Liu Lung asked after a moment, puzzled.

"How many times did I tell you that old man is dangerous?"

"How many times? I do not know."

"Oh, you unworthy fool. Don't you know that you have been treating a thief like a brother? He is going to take our place and drive us out to the street one of these days!"

"En—n?"

Liu Ma leaned closer to his ear and said, "I say the

old man is going to rob you of your job and your family; he is going to occupy everything you have, don't you know that, you fool?"

Liu Lung winced and picked his ear again. "Occupy everything I have? Even you?" he said. "No, he won't."

"Oh, you unworthy fool," Liu Ma said despairingly. "You do not even care, you ungrateful rotten old bone!"

"En—n?"

Liu Ma shouted, "I said you are an ungrateful rotten old bone, a deaf, dumb old turtle!"

"Oh, I heard that before," Liu Lung said.

"Oh, I am miserable," Liu Ma lamented. She decided to talk to Liu Lung again in the morning. She knew that she wouldn't get anywhere with him when he wasn't wide awake, and she might wake up the whole house by shouting at him. She hid the gold clock under a table and undressed herself. When she climbed into the bed, Liu Lung was snoring again.

Next morning, when Liu Lung learned of his wife's scheme, he was horrified. But Liu Ma wouldn't give up; she cajoled, threatened and reasoned with him until he finally consented to do what she had planned. He got dressed, hid the clock under his blue cotton gown and hurried out of the room. With a sigh, Liu Ma went back to bed and waited patiently for the result.

Before breakfast, she got up, dressed, washed and went downstairs as though nothing had happened. In the middle hall Liu Lung was mopping the furniture. When he saw her, he jumped and started working more energetically. "Hum," Liu Ma said, pretending that everything was normal, "have you ever thought of sweeping the floor? Must you always take the easy work?"

"En—n?"

Liu Ma didn't expect him to hear it anyway, so she ignored his question. She made a gesture and said, "Come here."

Liu Lung went to her and she whispered into his

ear, "I forgot to tell you. Do you know what the Old Master said before he went to bed last night?"

"Yes."

"What did he say?"

"He said he wanted to sleep."

"Oh, you stupid! Listen, he said we were no good. He said none of us was as hard-working as that old turtle Old Man Li and his daughter! Did you know that?"

"No."

"Well, you know it now. That old beggar wants to rob you of your job; didn't I say that?"

"You said it."

"Well, was I wrong? Are you convinced now that everything I told you is true?"

"Yes, yes, everything you said is true."

"Now you should understand that little scheme I told you to carry out is for your own good, don't you?"

"I—I—I—" Liu Lung gaped.

"Don't open your mouth so wide and say nothing but I, I, I!"

"I, I, I did not do it, Liu Ma," Liu Lung stammered.

"What?" Liu Ma shouted. She quickly controlled her rage, lowered her voice and said, "You did not do it, heh? After I planned it one whole day and now you have the gall to tell me that you did not do it."

"I—I could not do it, Liu Ma."

"Hum, you could not do it! I sweated every day and you could not even do an easy thing like that! Where is the thing I gave you this morning?"

"Don't do it, Liu Ma."

"So you tell me not to do it. So you still want to treat that old beggar like your own ancestor. Where is the clock?" She grabbed Liu Lung and barked into his ear, "Give it back to me! Give it back to me, I said!"

Liu Lung picked up a parcel from under the table and handed it to Liu Ma. "Here."

Liu Ma snatched the parcel and glared. "So you want to put it back, heh? You want to be the gentleman, I the thief, heh?"

"Don't do it, Liu Ma," Liu Lung said.

"Don't worry," Liu Ma said, hiding the parcel quickly under her blouse. "You go ahead and treat that old turtle like your own ancestor. I am not going to hurt even a hair of his. I have other use for the clock!" With a snort she hurried upstairs. Liu Lung was bewildered for a moment; suddenly he dashed after his wife and pleaded, "Don't do it, Liu Ma. Don't do it . . ."

10

Old Man Li loved the back yard as much as the cook loved his kitchen. He spent most of his time in the yard tending the flowers. The yard had looked like a garbage dump before; now that Old Man Li started taking care of it everything seemed to come alive again. The dying peach tree was in bud; the few small bamboos which Mr. Poon, the former owner of the house, had planted, stopped shedding their leaves; the grass began to turn from yellow to green; the yulan flower, the camellias and the azaleas that had been planted along the dilapidated hedge, were all budding and blooming. Old Man Li watered them every day and cooed at them as though they were sick babies. He weeded all the wild grass, repaired the hedge and painted it crimson. It would be wonderful, he thought, to turn the place into a little tea garden; while having a cup of jasmine tea in a comfortable rattan chair with a few friends, one would smell the fragrance of the flowers and listen to the birds singing. The sun would be warm and the gentle breeze would rustle the bamboo leaves. It would be just like General White's garden in China; everything would be neat and clean; he could see General White sitting in it now, sipping his tea and puffing on his pipe.

As Old Man Li was working in the yard and visualizing what he was going to build, he suddenly heard Liu Ma's wrangling voice and immediately the beautiful illusion vanished. He straightened up and wiped his forehead with the back of his hand. *"Shew,"* he said to himself, "with her around, this place is only good for a fish market."

May Li came into the yard and said excitedly, "Father, Liu Lung is begging his wife again!"

"Well," Old Man Li said, "when the wife is large and the husband small, that is not unusual."

"I wonder what trouble it is this time," May Li said. "Maybe Liu Lung did not give her his salary; maybe he wants his wine flask back. Remember this, May Li, there are many kinds of unhappy marriages—with the husband and wife throwing rice bowls at each other is one kind; with the husband running after his wife begging and imploring is another; with the wife running after the husband swinging a broomstick is a third. I have seen them all; but nothing is worse than a wife being too nice." He shook his head with a deep sigh. "Such a wife can make you think of her day and night as if you were bewitched; she can tear your heart to pieces when she passes away . . ."

"Oh, father," May Li said hastily, "mother died fifteen years ago, why must you still let it torture you? From now on I shall never mention anything that would remind you of a good wife. Let us go knock at Old Mr. Wang's door and tell him that I have come back."

"It is still too early, May Li," Old Man Li said. "Old Mr. Wang does not get up until the sun has reached the top of this peach tree, see?"

"I am going to wake Old Mr. Wang up and ask him what makes him think I have kidnapped his son."

"Oh, easy, easy," Old Man Li said. "We can ask him that later, can't we? *Shew,* you certainly act like an ant on a hot stove."

"I am very unhappy when people think that I am a bad girl," May Li said.

"Let us wait until he gets up. After he washes himself and has his ginseng soup, he will be in a good mood, then we shall go in and tell him politely where you went and what you did last night. Let us sit down and wait." With a grunt he sat down on the steps of the porch. "Well, you have not finished telling me what you did yesterday. Come, continue your tale."

May Li sat down beside him. "All right, where was I?"

"You have finished describing the soup of that delicious foreign dinner. Omit the dinner, May Li. It will do me no good except make my mouth water. Tell me where you went after the dinner."

"We went to a dance hall; there we saw many foreign foreigners."

"Foreign foreigners? What are they?"

"Oh, they are people from other foreign countries. One of them danced with me. He smiled good. The dance hall was full of them; they very friendly. Mr. Wang met a good friend there."

"A foreign foreigner?"

"No, he is Chinese, but he has a foreign foreign wife. She can speak only one sentence of Chinese, 'I am gluttonous.' That is the only thing she can say. She said it twice to Mr. Chang." She laughed.

"Well, maybe it is a foreign foreign custom for a wife to say such things to her husband. What else did you do?"

"We danced until after midnight," May Li said. "Then we said good-bye to Mr. Chang and his wife. Then Mr. Wang took me to his car, and we. . . . Oh, I forgot to tell you where we went before the movie. He took me to his foreign university to see what he has been studying. Father, have you ever seen an invisible animal?"

"Invisible animal? Never even heard of it."

"It is a kind of animal which you can not see without a magic glass."

"Magic glass? What is it?"

"It is a glass that looks like an anti-aircraft gun.

217

Through this glass you can see the invisible animals. Oh, I saw hundreds of them, swimming in a drop of water on a little glass plate. They have different shapes; they have no eyes, no mouth, no legs, but they can walk and swim. I swear I never saw such odd-looking things before! Mr. Wang says they are everywhere. Maybe there are thousands of them right in this yard."

Old Man Li looked around furtively as though there were such animals creeping beside him. "I do not see anything," he said.

May Li laughed. "Oh, father, you cannot see them unless you have a magic glass. Let us go see Old Mr. Wang. Maybe I shall have to tell the whole story all over again when I see him." She jumped up and started for the door.

"Wait, wait," Old Man Li said hastily, "let me go first. You have no manners." He rushed ahead of her and the moment they entered the middle hall he added, "May Li, remember this, Old Mr. Wang's spleen was on fire yesterday. When you see him, do not argue. Be very polite and agreeable, understand?"

"I don't have to be too polite," May Li said. "He called me a kidnapper."

"May Li, our sage has well said . . ."

"All right, father, our sage has said, 'Do not sail against a storm.' "

"Our sage is never wrong," Old Man Li said. "You wait here, I shall go and knock on his door." He went to Wang Chi-yang's door, raised his hand, but couldn't bring it down. "May Li," he whispered, "can't we wait until he coughs?"

"Oh, father," May Li said despairingly, "you look like a mouse trying to pay a visit to a cat . . ."

"What are you two doing here?" Liu Ma said, entering the middle hall from the dining room, eyeing them suspiciously.

"Liu Ma," Old Man Li said, "here is my daughter. Do you know where she went? Mr. Wang took her to his university, then to a movie, then to a foreign restaurant . . ."

218

"Am I a kidnapper?" May Li asked. "Am I?"

"Beggar maid," Liu Ma said. "You keep away from the Young Master!" With a snort she went to the kitchen.

"Tell your Old Master that the kidnapper has come back," May Li shouted after her. "Tell him . . ."

"May Li, May Li," Old Man Li stopped her hastily. "Don't shout like that!"

May Li went to the door and mimicked, "Beggar maid, you keep away from the Young Master!" Then she put her tongue out at the door.

"May Li, May Li," Old Man Li said, "stop this! *Shew!* You certainly are an ill-tempered wench, just like your mother. *Shew!*"

"That old hag! She always gives me advice!"

"May Li, I would give you the same advice if I saw you yesterday. You should have seen the old Mr. Wang, he was really angry! Remember, good medicine is bitter, sometimes it is the same with good advice . . ."

"Not her advice."

"Words of advice are like grandmother's peanuts, May Li, some good, some rotten. But it is always good manners to accept them. If you find them good, eat them; if you find worms in them, throw them away. When you are asked how are the peanuts, you say wonderful just the same. If you have learned this, you will have no trouble with ill-tempered old hags. Now let us go see Old Mr. Wang."

Wang Ta came into the middle hall. He had slept well last night. The moment he was awake he had started thinking of May Li. The "well-done" kisses last night has sweetened his thoughts, and Chang's marriage had helped him create in his mind a beautiful picture of his own married life. This morning he was going to propose marriage. He came into the middle hall whistling merrily. When May Li saw him, her face brightened. She promptly forgot about the old Mr. Wang and greeted Wang Ta cheerfully. "You are early this morning, Ta."

"You are even earlier," Wang Ta said, smiling. "In

China I usually got up very early. My room was next to my father's and his cough was an accurate alarm clock."

Old Man Li was glad that May Li's interest was diverted. He came to Wang Ta and said, "Your father coughs badly, Mr. Wang. *Shew,* even Liu Lung can hear it in the back yard. You should advise him to do something about it."

"He has done too much," Wang Ta said, sitting on the kang. "In China he drank ginseng soup day and night; he washed his chest with hot water every afternoon; he told Liu Ma to beat his shoulders any time she was available; he took all kinds of patent pills compounded of materials ranging from rice to fishbones. . . . He did everything except one thing—go to a Western doctor and have his lungs examined."

"He has not taken the right medicine," Old Man Li said. "I have a wonder cure for cough called the Eight Diagram Pill. Last year May Li had a cough, the pill cured it just like a gale blowing out a candle. Didn't it, May Li?"

"Er—er—yes, father," May Li said hesitantly.

Wang Ta laughed. "Old Man Li, if there is any such pill that can cure a cough like a gale blowing out a candle, a good many cough doctors will have to change their profession."

"Well, according to the ancient doctors," Old Man Li said, "a cough is caused by cold in the throat and heat in the lung; the positive and the negative . . ."

"The modern doctors have different opinions," Wang Ta interrupted. "We believe it is caused by germs, which you cannot see with your normal eyes."

"Father," May Li said excitedly, "that is what I have told you! The invisible animals!"

"Yes, the invisible animals," Wang Ta said, laughing. "They can only be seen through the magic glass."

"Well, it sounds like evil spirits," Old Man Li said.

"They are evil spirits," Wang Ta said. "But they are the kind of evil spirits who are not afraid of a Taoist priest."

"Father," May Li said, "I saw something else . . ." She suddenly put her handkerchief over her mouth and held her breath for a moment. "I saw something else . . ."

"What is it?"

"A human body—cut up into pieces—soaked in a big tank . . ." She stopped and made some throaty noises behind her handkerchief.

Quickly Wang Ta fumbled in his pocket and dug out the package of chili pepper and handed it to her. "Here, lucky I still have it."

"Human body, all cut up and soaked in a big tank?" Old Man Li asked. "*Shew,* this is the biggest nonsense I have ever heard early in a morning!"

"That is true, Old Man Li," Wang Ta said. "We have cut that body."

"You?"

"Yes, we. If we do not cut human bodies, we cannot learn how to be a doctor."

May Li made a queer noise and quickly she threw another chili pepper into her mouth. She chewed it and tears started pouring out of her eyes. Suddenly she jumped up from the kang and dashed toward the kitchen. Wang Ta followed her. In the kitchen she pushed the cook aside, turned on the cold-water faucet in the sink and thrust her mouth toward it. Wang Ta opened the icebox and pulled out an ice tray. He knocked the ice cubes out of the tray in the sink and stuffed a piece of ice into May Li's mouth. May Li held the ice in her burning mouth and sighed. "Feel better?" Wang Ta asked.

May Li nodded her head.

"Good. I have something to tell you. Let us go to the back yard and talk it over in private." He took her hand and they went to the porch in the back yard and sat down. "May Li," Wang Ta said, "will you marry me?"

May Li swallowed the ice, almost choking.

"Oh, you should not have swallowed that!"

May Li coughed, her face red. "When I want to say yes," she said breathlessly, "I do not want to spit out anything."

Wang Ta laughed. "Good," he said, patting her back to help the ice descend, "I like a wife whose words and deeds conform."

11

It was one of those rare days when Wang Chi-yang was completely happy. When he woke up from his afternoon nap he stayed in his bed and enjoyed the peace of his mind and a strong sense of achievement. He had met Dr. Ling and the professor had successfully made the match; that alone was a memorable event which Old Master Wang would cherish in his memory for the rest of his life. His sister-in-law had brought the geese to Mr. Loo's house and the engagement was properly acknowledged by both families. This had all been smoothly carried out within a day and a half and strictly according to the ancient tradition of China. The Year of the Horse had an excellent start. He was grateful to heaven and decided to make a handsome contribution to the Buddhist church when he took his routine walk on Grant Avenue next time.

He coughed for a few moments and thought it was about time to get up. He struggled out of his mosquito net, moved to a rattan chair, wiped his face with his hands, grunted and groaned until the slight dizziness that always accompanied an afternoon nap completely disappeared. Then he went to his bathroom to rinse his mouth and wash his hands.

After he had finished his afternoon toilet and trimmed his mustache, he thought of calling Wang Ta into his room and telling him of his engagement. But when he decided that the announcement should be made properly in the middle hall, he put on his best satin jacket, cleared his throat, and came out of his room.

In the middle hall May Li was shining his water pipe and Wang Ta was reading a magazine. They stood up and greeted him politely. Old Master Wang was pleased. He went to the kang, coughing a little, and sat down majestically. "May Li," he said, "give me the water pipe."

"Yes, Old Mr. Wang." May Li handed him the pipe with both her hands and then lighted a paper spill for him.

"Hm," Old Master Wang said, after he had smoked the first pipe, "I am quite pleased with your work in this house. The tobacco tastes better since you started changing the water in the pipe every day."

"Thank you for your good words, Old Mr. Wang," May Li said cheerfully.

"The pipe also looks cleaner and brighter since you came," Wang Chi-yang said. "The other lazy servants never bother to shine it unless I am in a fit of temper. Now it is different. I am quite satisfied, hum, humph." He showed his satisfaction by nodding his head a few times at nobody in particular, then went on smoking. Liu Lung brought in a kettle and poured hot water into the Old Master's Kiangsi teapot.

"Father," Wang Ta said, "how is your cough?"

"As usual, as usual," Wang Chi-yang said. "Wang Ta, tell Liu Lung to bring my ginseng soup. It soothes my throat and I decided to drink one more bowl of it every day."

"Liu Lung, hey, Liu Lung," Wang Ta said, making a hand gesture. Liu Lung nodded and went out.

"Hm, humph," Wang Chi-yang said, nodding with approval, "your hand talk with Liu Lung is not bad. You can teach Liu Ma how to do it, so there will be less noise in this house." He coughed and turned to May Li. "Do you know how to beat the shoulders?"

"Yes, Old Mr. Wang. I used to beat my grand-mother's shoulders when I was little."

"Come and beat mine, see if you can beat better than Liu Ma."

May Li went to the kang and beat Old Master Wang's shoulders with her palms with a fast and flowery rhythm. Old Master Wang grunted and groaned with pleasure.

"Father," Wang Ta said, "you should go to a hospital and have your lungs examined. I remember that you have been coughing ever since I could walk."

"Do not tell me to go to a modern hospital," Wang Chi-yang said. "I do not trust the modern doctors."

"Modern medicine is accepted all over the world except by the backward savages, father. I am sorry you do not believe in it. Please go to see Dr. Liu at Tung Wah Hospital."

"Hold your tongue," Old Master Wang said, slightly irritated by Wang Ta's blunt words, "it is enough that you study this modern medicine, but do not try to bring it home to deceive your own father. Look at these quacks in a modern hospital. Before they ask you where the ailment is, they first dig into your mouth with sticks and bars as if they were excavating a tunnel. When they kill a patient—that is what they always do—they put the blame on germs. One of those wretches in a hospital in Hunan even had the gall to suggest that I might have germs in my lung; outrageous!"

"That doctor in Hunan might be right," Wang Ta said. "Many people in our town in Hunan died of tuberculosis."

"Wang Ta," Wang Chi-yang said heatedly, "I have no objection to your making a living with the modern medicine in the future, but I shall not be pleased if you try to preach it to me!" He coughed. "May Li, beat a little faster."

"Yes, Old Mr. Wang," May Li said, beating his shoulders in a faster tempo. "Shall I beat a flower song for you, Old Mr. Wang?"

Wang Chi-yang grunted. "Go ahead. Beat the song."

May Li changed the rhythm and started beating a song. Old Master Wang closed his eyes and groaned, a faint smile climbing on his serene face. "Hm, hm," he mumbled, "not bad, not bad. What is this song called?"

"The Song of the Hoe," May Li said.

"Hm, hm. Sing it to me, sing it to me."

May Li beat the overture and started to sing:

> " 'With our hoe we till the fields, hei!
> Rid the fields of the wicked weeds, hei!
> Yi-ya-hei, ya-hu-hei!
> Rid the field of the weeds—
> Ya-hu-hei, ya-hu-hei!
> Our ancient nation must arise, hei!
> With our hoe once more we'll be free, hei!
> Yi-ya-hei, ya-hu-hei!
> With our hoe we'll be free—
> Ya-hu-hei, ya-hu-hei!
> Heaven sent us our great Sun Yat-sen, hei!
> Calling us with our hoe to arise, hei!
> Yi-ya-hei, ya-hu-hei!
> Calling us to arise—
> Ya-hu-hei, ya-hu-hei!
> Our revolution shall succeed, hei!
> Yi-ya-hei, ya-hu-hei!
> With our hoe we'll be the victors,
> Ya-hu-hei, ya-hu-hei!' "

"Hm, humph," Old Master Wang said, grunting and nodding his head, "not bad, not bad. From now on I shall let you beat my shoulders and sing this Song of the Hoe two or three times a day, do you hear?"

"Yes, Old Mr. Wang," May Li said.

"Hm, I am quite satisfied, quite satisfied. Your father's work here also pleases me. I have noticed that the trees and flowers have grown a little faster since he came, and the back yard no longer looks like a neglected graveyard . . ."

"That is because we owe you so much, Old Mr. Wang," May Li said. "Even the plants feel grateful for us."

225

"Well said, well said," Wang Chi-yang said, more pleased. "I have also noticed that you and your father are the first ones to get up in the morning. The spring is coming, the days will be longer. This is a new year's beginning. The late mistress used to say, 'Everybody should rise with the sun and work until after the sun retires behind the Western Mountains.' Although we are living in a foreign country now, we still should observe our own good ways of living. Wang Ta, do you hear?"

Wang Ta was reading his magazines. "Yes, father."

"As the spring is approaching," Wang Chi-yang went on, "your aunt and I have worked out some new plans for you for the new year. You throw that magazine away and please lend your ears to me!"

"Yes, father," Wang Ta said, putting the magazines away. "What new plans?"

"May Li," Wang Chi-yang said, "it is enough beating for today. You may go now."

"Yes, Old Mr. Wang." May Li cast Wang Ta a tender glance and left the middle hall.

Old Master Wang cleared his throat. "My son, Confucius has said, 'There are three major offenses to the ancestors; lack of descendants is the worst.' Now you are almost thirty, it is time for you to take a wife."

Wang Ta was somewhat surprised, for that was exactly what he had planned to talk to his father about. "I have thought of that, father. I am happy to say I have finally found the right girl whom I . . ."

"Finding the right woman is not your business," Wang Chi-yang said bluntly. "That responsibility rests on the shoulders of the parents who are more experienced in this matter."

"Do you mean—do you mean you have already chosen a wife for me?" Wang Ta asked.

"Yes, we have," Wang Chi-yang said, his voice softened, and there was almost a smile on his face. "Your aunt and I have found the right woman for you."

Wang Ta managed to control his rising anger; he paused for a moment before he spoke. "Father, I shall try to stand your telling me what to eat and what to wear, for I can spit out the food I do not like, and I can change the clothes that do not fit me. But a wife is like a man's shadow; if you do not mind, I would like to choose her myself."

"You young people are never careful," Wang Chi-yang said, displeased, but trying his best to keep the conversation pleasant. "I have seen the younger generation change their wives more often than they change their clothes. That is why the parents must make the choice."

"Father, this is the only thing I shall not tolerate. Our points of view are different, probably they are thousands of miles apart. No, I would rather die as a lonely bachelor than be tied down to a dumb, ugly old strange woman . . ."

"She is not dumb, ugly or old," Wang Chi-yang interrupted him hotly. "She is the second daughter of Old Mr. Loo, a good friend of your aunt's, a poet and a scholar, highly regarded in Chinatown for his scholastic achievement . . ."

"You see, father, our points of view are so different. You talk as though it was the father, not the daughter, whom I am supposed to marry."

"My intention is to tell you that the girl is raised in a respectable house with a high door . . ."

"So much the worse! A girl raised in such a house usually spends half her life in bed, half her life admiring herself in a mirror. If I married her, I would probably spend all my life regretting—"

"Hold your tongue!" Wang Chi-yang said, surprised by his son's boldness. "She was born under the zodiac sign of the rat, you under the zodiac sign of the sheep. Mr. Foon, the leading physiognomist in Chinatown, said this is a perfect match, no conflict in life."

"I do not believe in zodiac signs," Wang Ta said. "If I did, I still would not be able to see how a sheep could get along with a rat. Father, I might as well tell you the truth, I have already found . . ."

Wang Chi-yang shot up to his feet and said angrily,

"I have already engaged you to Old Mr. Loo's second daughter, and Mr. Loo has agreed to marry her ahead of her older sister. That is a big face he has bestowed upon us. You are going to marry her on the fifth of the fourth moon. That is a lucky date chosen by Mr. Foon, the leading physiognomist in Chinatown."

Wang Ta was stunned for a moment. He would never have antagonized his father so boldly if he had not been in love. Now that his own marriage plans faced the threat of being wrecked, he surprised himself by being more bold.

"Father," he said, starting for the door, "I am not going to marry anyone on the fifth of the fourth moon. I advise you to worry more about your own cough than my marriage!" He went out of the house, slamming the front door.

"Oh, rebellious dog," Old Master Wang said furiously without losing his dignity. He paced the floor trying to control his rage. "Ah, the younger generation," he mumbled to himself, "rebellious! Outrageous! They have no manners, no respect for their elders! Some day they will have the gall to cut their own father's throat!" While he was walking about and mumbling, Wang San sneaked by the middle hall through the hallway and tiptoed toward the front door. "Stop!" Old Master Wang said. He was in a bad mood and he was looking for somebody to scold. "Where are you going?"

"I am going to visit my aunt, father," Wang San said timidly.

"Nonsense! You visit your aunt every day, and she has never seen even your shadow since the New Year's Day. Come in!"

Wang San came into the middle hall reluctantly. "If you go to the street to play with the street urchins and disgrace my ancestors again," Old Master Wang warned, "I shall lame both your legs. Do not stand there like a little idiot! Go back to your room and study Confucius!"

"I have studied Confucius the whole afternoon, father."

"Come here! Recite the first chaper of Lung Yu. Go on, chapter one!"

Wang San took a step forward and tried, "Confucius says . . . Confucius says . . . Confucius says . . ."

"Is this what you studied the whole afternoon? Your hand!"

Wang San stretched out his right hand; Old Master Wang brought out the bamboo stick from behind the kang and whipped Wang San's hand twice. "Recite chapter two. Go on. Chapter two!"

Wang San swallowed hard. "Confucius says . . . Confucius says . . . Confucius says . . ." He stopped and automatically put his hand out to receive more punishment. Old Master Wang whipped his palm three more times. "Chapter three," he commanded.

This time Wang San didn't even try to recite anything. He simply put his other hand out. Old Master Wang pointed a finger to a corner and said, "I am not going to break my bamboo stick on your animal paw. Stand there!"

Wang San obediently went to the corner and stood there, facing the wall. "You are going to stand there until bedtime," his father said; "see if that will help you recite the Books of Lung Yu better tomorrow."

Old Master Wang's mood wasn't getting better after he had punished Wang San. He smoked a few pipes of the best Fukien tobacco, cast a glance at his second son, who was standing in the corner rigidly like a soldier at attention, then he rose and went back to his room to tend his miniature garden, hoping that the beauty of nature would cure him of his bad mood. He had been happy this morning; it irritated him very much that such rare happiness had lasted only a few hours. Suddenly he missed his wife again. While tending his miniature garden he thought of his wife and felt a strong nostalgia for his old home in China. The fact that he was now living in such a faraway foreign country and his house was full of strangers, including his sons, made him more unhappy and lonely.

After he had watered the trees and fed the goldfish,

he practiced his calligraphy for a while, and he was still depressed. Suddenly he heard Liu Ma greet his sister-in-law in the middle hall. This time he didn't wait for Liu Ma to come in and announce Madam Tang's arrival. He wanted someone to talk to and was glad that his sister-in-law had come. He quickly put his brush and paper away and went to the middle hall to meet her.

"My sister's husband," Madam Tang said the moment Wang Chi-yang had stepped into the hall, "please tell Liu Lung to go to the house of Loo and bring the two geese back."

Wang Chi-yang was shocked for a moment. "What do you mean?" he asked, going toward the kang.

"Mr. Loo's second daughter just rebelled," Madam Tang said, throwing herself on the other side of the kang heavily. "She just told her father that she is already secretly engaged to a white American. They are going to get married immediately. Her father tried to forbid the marriage but the girl said that she is over twenty-one and she can marry anyone she wishes."

Wang Chi-yang grunted. Somehow he felt slightly relieved, for the prospect of taming Wang Ta and making him accept the girl had been a burden on his mind.

"Besides," Madam Tang said, fanning herself with her handkerchief rapidly, "that girl has been insulting. She said that even if she was not engaged, she would not allow herself to be thrown at anybody in town. Her father told her that Wang Ta is from a wealthy family. Do you know what that girl said? She said in that case Wang Ta must be a good-for-nothing playboy whose only use in the world is to turn food into manure. Just imagine a young girl saying such a thing! I suggest that you tell Liu Lung to go to their house and bring back the geese immediately! And you can forget about the Friday invitation."

Wang Chi-yang cleared his throat. "What did I tell you, my wife's sister?" he said. "The younger generation is all spoiled. However, I am glad that this girl has objected to this marriage. My dog son, Wang Ta, has just refused to marry her, too."

"Has he?" Madam Tang said, her face brightening, then she triumphantly brought her palm down on the low table on the kang and added, "He has done the right thing! We must let that vulgar girl know that she was turned down first!"

"Oh, what difference does it make now?" Wang Chi-yang said. "One crow is not darker than the other. Both are spoiled eggs of the modern times."

"My sister's husband, after I heard what that vulgar girl just said to her father, I began to realize that Wang Ta is a hundred times more cultured than she is. I just pity that white American man who is going to marry her. Now, even if she crawls to this house and begs you to take her, I would still advise you to kick her out with both your feet!"

Wang Chi-yang grunted. "Tell you the truth, a moment ago I almost had a good mind to kick Wang Ta out and disown that unfilial dog."

"All right," Madam Tang said, "let bygones be bygones. Fortunately no servants know of this unpleasant experience. If anybody knows, we must see to it that he does not gossip about it in Chinatown." Suddenly she spotted Wang San in the corner; she pointed a finger at him and asked, "What is the meaning of that?"

"I am giving that little devil some standing punishment."

"What crime did he commit this time? Did he steal again?"

"No; laziness, an offense worse than theft."

"He has just reached the lazy age. It is natural, my sister's husband; nobody can help it. Please let him go. I hate to see my sister's own flesh and blood suffer this stiff, uncomfortable posture . . ."

Wang San turned and asked anxiously, "May I go now, father?"

"Go back to your room and study Confucius," Old Master Wang said. "If you can not recite the Books of

231

Lung Yu again tomorrow, you shall stand there one whole night, I am giving you this warning. Get out!"

Wang San instinctively dashed toward the front door, but before he reached it Old Master Wang thundered, "Stop! That door is to the street!" He pointed at the stairway. "That door is to your room!" Wang San turned back and climbed up the stairway sullenly.

"How do you expect this boy to earn a living if he can only recite Confucius in the future?" Madam Tang asked.

"I do not expect him to earn a living," Wang Chi-yang said. "I shall die in peace if he could only recite a few pages of Confucius without mispronouncing too many words. Right now all he knows about Confucius is his name."

"My sister's husband, do not forget that we are living in a modern world."

"My wife's sister, by your custom, you seem to belong to the modern generation; but by your age, you can not deny that you are still a member of the old. Please tell me honestly, have you not missed the good old days? Those days when children were respectful and obedient, virtues were high, life was serene and peaceful . . ."

Madam Tang liked the good old days in China, but she also found many new comforts in the modern world. To her a combination of the old and the new would be ideal. She wanted to speak her mind but she didn't know how to begin. Suddenly the front door was flung open and Wang Ta burst in from the street. In his hand was a microscope, which he brought into the middle hall and dumped on the low table on the kang in front of his father.

"Father," he said breathlessly, "in order to show you what germs look like, I have brought you a microscope. Please take a look into it. And I have also made an appointment for you with Dr. Liu at Tung Wah Hospital on Jackson Street to have your lungs examined. If you do not go to see him tomorrow, he will come to see you. But please take a look into the microscope first."

Wang Chi-yang flinched from the microscope. "Take it away," he said angrily. "I am not interested in any of your foreign black arts. Take it away!"

"Father, I must convince you that the world is different now. You are still living in an old—"

"The world is changing from bad to worse," Old Master Wang interrupted him. "The world is ruined by you young fools! Take this thing away or I will throw it into the gutter!"

"Wang Ta," Madam Tang said, "your father is in a bad mood today. Take this monstrous-looking thing away and keep quiet."

"Father," Wang Ta said, "I just bought this microscope from a downtown store. I shall leave it here. If you are wise, you will take a look into it and go visit Dr. Liu at Tung Wah Hospital; if you insist on being stubborn, you may throw it into the gutter as you wish. It costs you a hundred and forty dollars. They will send you the bill."

"Take it away," Wang Chi-yang said. "I say, take it away!" But Wang Ta ignored him and went out of the house, slamming the door. At this moment Liu Lung was bringing in Old Master Wang's ginseng soup. When the Old Master saw him he shouted, "Liu Lung, take this thing and throw it into the street!"

"My sister's husband," Madam Tang said hastily, "please calm yourself. This microscope costs you a hundred and forty dollars, you can not just throw it to the street. I shall find out where he bought it and return it to the store at a discount." She rose from the kang and started for the front door. "I am going to talk to that mad boy."

After Madam Tang had left hurriedly, Liu Lung was puzzled and frightened. "Old Master," he asked timidly, "throw this good ginseng soup to the street?"

"Take it away, you fool!" Old Master Wang shouted. He was getting angrier now. "What happened to the cook? What happened to my dinner? Where is Liu Ma?"

"I am coming," Liu Ma said, hurrying into the mid-

233

dle hall. "I am coming. The dinner is ready, Old Master."

"Why did you not announce it sooner? Must I starve in my own house? Take a look at the clock and see what time it is. . . . The clock! Where is the clock?" Wang Chi-yang hurried to the table and looked, trembling with rage. "The clock is gone. Who has stolen it? Who has stolen the late mistress' gold clock? . . ."

12

Madam Tang had not slept well last night. The quarrel in the House of Wang had been bothering her. She looked at her watch, 3:30 P.M. She decided to go to her brother-in-law's house to see how things were going. Wang Chi-yang ought to be out of his bed by now, she thought. She never took an afternoon nap and this sleeping habit in the House of Wang irritated her. She waited twenty more minutes before she started in hopes that Wang Chi-yang would be wide awake when she arrived.

It was one of those foggy afternoons; everything seemed a bit gloomy. Far out in the Bay a foghorn tooted. Foghorns always made Madam Tang feel depressed; she welcomed the thundering noise of the jet planes any time, it wasn't too pleasant but at least it was an indication of fine weather. She wondered why people must make foghorns sound so melancholy; poor weather itself is melancholy enough.

"How are you, madam?" Liu Ma greeted her as she arrived at the House of Wang.

"Not good, not bad," Madam Tang said. "Serve me with some hot tea. Oh, I hate these chilly afternoons."

"Yes, madam."

Madam Tang went into the middle hall and the first thing she saw was Wang San, an eyesore that added depression to her already dejected mind. The boy was sluggishly standing in a corner, facing the wall, apparently suffering from another long standing punishment. "Well," Madam Tang said with a deep scowl, "have you failed to recite Confucius again?"

"No, my aunt," Wang San said, shifting his legs restlessly.

"Then what are you standing there for? Practice?"

"No, my aunt. The gold clock is gone."

Instinctively Madam Tang's eyes darted toward the table. A pain gnawed at her heart when she saw her sister's clock was no longer there. She went to Wang San, her hands on her hips, and demanded, "You incorrigible rascal, how could you steal your own family treasure?"

"I didn't steal it."

"Nobody else has the gall to touch that gold clock. You are the only reputed thief in this house. Tell me where have you sold it?"

"I did not sell it."

"You must have sold it to one of those greedy pawnbrokers on Kearny Street. Listen, if you tell me the truth, I shall ask your father to shorten this punishment."

"I didn't steal it," Wang San said.

"Wang San," Madam Tang said hotly, "I am ashamed of my sister for having brought you into this world. You not only steal, but also lie! You are indeed a disgrace to the House of Wang!" She opened her handbag, fished out a five-dollar bill and brandished it it front of Wang San's face. "See here, this is five dollars. If you tell the truth, the money is yours; if you don't, the money will go right back into my bag. If your father makes you stand here for three days without food or water, do not expect me to say a word for you."

She looked at Wang San expectantly. Wang San looked at the banknote, swallowing hard, apparently fighting a battle within his mind. After considerable struggling, he finally triumphed over the devil of temptation. "I didn't steal it," he said, turning his head away.

Madam Tang tossed the bill back into her bag and snapped it shut. "Incorrigible," she said. "Standing punishment is too good for you. If your mother were still alive, she would make you kneel on a washing-board instead of standing on a floor." She went to the kang and sat down angrily. Liu Ma came into the hall with the hot tea. "Has the Old Master awakened yet?" Madam Tang asked.

"He did not nap today," Liu Ma said, serving her with the tea. "He is very upset about the clock."

"Tell me, when was this clock stolen?"

"I do not know, madam," Liu Ma said. "I do not have the faintest idea who has the gall to steal it. The Old Master thinks it must be Young Master Wang San, but I do not think so."

"Why do you not think so?"

"There are so many people coming and going, how can anyone tell whose hands are clean and whose hearts are not black?" She cast a glance at the doors, then leaned forward toward Madam Tang and whispered, "Madam, do you know what Liu Lung saw the day before yesterday? He saw two people whisper in the back yard, then he saw them sneak into this hall."

"Who were they?"

"Liu Lung said it was dark, but one looked like an old man and the other a girl." She poured more tea into Madam Tang's cup. "But I do not think so, madam."

Madam Tang picked up her tea, sipped it and then nodded her head pensively. "Hm, very possible."

"I said to Liu Lung," Liu Ma whispered enthusi-astically, "they have plenty to eat in this house, why should they steal? Liu Lung said perhaps they are used to borrowing things at night. He said a lot of people are like that; when they see expensive things, their hands just begin to itch."

"Hm," Madam Tang said, nodding, "perhaps Liu Lung is right."

"Madam, do you know what else Liu Lung saw? He saw that beggar maid hide something from him this morning. Do you know what it was? Young Master Wang Ta's foreign pen!"

"What? Did Liu Lung really see that pen in the girl's hand?"

"Madam, Liu Lung is as deaf as a stone, but he has a pair of eyes as sharp as an eagle's."

Madam Tang put down her teacup heavily. "Yes, it is positive that the girl has stolen the clock!"

"Madam," Liu Ma whispered, "please do not tell anybody that Liu Lung saw all these things. If it goes to the ears of that cunning old man, heaven knows what poison he is going to put into Liu Lung's tea. I have told Liu Lung to hide our money, add an extra lock to our trunk, and keep his mouth shut."

"I knew these people are not to be trusted," Madam Tang said. "But the Old Master never listens to me."

"You better take care of your own expensive things while you are in this house, madam. I still say that old man knows some sorcery. He can move things around without touching them."

"Nonsense, there is no such thing," Madam Tang said; nevertheless, she removed her handbag from the low table on the kang to her lap. "Liu Ma, check everything in the house and see if anything else is missing."

"Yes, madam. I am going to find it out. Liu Lung said that beggar maid has her luggage hidden under her bed and covered with a blanket. I am going to examine it some day. Who knows if that gold clock is not in her bag?"

"Ask the Old Master to come here."

"Yes, madam."

After Liu Ma had left, Madam Tang lighted a cigarette and puffed on it vehemently. Of all petty crimes she hated theft the most; she was determined to catch the thief and restore her sister's clock even if she had to hire all the private detectives in San Francisco to do it. She wasn't so sure that May Li had stolen it; it seemed to her that the smiling Old Man Li looked more like a thief. However, she was not going to make any accusation until there was evidence. May Li has Wang Ta's fountain pen, she thought. That was something to be studied, too.

Wang Chi-yang came into the middle hall, coughing. Madam Tang eliminated the usual greetings and expressed her sorrow. "My sister's husband, I was shocked when I learned that my sister's gold clock was stolen."

"The gods are punishing me for having raised this unfilial son Wang San," Wang Chi-yang said, sitting down on the kang with a deep sigh. "He can not recite a word of Confucius; he steals the fruits of the god of longevity; now he even has the gall to steal the family treasure."

"My sister's husband, punishing the innocent or rewarding the villainous is an unforgivable mistake. I have just questioned this boy, and I found that his answer is reasonable and innocent, therefore I doubt that he is the real thief."

"For fifty years not even a straw has been stolen in the House of Wang," Wang Chi-yang said with another sigh. "Since this unfilial dog was born, things began to disappear quite often. Who else could have stolen the clock?"

"I just want to tell you something which your prejudice may not allow you to believe," Madam Tang said gravely, pointing her ivory cigarette holder at her brother-in-law, "but it is true. That servant girl you hired has stolen Wang Ta's gold fountain pen. Liu Lung saw it; he is deaf, but he has eyes as sharp as those of an eagle. He also noticed that the girl's luggage, hidden under her bed, is covered with a blanket. My sister's husband, some day your house will be stripped barren by thieves and yet you will still punish your own son for the crime!" She looked at Wang San and shook her head sadly.

Wang Chi-yang rose from the kang, went to the door and called, "Old Man Li! Old Man Li, May Li, come here!"

"My sister's husband," Madam Tang said, "you might as well tell everybody to come. That is the proper way to question a suspect."

"Liu Ma, Liu Lung, Lao Feng," Old Master Wang called. "Come here, all of you!"

"Did I not warn you before?" Madam Tang said. "Now you can see what is happening. One misfortune after another."

"All the troubles have been brought into the house by Wang Ta," Old Master Wang said gruffly. "Nobody but that unfilial dog is to blame." When he returned to the kang, Old Man Li and May Li hurried into the middle hall from the back yard. "Did you call us, Old Mr. Wang?" Old Man Li asked.

"Yes," Wang Chi-yang said. "Do you know that the late mistress' gold clock has been stolen?"

"Liu Ma has told us," Old Man Li said. "I feel sorry for the thief. He has stolen under the staring eyes of the god of longevity. Even if he escapes the law, he will never escape the celestial punishment."

"When did you last see the clock?" Old Master Wang asked.

"Well, it is hard for me to remember exactly," Old Man Li said. "You see, I never look at a clock; the sun and the moon are good enough to keep time for me; besides, I can not read the queer marks on a clock. May Li, when did you see it?"

"I saw it day before yesterday," May Li said. "And I wound it, too."

"You are supposed to wind it every morning," Madam Tang said. "Did you not discover that the clock was missing yesterday?"

"Yes, but I thought Old Master Wang had removed it from the table here. It is not too safe to leave a gold clock in the middle hall . . ."

"Liu Ma," Madam Tang shouted at the door, "what are you standing there for? The Old Master wants you to come here, all of you!"

Liu Ma pulled her husband out from behind the

239

door. "You coward," she said, pushing Liu Lung toward the middle hall, "you are not the thief, why are you so frightened? Go in, go in!"

"Where is the cook?" Madam Tang asked.

"The cook went out shopping," Liu Ma said.

"Liu Ma," Old Master Wang asked, "when did you last see the clock?"

"It was there yesterday," Liu Ma said, then hurriedly she added, "Liu Lung saw it too. Did you not, Liu Lung? He saw it. He said it must have been stolen during the night."

"My sister's husband," Madam Tang said, "if the clock was stolen during the night, the thief could not possibly be from outside, for the doors were locked and no windows were broken, and nobody heard any noise."

"Did anybody hear any noise during the night?" Old Master Wang asked.

There was a moment of silence. "I did not hear anything," Old Man Li said. "Did you, May Li?"

"No," May Li said.

"Neither did I," Liu Ma said hastily. "I always sleep like a log; even Liu Lung's snore can not wake me up."

"Wang San," Old Master Wang said, "did you hear any noise?"

"No," Wang San said in English, then he quickly realized the mistake and added in Chinese, "No."

"That is all the Chinese you can say now, is it?" Wang Chi-yang said angrily. "Now, get out!" Wang San, whose mind was already on the Chinese playground on Sacramento Street, bolted out of the room.

"My sister's husband, you can save your breath, the thief is definitely not from outside."

"Liu Ma," Old Master Wang said, "you have been working for the House of Wang for more than twenty years; there has never been a case of theft except for some fruits and cakes stolen by rats and chipmunks; therefore I trust that you would not suddenly do anything ungrateful and disgraceful. And as for your husband, he is as deaf as a stone, not qualified to be a burglar at all. Now I want you to tell me who the thief is."

"Liu Lung said he saw a girl's shadow talking to somebody in the back yard one night last week," Liu Ma said, then she hastily added, "but I was asleep."

"May Li, was that you?" Old Man Li asked.

"Yes," May Li said, "have you forgotten already, father? You and I were enjoying the moon in the back yard, and you were telling me about the flowers . . ."

"Liu Ma," Madam Tang said, "tell the Old Master exactly what Liu Lung saw."

"Liu Lung said it was dark, there was no moon that night; he said he saw two people whisper to each other, then sneak into the middle hall." She turned to Liu Lung and shouted, "Why are you so frightened? Nobody is going to poison you!"

"En—n?"

"Oh, shut up!" Liu Ma said.

"Well, if he saw two people talk," Old Man Li said, "it must be May Li and me; if he saw people whisper, they must be somebody else. We never whisper."

"Whispering is only done by people who have secrets," May Li said. "My father and I have no secrets, so we always talk aloud."

"Young girl," Madam Tang said, "it is ridiculous to hide your secret by saying high-toned words and by looking so upright. Somebody saw you in possession of a gold fountain pen, is that true?"

"Yes, Mr. Wang gave it to me."

"Madam Tang," Old Man Li said, "allow me to say a word. May Li and I are god-fearing country people. We would not look at a gold brick on a roadside even though we are poor; we would not even touch a grain of rice in other people's bowls even if we were starving . . ."

"Old Man," Madam Tang said, "I have never wronged anyone in all my life; punishing the villainous and rewarding the innocent is always my motto. If you are innocent, you have nothing to fear. My sister's hus-

241

band, I suggest that we examine their luggage. It is the only way to find out."

"You can not examine our luggage!" May Li protested.

"Madam Tang," Old Man Li said, "my daughter and I came into this house at the invitation of Mr. Wang. We did not come here to steal. Examining one's luggage is a great insult. We are poor people, but we love our face more than you love your family treasure. It can not be done."

"You see?" Madame Tang said to her brother-in-law, with a meaningful nod of her head, "they refuse to have their luggage examined."

"You have no right to examine our luggage," May Li said. "Nobody has the right to examine our luggage!"

"Young girl," Madam Tang said sharply, "nobody is allowed to talk wildly in this house!"

"Calm yourself, May Li," Old Man Li said, patting her on the shoulder, "calm yourself."

"Old Man Li," Wang Chi-yang said, "you and your daughter look like honest people. I have trusted you and treated you well. But, after all, you are two strangers my son picked up on the street. I know nothing of your background and your pedigree; it is natural for us to be suspicious. If you are really as innocent as you look, you should not object to the inspection. Now, here is a good chance for you to prove your innocence. Bring your luggage here and let us have a look. If we find nothing that does not belong to you, I shall give you twenty dollars as a compensation, and I shall allow nobody to say a word about it so that you will not lose your face . . ."

At this moment Wang Ta came home. He was somewhat surprised at this unexpected gathering in the middle hall, but he was glad, for he had something to say and he wanted everybody to hear it, especially his father. He went straight to May Li, took her hand and said, "May Li, the Reverend Han of the Presbyterian church has promised to marry us. I am taking you to apply for a marriage license."

The information was so shocking that everybody in the room was dumfounded for a moment; finally Madam Tang found her voice. "Are you crazy, Wang Ta?"

"My aunt," Wang Ta said, his voice none too polite, "I have decided to marry May Li. From now on please do not bother to look for a wife for me . . ."

"Madman," his aunt interrupted him hotly, "can't you see what has happened here?"

Wang Ta cast a glance at the others. "What has happened?"

"Your mother's gold clock has been stolen. We are trying to find the thief."

"Ta," May Li said, "they suspect that my father and I have stolen the clock, because someone saw me use your foreign pen."

"Father, this is ridiculous," Wang Ta said angrily, "I gave her that pen as a present two weeks ago . . ."

"You see?" Old Man Li said triumphantly. "Did my daughter steal the pen? Did she? Mr. Wang, now they want to search our luggage for the gold clock!"

"Father, how can you accuse people of stealing without evidence—"

"We are trying to find the evidence," Wang Chi-yang interrupted him sharply. "I am the master of the house! I want to examine their luggage and nobody is to stop me! Liu Ma, go bring their luggage here!"

"Wang Ta," Madam Tang said, "why cannot you respect your father like a well-bred son? Your mother always believed in the ancient virtues, especially filial obedience . . ."

"May Li," Wang Ta said, "I believe that you did not steal the clock. Let them examine your luggage. My luggage has been ransacked by customs officers more than a dozen times. No matter where I go, they always suspect me to be a smuggler . . ."

"Liu Ma," Wang Chi-yang shouted, "did you hear me? Go bring their luggage!"

Liu Ma turned to Old Man Li and said, "Old man,

you'd better come with me. I never touch anybody's property without its owner watching."

"You don't have to touch it," Old Man Li said. "We shall bring it here ourselves. You just come and keep your sharp eyes on us. May Li, Mr. Wang is right, let them examine our luggage, *shew!* Our sage has well said, 'If nothing wrong is done, there is no need to fear the ghost knocking at your door at night.' Come, May Li." He started for the stairway; May Li followed him. Liu Ma turned to follow but suddenly she remembered her husband. "Liu Lung, come with me."

"En—n?"

"Follow them, you lazybones!" she shouted, pushing him toward the stairway.

"Father," Wang Ta said, "wronging innocent people is worse than stealing. This is the most disgraceful thing that has ever happened in this house."

"That is my decision," Wang Chi-yang said. "I suspect them and I want to examine their luggage, that is all!"

"I do not understand you, father. You liked them. You were kind to them and treated them well. All of a sudden you think they are thieves and destroy all the good will and friendship you have built."

"Stop using the word 'friendship.' I never tried to build a friendship between them and me and I do not need it."

"Wang Ta," Madam Tang chided, "if your poor mother were still alive and could see you now, she would never believe that she had borne a rebellious son like you. You are so changed; I wonder why."

"Perhaps I have become wiser, perhaps I can not stand all these old-fashioned—"

"Listen, listen," Madam Tang interrupted, "your father and I have lived thirty years longer than you have; no matter how old-fashioned we are, our judgment and wisdom will still be better than yours. Take choosing a wife, for instance; how could you choose a better girl than we could, while you have no experience with females at all?"

244

"That is what you think, my aunt," Wang Ta said, turning away from her.

"Listen to me," Madam Tang said hotly, "your father and I engaged you to an excellent girl whom you could never find yourself, but you did not trust us, you turned down this match. You have thrown your future and your happiness to the mud. Now you are going to ruin your own life by marrying a servant girl whom you picked up on the street . . ."

"That is enough, my aunt," Wang Ta said. "I can take care of my own life perfectly well, if you will please stop looking for an excellent wife for me. You and my father have run the first part of my life, now I do not see why I should not have the privilege to manage the second part of it myself . . ."

"We have no time to talk about your life this moment," his father interrupted him. "We are busy locating your mother's gold clock, which is more precious than your worthless life!"

They waited quietly until Old Man Li and May Li returned to the middle hall with their luggage. Liu Ma and Liu Lung followed them closely. Old Man Li dumped his worn-out traveling bag in front of Wang Chi-yang and said, "All my belongings are in this bag. I have not touched a thing inside. Liu Lung can be my witness. If you do not mind dirtying your hands, please examine it."

"Liu Lung," Old Master Wang said, "take the things out of the bag."

"En—n?"

"The Old Master wants you to pour the things out of that sack," Liu Ma shouted into her husband's ear.

"Oh," he said. He picked up the bag and turned it upside down. Old Man Li's gong, whip, his beard and a few threadbare clothes fell out on the floor. Madam Tang inspected the contents of the bag with a help of her foot.

"Here are my pockets," Old Man Li said. He busily went through his own pockets and brought out a handkerchief, an old wallet, his wine flask and a few other cheap articles. He put them on the floor and searched himself again. "Here is my coat, there is nothing hidden in it." He took off his coat and shook it like a magician, then he threw his coat on the floor and started searching his shirt and trousers. "There is nothing hidden in my shirt, nothing in my trousers, nothing in my shoes . . ."

"That is enough," Old Master Wang said. "Liu Ma, take the things out of the girl's luggage."

Liu Ma turned to May Li and said, "Before I touch your bag, tell the Old Master that I have not touched a thing of yours. When the inspection is over, do not try to tell me that you have lost any of your junk."

"Please don't worry," May Li said heatedly. "I would not care even if you have stolen everything I have. Steal anything as you please. But you can not steal the thing which I value the most—that is my clean conscience!"

"We have no time to waste in talking," Wang Chi-yang said. "Liu Ma, pour the contents out of that bag."

"Yes, Old Master." Liu Ma picked up May Li's bag, turned it upside down and shook it roughly. Some small articles fell out first—combs, a hand mirror, a few bottles of perfume, shoes, towels; then her flower drum, then her clothes, and finally the gold clock, which tumbled and rolled and landed at Old Master Wang's feet. Madam Tang leaped up from the kang and picked it up quickly. "Look, my sister's husband," she cried. "Look, everybody! What is this? Is there anybody in this room who did not see the clock fall out from that girl's bag?"

Wang Ta was so surprised that he shot a quick glance at May Li, who was staring at the clock in Madam Tang's hand, petrified. "No, no!" she suddenly cried. "I did not steal it . . ."

"Young girl," Old Master said sternly, "you have stolen the gold clock, nothing can hide your crime now!"

"I swear I did not steal it," May Li said. "Somebody else stole it! Somebody else stole it and put it in my bag!"

"What nonsense!" Liu Ma said. "Would a thief steal an expensive gold clock and give it to you? Is there any such a fool? Old Master, no wonder she did not want to have her bag examined!"

"I did not steal it! I swear to heaven I did not steal it . . ."

"All right," Madam Tang said, "if you insist that you did not steal it, we shall call the police and they will give you a trial. You can prove your innocence to them . . ."

"Madam, madam," Old Man Li said hastily, frightened, "please do anything but call the foreign police! We do not speak their language, they will not understand us and they may deport us! May Li, no matter what crime people put on you, it is only like some dirty clothes you are wearing; a clean conscience is all that is necessary and matters." He turned to Wang Chi-yang and added, "Old Mr. Wang, heaven is above and has eyes. My daughter has never touched anything that does not belong to her. Her heart is as clear as the dew on a lotus leaf. Now you have found the clock in her bag, you have pointed a knife at her throat. There is nothing a helpless girl can do but put herself at your mercy." He bowed and started gathering up his belongings on the floor and stuffing them into his bag. May Li covered her face with her hands and sobbed.

"My sister's husband," Madam Tang said, "stealing is a crime which can not be encouraged."

"Father," Wang Ta said, "we are all refugees from the Mainland China. Please have some consideration. You do not want to have them deported because of a rusty old clock."

"Hold your tongue!" Old Master Wang said angrily. "Do you still have the face to defend them? It is you who have brought me all this trouble! Old Man Li, you and your daughter are ungrateful and mischievous. I could call the foreign police and have you deported, but I am not a hard-hearted man. Now, pack your things and be off, and stay away from Chinatown."

"Old Mr. Wang," Old Man Li said, "we shall not

come near this town again even if we are invited with sedan chairs and firecrackers, *shew.*" He picked up his bag and said to his daughter, "May Li, let us go. Let us go back to Los Angeles."

May Li put her things into her bag, sobbing. After she had packed, she fished the fountain pen out from her bosom. "Mr. Wang, here is your fountain pen, I am returning it to you."

"You may have it," Wang Ta said.

May Li looked at him; her lips trembled and fresh tears welled out of her eyes. Suddenly she dashed toward the table, tossed the fountain pen on it, picked up her bag and ran out of the house, crying.

"Mr. Wang," Old Man Li said to Wang Ta, "I thank you for your kindness for inviting us to stay with you, but the insult we received in this house shall take months to be forgotten, and my daughter's heart which you have broken shall take years to heal." He flung his bag over his shoulder and strode out of the house.

Liu Lung watched him go, gasping, then he turned to Wang Chi-yang and tried to say something but his tongue couldn't function. Suddenly he gave up the effort and hurried out of the front door.

"What is the matter with him?" Madam Tang said, puzzled.

"Please don't mind him, madam," Liu Ma said. "He is bewitched by that old man."

"My sister's husband," Madam Tang said, "you can see now that it is dangerous to take strangers into a house. I hope this will serve you as a good lesson."

"Madam," Liu Ma said, "did I not tell you before that they looked like thieves to me? The way they sneaked and the way they whispered to each other made me think they were going to steal something a long time ago. I told you before, Old Master, nobody could bring a bit of dust out of this house if I have kept my eyes on him."

"The clock is restored," Wang Chi-yang said sternly; "this unpleasant incident is all over. From now on nobody is to remind me of it. Wang Ta, I want to make

248

this clear to you: this is my house, nobody is allowed to invite people to stay here without my permission . . ."

Before he finished, Liu Lung returned hurriedly. He looked more uneasy than before; he went to Wang Chi-yang and once more his mouth worked like that of a fish, but no sound came out. "Liu Lung," Madam Tang said, "what is the matter with you?"

"What are you trying to do?" Liu Ma shouted. "Oh, you lazybones, get out and try to find some work to do!" She started pushing Liu Lung toward the kitchen. "Get out!"

"Old Master. . . . Old—Old Master!" Liu Lung said. "That girl did not—she did not . . ."

"Get out, get out!" Liu Ma cried, pushing him angrily.

Wang Ta quickly stepped between them. "Liu Ma, leave him alone! Liu Lung, what did you say?"

"She did not steal the clock," Liu Lung said, his voice trembling. "Liu Ma stole it. She stole it and put it—"

"Shut up!" Liu Ma shouted. "You ungrateful old beast, are you mad?"

"Let him talk!" Wang Ta said sharply.

"She stole it," Liu Lung said. "She told me to put it in Old Man Li's bag. I did not do it. She—"

Liu Ma grabbed him and slapped him. "Shut up, you old beast! Oh, Old Master, this deaf old turtle is mad; he must have been bewitched by that old man . . ."

"Old—Old Master," Liu Lung said desperately, "she put the clock in the girl's bag. She did it! She did it!"

"Get out, you ungrateful old beast," Liu Ma cried, slapping him again, "get out!"

By this time Wang Ta had brought the bamboo stick out from behind the kang. He thrust it in Liu Lung's hand and said, "Liu Lung, beat your wife, beat her!"

Liu Lung grabbed the stick. Suddenly a wild look came to his face. Liu Ma flinched from him. "What are you going to do? I dare you to touch me, I dare you . . ." Liu Lung stepped forward and slashed his

wife with the stick. Liu Ma tried to fight back but Liu
Lung whipped her so violently that she finally re-
treated toward the door, shrieking and swearing. Liu
Lung chased her to the back yard and presently a
sound beating was heard.

"Wang Ta," Madam Tang said, "go stop that beast
beating his wife."

"Stop him? No!" Wang Ta said. "This is the first
time that bamboo stick has been put to its right use."
He left the middle hall hurriedly.

The beating and screaming went on. Madam Tang
got up from the kang and walked up and down nervously. "My sister's husband, this is the most horrible
thing I ever saw. Allow a man to beat his wife like a
wild dog . . ."

Old Master Wang poured himself a cup of tea and
said quietly, "This is his own privilege; I am in no position to interfere."

"This is your house," Madam Tang said. "Such a
scandalous thing will spread all over Chinatown in
two days. Just think of your reputation, my sister's husband."

"I have loved my reputation above everything,"
Wang Chi-yang said gravely. "Today I begin to feel
that my reputation is like an artificial flower. I wonder
if it is worthy of any more care."

"What makes you sound so pessimistic? You are
changed all of a sudden."

"My wife's sister," Wang Chi-yang said with a deep
sigh, "you are the closest relative I have, let me be
frank with you. I have done many wrongs in my life,
but I have always managed to conceal them very well.
Many people believe that I am a perfect gentleman,
having no flaws either in thoughts or in conduct. But
today Old Man Li said something that somehow awakened me. My wife's sister, it would really be happier if
one could be like Old Man Li, wearing rags on top, but
having a clean conscience."

"Ah," Madam Tang said, fanning herself rapidly
with her handkerchief, "now you even wish to be in

that old man's shoes. You are changed indeed!" Suddenly she saw Wang Ta come down the stairway with a suitcase and his overcoat. "What? Where are you going?"

Wang Ta came into the middle hall. "Father, I am going away."

"Do not be foolish, Wang Ta," Madam Tang said.

"I have decided it is better for me to be independent," Wang Ta said. "Please do not try to stop me."

"Where are you going?" Wang Chi-yang asked, coughing.

"I am going to join Old Man Li and his daughter. I am going to tell them that we are the real thieves, we have stolen their happiness. I am going to beg their forgiveness and ask May Li if she still cares to marry me . . ."

"Oh, stop this madness," Madam Tang said. "I cannot stand this nonsense!"

"My aunt, you do not have to stand for it any more, for I shall never see you again. Frankly, I am disgusted with this house and everybody in it!"

"Get out!" Old Master Wang said angrily.

"My last advice, father. You are a sick man, both socially and physically. If you still insist on being blind, you will . . ."

"I do not want your advice!" his father shouted. "Go starve yourself! I am glad that you will leave me here to enjoy a few years of peace! Never come back to my house again, you ungrateful dog."

Wang Ta hurried out of the house, slamming the front door. When Wang Chi-yang's cough subsided, he turned to his sister-in-law quickly. "My wife's sister," he said painfully, "please go find out where he is going."

"He is not going anywhere," Madam Tang said. "If he does not want to come back here, he is going to stay with me." She grabbed her purse and left.

Old Master Wang groaned and grunted and took a sip of tea to soothe his still itching throat, then he sat on the kang quietly for a moment. Suddenly an unbearable loneliness closed in on him. He felt as though he were sitting all alone in a small boat on a vast ocean, without a speck of land in sight, with dark clouds looming in the distance. He didn't know that with Old Man Li, May Li and Wang Ta gone, the house could be so empty and forlorn, like a frightful endless dark ocean. With a shiver he quickly rose from the kang and went back to his room.

He didn't know why but his bedroom also looked deserted now. It had been cozy and warm before and he had always felt secure and comfortable in there; but now it resembled another lonely ocean, with every article in the room reminding him of how forlorn he was. At his age he should live in a house full of off-spring. Not that he wanted many chattering relatives to bother him, or waves of children tottering in and out of his room, but he must have a feeling that he was not alone, a feeling that he was forever surrounded by his own flesh and blood. The cry of a baby in the next room, the laughter of a teen-age daughter, the scolding of his wife, or even the quarreling of two daughters-in-law would provide a house with life and warmth that was so necessary to a man of his age.

For a moment he sat at his desk and let this terrible loneliness gnaw at him. When he could not bear it any longer he took out his brush and paper and practiced calligraphy. It was no use. He tried to tend his mini-ature garden, but the work only increased his unhappi-ness. He must do something positive to relieve himself of this depression.

When he came out of his room again, Madam Tang had returned to the house. "He is gone," she said breathlessly, fanning herself with her handkerchief. "He wants to go into the grocery business with a friend. He is just as stubborn as you are. Are you going out, my sister's husband?"

"Yes," Wang Chi-yang said, putting on his black satin cap. "I am going to see Reverend Han of that foreign church he mentioned."

"What for?"

"Do you think that lunatic can really make a living and support a girl and an old man? They will starve to death in a few weeks if I do not find some way to give him this." He showed his sister-in-law a check that he had just written.

"What? Five thousand dollars?" Madam Tang said, frowning. "He will throw it into the gutter. Oh, my sister's husband, he did not want your money. Did he not say that he wants to be independent? He is going into the grocery business. You'd better tear this check up before it falls into the hands of somebody else."

"Perhaps you are right," Wang Chi-yang said after a moment, tearing up the check. "He seems to hate my money. But I should give Reverend Han some money for the wedding. I do not want the wedding to look too shabby."

"Ah, Wang Ta will take care of it himself. Perhaps he will not go to see Reverend Han at all. He is anxious to go into the grocery business with a friend in Los Angeles." She stopped fanning herself and asked seriously, "Do you really approve of this marriage?"

"To be frank with you, my wife's sister," Wang Chi-yang said, "when that unfilial dog said that he was going to ask May Li whether she still cared to marry him, I was kind of pleased."

"Ah, you have changed indeed, my sister's husband," Madam Tang said. Now she realized that Wang Ta, her favorite nephew, had sworn he would never return; she felt a sudden pang. Despite the fact that he had refused to have anything to do with her from now on, she had never missed him so much before. She felt a strong urge to do what her brother-in-law had just intended to do—give the boy some money in some roundabout way. The rascal had the ill luck to fall in love with a girl poor as a nail, plus an old father who had nothing but a wine flask to his name. They might really starve if she did not take care of the matter. "Well," she went on, "the boy has set his mind on marrying that girl, there is nothing we can do about it anyway. He is as stubborn as a mule. Hm, grocery business. Perhaps it is some business worth looking into." In an effort not to betray her secret desire, she decided not to say a word more, quickly picked up her purse and started for the door.

"Are you going so soon?"

"Yes, I am busy," Madam Tang said and hurried out of the house without looking back.

Old Master Wang stood in the middle hall for a moment, feeling very old and tired. For the first time in his life his stubbornness, which had been his strongest fort, began to tumble down. He picked up his cap, put on his satin jacket and went out of the house. He wanted to see Chinatown and let the familiar signs and smells remind him of his home town in Hunan Province. He couldn't stand this feeling of being alone and deserted in a foreign land. He wanted the feeling of familiarity and intimacy, the consciousness of still being among his countrymen.

Walking along a side street toward Grant Avenue, he thought of his remaining years and was glad that he could see the end of his journey in the not too distant future. Perhaps in ten years he would be gone and everything would be forgotten. He realized now that this was a world of the younger generation and that the best way to conduct himself was to live in it like a polite guest, taking what was offered to him and being content with it. He nursed a faint fear that the younger generation, which seemed to be rebellious and undisciplined and totally lacking filial piety, was going to ruin this world. He was glad that he was not going to live long enough to see it. But he managed to console himself with the fact that Wang Ta, perhaps the younger generation as a whole, did have a sense of fairness and uprightness, as Wang Ta had demonstrated a while ago. Wang Ta's attachment to May Li and her father, his decision to follow them, apologize to them and to live with them, all seemed to him the right thing to do. Perhaps it was the only move that would help relieve him of his guilty feeling, the most uncomfortable feeling of having wronged some innocent people.

The inhabitants in Chinatown were quietly working as usual. The man at the noodle factory was there, grinding a hand machine; the seamstress was there, sewing away, bending over her work fourteen hours a day, her children playing at her feet; the barber was in his shop giving a customer the elaborate treatment, shaving his face and trimming the hair in his nostrils. The grocer was patiently watching a housewife select the salted fish, the thousand-year-old eggs, the taro roots and the dried seaweed, his abacus ready; the retired old man was still sitting in his store that sold nothing, reading the Chinese newspapers from cover to cover, perhaps for the third time, till new ones were delivered to him in the late afternoon. The restaurant was not crowded, with a few customers sitting at the counter sipping tea and picking their teeth.

On Grant Avenue the cars crawled like an endless parade. There was the Chinese tranquillity and patience; nobody seemed to be in a great hurry, and nobody could be even if he wanted to. The herb merchant, sitting behind his shiny counter, his hands in his sleeves, watched the street without an expression on his face. As Old Master Wang passed the herb store he wondered what the herb doctor was doing inside. Perhaps he was reading the ancient medicine book, or practicing his calligraphy, or diagnosing the case of a patient, or just sitting behind his desk serenely, meditating. He was the only man in Chinatown with whom Old Master Wang could easily identify himself. He was old-fashioned, full of classical learning, with emphasis on calligraphy and the beauty of composition. He was the one who also hated change and always dreamed of going back to the old village in China, to die in China, and be buried in a good coffin, with numerous offspring visiting his grave every spring, making offerings and burning incense for him.

As Old Master Wang passed the herb store he wondered if the herb doctor also had identical problems. He controlled a strong desire to drop in and pay him a visit. It was no use having their old-fashioned ideas strengthened with further association, he thought. He hastened his steps and turned on Jackson Street, feeling like a man who had just betrayed his best friend. He felt very sad about what he had just seen and thought. Perhaps in fifty years most of the familiar sights and smells in Chinatown would be gone. Perhaps there would be no more clatter of mah-jongg behind closed doors, no more operatic music of drums and gongs, no noodle factories, no old-fashioned barbershops with all the traditional services, no more retired old men reading Chinese newspapers, no more grocers with abacuses, no more thousand-year-old eggs, taro roots or dried seaweeds. . . . For this was the world of the younger generation, everything was changing, slowly but steadily. Even he, old-fashioned as he was, was now deserting his herb doctor, his best friend and the only man in Chinatown with whom he could happily associate.

On Jackson Street on the corner of Stockton Old Master Wang sighted the massive building. He had passed the seven-story building numerous times but had never looked at it. He had always regarded the building as an ill omen and had always quickened his steps when he passed by it. Now he stopped in front of it and looked at it for a long time. He looked at the red lacquered sign with these characters: Tung Wah Hospital. It was an impressive sign, hanging under the red-tiled pagoda roof. The characters were well-written, although lacking strength in some strokes, but on the whole they were the product of years of patient practice in the Sung School. Then he looked at the revolving door, braced himself a little, took a deep breath, mounted the marble steps and entered the building.